N(
EV(
S(X
AT A
WEDDING

BOOKS BY TRACY BLOOM

No-one Ever Has Sex on a Tuesday
No-one Ever Has Sex in the Suburbs
No-one Ever Has Sex on Christmas Day
The Last Laugh
Dinner Party
Single Woman Seeks Revenge
I Will Marry George Clooney by Christmas
Strictly My Husband

NO-ONE EVER HAS SEX AT A WEDDING

TRACY BLOOM

Bookouture

Published by Bookouture in 2019

An imprint of StoryFire Ltd.

Carmelite House
50 Victoria Embankment
London EC4Y 0DZ

www.bookouture.com

ISBN: 978-1-78681-837-9
eBook ISBN: 978-1-78681-836-2

'Will all of you witnessing these vows do all in your power to support these two and their marriage?'

The congregation, or wedding guests then respond,

'We will.'

Chapter One

The Marriage of Craig Bellamy and Abigail Fletcher

Cressington Manor, Leeds

Katy lowered herself slowly down onto the sofa in the corner of the hotel suite and watched as the two best friends went into battle.

'Did you choose these, Braindead?' asked Ben in frustration as he failed to get the cravat to sit straight under his friend's collar.

'No,' replied Braindead. 'I just said to Abby I'd wear anything but I don't really like ties so I left her to it. I had no idea this was an option. Why do I have a handkerchief around my neck?'

'Moron,' muttered Ben under his breath.

'Shall we cut out the insults today?' Katy shouted over.

'Yes,' agreed Braindead. 'And that includes calling me Braindead,' he told Ben.

'But I always call you Braindead. I'm just supposed to start calling you Craig, am I, just because it's your wedding day? I can't call you Craig. I never call you Craig.'

It was true. Ben had known Braindead since they were at school. There was no recollection of exactly when he first came up with the

nickname but it was affectionate, of course. Braindead was far from
brain dead. In fact, he was probably the most intelligent person Ben
and Katy knew – he just had a funny way of showing it.

'Craig it is today,' announced Katy, hauling herself up and coming
over to take over the spectacularly appalling mess the cravats were now
in. She was four months pregnant, married to the best man and, for her
sins, acting as mother of the bridegroom to Braindead – sorry, Craig.
Her stomach was doing somersaults with nerves from the desire to be a
fitting support to her husband's best mate, the baby was literally doing
somersaults, and the bridegroom and best man were bickering like
children. Not to mention that she couldn't help feeling very anxious
that her three-year-old daughter Millie was probably causing havoc in
the bridal suite with the excitement at being a bridesmaid and without
either parent there to calm her down. This wedding was shaping up
really well already.

'Now,' she said, smoothing down Braindead's collar, 'you look the
part. Your mother, I'm sure, would have been very proud.' She looked
at Braindead and couldn't prevent a tear instantly springing to her eye.
Being pregnant whilst replacing a dead mother was not something her
hormones were prepared to handle in a dignified manner.

'Don't be daft,' grinned Braindead. 'She would have said I looked
like a right tool dressed like this!'

'Well, I think you look very handsome,' said Katy, still trying to
fight back the tears.

'Well, it's a good job it's you standing here then and not my real
mum,' said Braindead, showing no emotion whatsoever.

Katy had never known Braindead's mum as she had died when he
was fifteen, way before Katy met him. Ben had told her that he only
saw Braindead cry once over her death. It was after the funeral when

he'd nicked a bottle of whisky from the wake and they'd hidden in the park and drank it between them. He'd cried then, he said. Even let Ben put his arm around him. Neither of them had ever touched whisky since though, and they had never spoken about Braindead's mum again either.

Katy wiped a tear from her eye. She had to pull herself together. It was her job to support Braindead, not make him sad. Not today. Today had to go well for him. She was his acting mum so she had to make sure he didn't screw it up. He was totally relying on her.

'So,' she said, looking at her watch, 'we should go downstairs in a minute. People will be arriving.'

'Really?' said Braindead, startled. 'It can't be that time already. I'm not ready.'

'What do you mean, not ready?' asked Ben. 'You are dressed up like a muppet. Of course you're ready.'

Braindead turned to look at him, a strange expression on his face.

'What if I'm not ready? Not ready to be... you know... a husband.'

Ben and Katy exchanged a look. They had been prepared for this moment. In the absence of his mother Braindead had often consulted Katy on the ways of the female mind so she had given some thought to how she would best advise him on being a husband, should he ask.

'I'll get the brandy,' said Ben, walking towards the mini bar.

Katy stood in front of Braindead and took both of his hands in hers. She cleared her throat.

'Listen to me,' she said gently, looking into his eyes. 'It's really easy to be a good husband and you *will* be a brilliant husband.'

'She's right,' said Ben, offering Braindead a glass with an inch of amber liquid in the bottom. He took it and threw it down his throat.

'But what do I do?' he asked, a slight tremble in his voice.

'We made a list,' said Katy, glancing over at Ben. 'We made a list of all the things you need to remember in order to be a good husband. We thought... well, we thought you might find it useful.'

'Of course,' cried Braindead, looking instantly relieved. 'A list! A list is great. A list is genius. Tell me what is on the list. I'm all ears.'

'Well,' said Katy, taking a piece of paper out of the pocket of her sky-blue dress coat that had fitted perfectly two weeks ago but was now straining over her bump. 'These are in no particular order, okay? I wanted to categorise it, but Ben said I was being anal so I'll just read them out as I wrote them down, shall I?'

'Just get on with it,' urged Ben, looking at his watch. 'We really need to be downstairs.'

'Right,' said Katy, clearing her throat again. 'How to be a good husband. Number one. Clean the toilet after you have used it.'

'Really?' asked Braindead.

'Really,' said Katy, nodding vigorously. 'It's so important. Much hostility can grow from the issue of toilet cleanliness. The most, in fact.'

'Okay,' nodded Braindead. 'Got that. Next?'

'Wash,' answered Katy. 'Keep yourself clean.'

'I'm pretty good at that,' he answered.

'You are not,' replied Katy and Ben in unison.

'Do you shower as soon as you get back from football?' asked Katy.

'Yes,' protested Braindead. 'Monday morning, I always shower.'

'When do you play football?' asked Katy.

'Saturday,' replied Braindead.

'Like I said, keep clean,' confirmed Katy. 'Share the chores,' she continued. 'Marriages are not glued together by gifts or soppy love messages or even grand romantic gestures, they are glued together by agreements on waste disposal and dishwasher duties.'

'Okay, if you say so. Understood,' said Braindead. 'I can do all that.'

'Good, that's the basics. Now listen closely to the following, because these are the tough ones. You must understand that neither of you is perfect. You *will* both screw up many times and so to be a good husband and to protect your marriage, you have to learn to forgive and forget.'

Katy felt Ben take her hand. She looked up at him gratefully. She understood only too well the importance of forgiveness to her own marriage. If it wasn't for forgiveness then she and Ben would not be married and certainly not standing here expecting their second child.

Braindead screwed his eyes up as though he was trying to make sense of what Katy was saying.

'Are you talking about the time when you had a one-night stand behind Ben's back?' he asked eventually.

Katy gasped. She felt Ben squeeze her hand.

'Well, yes, that is a very good example,' she replied. 'Of course, as you remember, we hadn't been going out long and we certainly weren't married. But, as you well know, Ben forgiving me for that stupid mistake meant we could go on to have a very brilliant, wonderful marriage.'

'I told him to forgive you,' added Braindead.

'I know,' Katy replied. 'And I am eternally grateful, but it is why *I* understand more than most how important it is to accept each other's failings and forgive them.'

'I get it,' said Braindead solemnly. 'Anything else?'

Katy swallowed, relieved to have got that one over with.

'Talk to each other,' she said. 'Communicate.'

'Have you met Abby?' asked Braindead, taking a step back and throwing his arms in the air in amazement.

'Good point,' agreed Katy. Abby could indeed talk for England. 'Did we forget anything?' Katy asked Ben.

'Always have sex on a Tuesday?' he replied with a grin.

Katy laughed. That had been Ben's chat-up line the first time they met. He'd asked her out and she told him she wasn't interested in him in that way so he said they would meet on a Tuesday then because no-one ever had sex on a Tuesday. He had some theory about it, which she had long forgotten. So they'd met on a Tuesday and she'd soon realised that she might have to change her mind about him. It was possibly a Saturday when they actually did have sex for the first time.

'Speaking of which,' asked Braindead, 'what are your tips for, you know… the wedding night shenanigans?'

'What do you mean?' asked Ben.

'Well, you need to perform, don't you, on your wedding night? Needs to be special. You actually need to do it to make it legal, don't you? It's like a law?'

'Well, we didn't,' replied Katy.

'What?' gasped Braindead. 'What do you mean?'

'We were just knackered, mate. And I think Millie kept getting up in the night so no chance there.'

'What? So you might not be married then?'

'You don't need to have sex on your wedding day to be married,' said Katy.

'Are you sure?' asked Braindead.

'Yes!' said Katy. 'Anyway, who on earth do you think is going to check?'

'I don't know,' replied Braindead. 'I thought you had to tick a box on your marriage certificate or something. I don't know, do I? I've never done this before!'

Katy looked at him in wonder. Maybe this was what happened when you didn't have a mother to ask the basic stupid questions. Maybe this was why Braindead could be so smart and then such an idiot sometimes. The fundamentals in life had never been covered.

'Of course you should try to have sex,' added Ben. 'I mean, it's ideal if you do, but it's not like you have to, not to seal the deal.'

'Wow,' said Braindead, sitting down heavily on the sofa. 'I'd... well... I'd... planned to make it really special, you know. Even looked stuff up on the internet.'

'Whatever you have looked up on the internet, don't do it,' said Katy, horrified.

'Really?' asked Braindead.

'No,' she said, shaking her head. 'Definitely not.'

'But I bought a—' started Braindead.

'Don't want to hear it, la, la, la,' said Katy, covering her ears with her hands.

'Okay, well maybe I can send it back. I think I kept the bubble wrap. As long as you are absolutely sure?' he asked.

'Really sure,' replied Katy, stepping forward to give him a reassuring hug. 'We are always here for you, you know that, don't you?' she added, starting to feel emotional again. 'And all those people downstairs, they all love you and are behind you every step of the way.'

'She's right, mate,' said Ben. 'It's going to be a great day.'

'I think you will find they are here for the free food and booze,' said Braindead with a grin. 'But anyway, I know with you two by my side nothing can go wrong, can it?'

Katy felt the baby kick in protest and a weird sinking feeling in her stomach.

'Of course not,' she replied. 'It will all go just like clockwork, I'm sure.' The baby kicked again.

Chapter Two

Ben

Ben took a sharp intake of breath as they stepped into the flower-infested room where Braindead was to be betrothed to Abby. Even to him it looked beautiful, with its avenue of ruby-red flower arrangements lining the aisle that ran down towards an archway of white roses and green foliage. It was stunning, romantic and grown-up. Words that Ben would never use to describe his buddy Braindead.

'Put one step in front of the other,' Ben said helpfully to Braindead when he appeared to be rooted to the spot in shock.

'What is all that stuff on the floor?' hissed Braindead.

'Petals,' Ben hissed back.

'Why?'

'I have no idea but go with it.'

'Okay. You never said I had to walk on petals. Did you walk on petals? Is that a thing?'

'No,' replied Ben. 'But you know we had a very different kind of wedding.'

'What on earth have you got around that man's neck?' came a cry from just inside the door. Ben looked up to see Daniel poised to welcome guests and hand out the Order of Service. He thrust the booklets at Ben and immediately began fussing with Braindead's cravat.

'Honestly, have you never done one of these before?' he sighed. 'Katy, what were you thinking, letting him come down the aisle looking like a dog's dinner?'

'I did the best I could,' mumbled Katy. 'I *am* pregnant.'

'Pregnant, shmegnant! That's your excuse for everything, young lady. You've got a free pass for looking shoddy today, Braindead hasn't.'

'I don't look shoddy, do I?' exclaimed Katy.

'All I can say,' said Daniel, 'is that you are supposed to hold the wedding inside the marquee, not be wearing it!'

Ben shook his head and tried not to laugh. He was about to tell Katy that she looked beautiful and she should ignore her acidic friend when Daniel started squealing like a demented piglet.

'I might faint with desire,' he said, throwing his hand to his forehead. 'Oh my goodness, I have come over all Jane Austen. Honestly, is it hot in here or am I seriously about to faint at the sight of the most gorgeous-looking human being that has ever attended a wedding in the history of weddings?'

'For goodness' sake, stop being so gay,' protested Katy.

Ben looked round to see the vision that was Daniel's boyfriend standing in the doorway. Gabriel was indeed standing there like a Jane Austen hero, hair flowing over his collar, his silhouette encased in a frame of white chrysanthemums and gypsophila.

'Daniel,' he cried, stepping forward. 'But you look so like a proper English gentleman today?' he said in his thick Spanish accent.

'And you look like… look like… well, words fail me,' said Daniel breathlessly, looking him up and down.

'Well, that's a first,' muttered Ben. He glanced over at Katy, who was pulling a face.

'This is my plus one,' Daniel announced spontaneously to a guest who had just arrived. 'Aren't I the luckiest man alive?'

The elderly gentleman in a pinstripe suit looked him up and down. 'I've just had my prostate fixed,' he announced. 'I can go for a piss again so I think you'll find that actually *I* am the luckiest man alive.' He reached forward and took an Order of Service from Daniel and strode down the aisle.

'I don't think he understands what I'm saying,' commented Daniel. 'I have been the dreaded "plus one" so many times I was thinking of charging an escort fee. Women were always ringing me up and saying – "I've just split up with my boyfriend and we were invited to a wedding so please be my plus one. A gay man would make the ideal companion." Talk about abuse of a friendship.'

'But you love weddings,' protested Katy.

'I know I do but it's so nice to be invited for my own sake rather than arm candy for desperate wannabe housewives!'

'I'd like to be a housewife,' announced Gabriel. 'Hard work, I think, but fun. I would enjoy breadmaking.'

Daniel gasped. 'Could he be more adorable?' he asked everyone.

'Well, you just remember you are only invited to this wedding because of me,' pointed out Katy. 'One of those pathetic females you just mentioned who used you so many times as their "escort". You only know Braindead because of *me*.'

'Correct,' agreed Daniel. 'I only know Braindead because it was he and I who were instrumental in dragging the two of you back together when "you know what" happened.'

Ben watched Katy's cheeks colour. He was right, of course. Daniel and Braindead had been the ones to talk Ben down from chucking in the towel on his relationship with Katy over the dreaded one-night stand but there was no need to mention it now. They were at a wedding, for goodness' sake!

'Speaking of the Devil,' said Daniel, looking towards the door again with a puzzled expression on his face. 'Is that Matthew? How interesting!'

Ben swirled around. Not Matthew, he thought. Surely not. Surely Braindead couldn't be really that... brain dead!

'Hello,' said Matthew, walking towards them.

Indeed, Matthew and his wife Alison had quite remarkably just arrived.

'Aww, thanks for coming, mate,' said Braindead, walking over and embracing the couple. 'I know it was last minute and everything but I wouldn't be here without you so it's only right that you are here. Matthew has been helping me with my accounts,' he told the stunned group staring awkwardly at the new arrivals. 'His tax evasion advice has paid for half the honeymoon and the Bon Jovi covers band.'

'It's *not* tax evasion,' urged Matthew, looking around guiltily. 'I keep telling you not to say it like that. That will get you and me into a lot of trouble.'

'Whatever you say, boss,' said Braindead, slapping Matthew on the back, 'but Bon Giovanni are appreciating my money a damn sight more than the Inland Revenue ever would, I can tell you.'

'Bon Giovanni?' whimpered a severely unimpressed-looking Alison.

'Yeah,' replied Braindead. 'The lead singer's grandmother is Italian, apparently.'

'Right,' said Alison. 'Do they sing the songs in Italian?'

'God no! Luke is a proper Yorkshire lad. Doesn't know a word of Italian. Although if you get him really drunk you can get him to do a version of "Living on a Prayer" entitled "Living on a Pizza". It's awesome.'

'I'm sure it is going to be the highlight of the entire day,' she grimaced. 'Let's just hope it doesn't end up like the last wedding we all attended together!'

Ben screwed his face up. He struggled to remember why on earth he would have attended a wedding with Matthew and Alison before this one and then it all came flooding back and he felt his face start to go crimson.

'It was… it was… highly entertaining,' he finally settled on.

'No, it wasn't,' bit back Alison. 'It was carnage.'

Ben and Matthew exchanged sheepish looks before pretending to study their Order of Services.

Alison was right.

It was carnage.

Matthew had chosen the occasion to tell Ben that he'd had a one-night stand with Katy at a school reunion they had both attended some time ago. The result had been a dirty scrap on the dance floor and the pair of them going home with their tails between their legs. Alison, in a severely pregnant state with twins, hadn't been told the cause of the fight. In fact, as far as anyone was aware, she was still oblivious to her husband's extra-marital indiscretion. Even if the rest of them weren't.

'Shall we sit down, Braindead?' said Ben, keen to move on. 'Abby should be here any minute and you need to look ready.'

'Do you know what?' replied Braindead, oblivious to the uncomfortable glances continuing between the group. 'I am ready,' he beamed. 'This is going to be the best wedding ever, I just know it. Let's do it, shall we?'

Chapter Three

Matthew

Matthew led Alison down the aisle then stepped aside to allow her into the row of white painted chairs. He sat down and breathed out.

He'd been genuinely chuffed that Braindead had generously invited him and Alison to the wedding last minute. There was no need really – he was just helping out with the basics with his tax. Easy stuff, to be honest. But nonetheless, he still felt honoured as the more he'd got to know Braindead the more he liked him. Braindead wasn't like the corporate types he met through work in their conforming suits and conforming views on the world. He had a weird, random, funny, bizarre mind and that was exactly what Matthew liked about him. After a hard day of making everything add up and make sense, he enjoyed the free-flow nature of Braindead's conversations.

'Red and white,' announced Alison, shaking her head as Matthew sat down.

'What?' he asked.

'You should never have red and white flowers at a wedding.'

'Why not?'

'They represent death.'

'What, like the Grim Reaper?'

Alison turned to look at him.

'Yes,' she hissed.

'Oh,' he said, looking down at his Order of Service.

'Do you remember our flowers?' asked Alison.

Matthew swallowed. Did he? Of course he didn't. Flowers? Were you supposed to remember flowers from your wedding day? Surely not. No man could be expected to remember flowers from their wedding day, could they?

'Of course I do,' he said, nudging her in what he hoped was a conspiratorial 'how could I ever forget our wedding flowers?' fashion.

'Which were your favourites?' she asked.

Favourites? Would he get away with saying, 'All of them'? Unlikely.

'Erm,' he said in a way he hoped indicated that he was thinking really hard about it rather than scanning his utterly flower-free set of memories.

'I know, I know, I know,' he said, wriggling in his seat, so pleased was he to stumble upon a vaguely flower-related memory. 'Actually, my favourite flowers were the hundreds of pink rose petals strewn all over our honeymoon suite. Do you remember those?'

'Of course I do,' replied Alison. 'I remember I picked every single one of them up whilst you snored for England in a star-shape formation in the middle of the bed so I couldn't get in. I slept in my dress on the chaise longue because I couldn't wake you up to help me get out of it. Oh yes, I really remember those pink rose petals.'

Matthew's shoulders slumped.

Neither of them said anything.

'You made up for it in Rome though,' Alison announced eventually.

Matthew's shoulders came back up.

'Well, when in Rome…' he said cheerily.

'Indeed,' she said, taking her turn to give him a conspiratorial nudge. 'Pity we never got to see much of the place on our honeymoon,' she added.

'Not a pity at all,' answered Matthew. 'I had the best view of Rome any newly married guy could wish for.'

They turned and grinned at each other. Matthew reached out and grasped Alison's hand. He looked into her eyes. He wanted to tell her that he thought she looked even more beautiful than she did on their wedding day but he wasn't sure if that would go down well. But in his eyes she did. The slight bulge at her waistline told the story of her bearing their four fantastic children, including a set of twins. The faint lines at the corners of her eyes showed the effort and passion she put into taking care of her family. The scratches on her wedding ring showed that it had stood the test of time just as their marriage had. He knew he was more in love with her now than on their wedding day because they had lived so much life together that it had made them stronger. He loved her then because of who she was, he loved her now because of what she had become. He was just about to tell her that when she asked a surprising question.

'Do you think we can escape after the speeches?'

'What do you mean?' asked Matthew.

'Well, it's not often we get a night off from the kids and a hotel room at our disposal, is it?'

Matthew felt his jaw drop. Was she really saying what he thought she was saying? She winked at him. Oh my goodness, she really was.

'You have to make the most of these opportunities, don't you? When you've got young children,' she continued. 'I've just written a whole piece on it on the blog. It's proved really popular. It's been shared over a thousand times.'

'You've written a piece on having sex at other people's weddings?' he asked, incredulous. When Alison had become a full-time mother she had transferred her skills from her previous HR career into helping other parents who were struggling with childrearing via a blog. So direct was her advice that it had gained a considerable following and she now even took on sponsors and advertisers. Matthew was extremely proud of her.

'Not weddings specifically,' said Alison. 'Just that when the kids are young you have to take the opportunity or make the opportunity. That's my advice. It's important to keep your marriage alive.'

'I couldn't agree more,' said Matthew. 'We can go before the speeches if you like?'

'Oh no,' said Alison, shaking her head. 'No, that would be rude. Let's stay and listen to the words of wisdom that I'm sure Braindead has to impart and then make a break for it. No-one will notice if we disappear for a bit. We hardly know anyone here, after all.'

'I love you,' he said, putting his arm around his wife and feeling a sense of utter contentment. Sex at someone else's wedding. What an absolute bonus!

Chapter Four

Ben

Ben glanced over at Braindead standing next to him, waiting for Abby to walk down the petal-strewn aisle. He noticed he was trembling ever so slightly and put his hand out to squeeze his arm.

'She looks amazing,' he told him.

'Does she?' Braindead asked. 'I'm not looking yet. What's she wearing?'

'A long white dress.'

'Helpful,' said Braindead. 'More info, please.'

'It's sparkly and I have to say there is an impressive cleavage on display.'

'That's my future wife you are talking about,' hissed Braindead.

'I know. I'm just saying it's kind of what you notice. It's impressive. She's here. Good luck, mate.'

Braindead turned to greet Abby and Ben allowed himself to breathe out. For some reason he felt even more nervous than on his own wedding day.

'Bloody hell Abby!' he heard Braindead say. 'You could park a Ford Cortina. Where have they come from?'

Ben took a sharp intake of breath. Now he knew exactly why he was nervous.

'Craig and Abigail, before you are joined in matrimony, I have to remind you of the solemn and binding character of the vows you are about to make. Marriage, according to the law of this country, is the union of two people, voluntarily entered into for life, to the exclusion of all others. Now I am going to ask each of you in turn to declare that you know of no lawful reason why you should not be married to each other—'

'Can I just ask a question?' said Braindead, interrupting the registrar.

The stern lady in a grey knee-length suit looked over the top of her glasses at him.

'Of course,' she replied. 'If you feel you must.'

'My friends told me you don't actually have to have sex on your wedding day in order to make it legal...'

Ben took another sharp intake of breath.

'You don't want to have sex with me!' exclaimed Abby.

'I do, yes, of course I do,' said Braindead. 'I just want to check because what if we forget or something and I don't want to wake up tomorrow and find out we are not really married. We can't afford to do this all over again just for the sake of not having sex. I mean, that would be stupid... and expensive.' He turned back to look at the registrar expectantly.

'Do you want me to answer your question now?' she asked.

'Yes, please,' nodded Braindead. 'I just want to be absolutely sure. It's important, isn't it?'

The lady pushed her glasses back up her nose, gave a bewildered glance at Abby and then turned to address Braindead.

'The law states that no, you do not have to have sex to make a marriage legal. However, if you don't have sex then you can annul the marriage should you wish, which is easier than a divorce. And just so you are aware, and if you should ever need this information in the future, this does *not* apply to same-sex couples.'

'Why not?' asked Braindead.

'I don't know,' the lady replied. 'I don't make the law.'

Braindead stared back at the lady. Ben held his breath.

'So the law doesn't care whether or not a gay couple have sex but it does if a non-gay couple does?'

'Basically, yes,' replied the lady. 'Shall we proceed?'

Braindead looked at her for a moment, clearly with things still on his mind. 'Just so I'm sure then, are there any other things I need to be aware of that could mean we aren't really married?' he asked.

'Not really the time to be asking, mate,' Ben hissed in his ear.

'Of course it is,' replied Braindead. 'I'm entering into a legal contract. I want to know it's binding.'

'If your wife did not properly consent to the marriage then the marriage could also be annulled,' said the lady in grey, her eyebrows raised high in astonishment at this unusual conversation. 'For example, if she was drunk when she agreed.'

'Of course she was drunk,' replied Braindead. 'It was a Friday night down the Rose and Crown.' He turned back to Ben. 'This is what I mean. This could all be a waste of time.'

The lady in grey turned to Abby. 'Did you properly consent to marry this man? Are you here against your will?' she asked.

'Of course not!' exclaimed Abby. 'I've been waiting my whole life for this moment.'

'Really,' replied the lady, raising her eyebrows further in the direction of Braindead. 'And, while we are at it then, do either of you have a sexually transmitted disease? You could annul the marriage if this was the case.'

'No!' said Braindead and Abby together.

'Not since...' began Braindead before Ben kicked him hard on the ankle.

'Then the only other thing we should check before we get on with the main ceremony and actually get you married is if Abigail here thinks it is at all possible that she could be pregnant with another man's child.'

The audience gasped. Ben bit his lip. He could feel nervous giggles coming on now.

'I am most certainly not pregnant,' announced Abby. 'With anyone's child. In *this dress*?'

'Excellent news,' replied the lady in grey. 'I can now declare that you are both eligible to get married and stay married. Congratulations!'

'Is this the moment when I get to kiss the bride?' asked Braindead.

Chapter Five

Katy

Katy knew she probably had the imprint of the loo seat on her backside by now. But it was a much better place for her, here in the ladies' toilets rather than standing for God knew how long, holding a glass of orange juice and praying the canapé tray would come her way if she looked pleadingly enough at the bored-looking waitresses, whilst everyone else got roaring drunk. She was beyond tired, beyond hungry, beyond the hideous craving for a drink to speed up the pain of an eight-hour day on her feet. She'd fled the library where drinks were being held, grabbed some bread rolls from the neatly lined-up baskets in the dining room and camped out in the toilets.

Once installed, she had released her poor baby bump from its hideous encasement of maternity tights and sternly told her yet-to-be-born child that his/her wedding must be to an American, where they were much more sensible about these kind of events. Wedding at 5 p.m., food at 7 p.m., dancing at 9 p.m. How marvellous compared to the long, drawn-out affairs of the British.

Katy knew she had the best seat in the house when, as she tucked into her second bread roll, in came the mother and sister of the bride, who had a blazing row about a corner cupboard that had not been allocated in Abby's father's will. It was a lively and colourful debate which left Katy wondering why no-one had corner cupboards any more as she brought up the Ikea website on her phone to find that even the ubiquitous furniture retailer didn't stock them. It made her feel nostalgic for the oak corner cupboard that used to hang in her parents' dining room, hiding the secret stash of Martini, Cinzano and Babycham. Katy sighed. She wondered what had happened to that corner cupboard in the aftermath of her parents' move to Spain some years ago. She wasn't sure if it had made the cut. After all, drinks didn't need to be hidden any more. Her parents had a bar in the lounge of their villa to entertain their expat friends, complete with a pineapple ice bucket and a glass full of paper umbrellas. She wondered fleetingly whether her parents had hosted Carlos at their in-house bar and if alcohol had a part to play in the lubricating of her mother's affair with the local bar owner. Perhaps her parents would still be together if they had kept the alcohol hidden in the corner cupboard.

She sighed again as she heard Abby's mum and sister leave. Both pretty drunk, she could tell. This do was going to get messy. It was written all over it and all she could do was pretend to enjoy it as she lugged over ten pounds of additional weight around the dance floor, regretting having taken advantage of the 'eating for two' rule. People should be banned from getting married when close friends were pregnant, she decided. It was just cruel. And of course this wasn't the only wedding she had to face this summer. If only. But she wouldn't think about that one today. One wedding at a time.

She hauled herself up from the toilet. She had to face the inevitable. Politeness in the face of much drunkenness. Her favourite thing. Not. She picked up her bag. Mustn't forget that. Her sobriety had put her in charge of keeping hold of the best man's speech. Ben had practised his in front of her the night before and it was a fitting tribute to his best friend, full of affectionate stories of their childhood together and funny anecdotes of Braindead's many fantastic one-liners. It glowed with Ben's love of his friend and she hoped that Braindead would appreciate it.

She also hoped that Braindead had at least put some thought into his speech. When she had asked him about it quietly he'd said he was going to be spontaneous. Just say how he felt in the moment. As a responsible stand-in mother, she had advised him to at least write a few notes, to be on the safe side. Just in case the moment rendered him speechless but he had assured her that there was absolutely no need: he wanted his speech to come from the heart, not a stack of prompt cards. She couldn't argue with that but still she had a slightly uneasy feeling about leaving Braindead completely to his own devices in front of a listening audience. His brain and mouth had a habit of disengaging and she just hoped that the seriousness of the occasion would prevent him from completely letting himself down and saying something he might regret for the rest of his life.

Chapter Six

Katy

Katy thought it was the biggest worry of all leading up to any wedding.

Where you had been put on the seating plan.

It's a caused anxiety for two reasons.

One, because it confirmed your status in relation to the happy couple. Were you in the 'fun friends' gang or the 'I'm not that fussed about you so I'll stick you with the boring relatives' gang?

And two, it confirmed whether or not the bride and groom actually wanted to talk to you on the day. Have they located you next to the top table or do they clearly not give a toss if they see you at all so have put you on the table next to the toilets at the back of the room?

Friendships can be confirmed and uplifted on the basis of wedding seating plans or, quite frankly, ended.

Katy supposed she had to feel lucky to be on the top table at Braindead and Abby's wedding. Well, she was the mother of the groom, after all, and her husband was best man and their daughter was a bridesmaid so they really had little choice but to include her. However, her placing on the said top table didn't feel quite so lucky, especially as it was a long, oblong table at one end of the room, making her feel like she was in the grand dining room at Hogwarts and cast as a snooty teacher rather than having fun with all the naughty pupils. Next to her was Millie, who had been placed on the end, presumably so she could wreak her nearly four-year-old havoc as far away from the happy couple as possible, and on the other side the slightly terrifying Erica, Braindead's sister, who was also acting as bridesmaid. Erica, in some bizarre twist of genetic engineering, was a model, much to Abby's distress. Abby had assumed from Braindead's description of his sister that she was maybe a catalogue model or a hand model as he had not made a big deal out of it. But remarkably, Braindead's sister turned out to be a model of the highest order: catwalks, magazine photoshoots for top brands, you name it. Could you imagine the disaster of planning your wedding and your future sister-in-law showing up with legs up to her armpits and cheekbones chiselled in Yorkshire stone?

'Why didn't you tell me Braindead's sister was a real model?' Abby had asked Ben after they had picked her up from the airport two days earlier on her flight in from Milan.

'I did say she was a real model.'

'You never said how stunning she is and she does real modelling, like designer clothes and make-up and stuff?'

'Does she?'

'Yes, she showed me her portfolio. Well, I made her – she didn't want to. I never thought that Braindead would ever have a sister who would look like that! He always calls her Eric and said she looked like a man!'

'Ah, well that's because she was such a tomboy when she was a kid. She's got really big hands. Have you noticed? She used to kick our ass snowballing when we were kids. She'd get those hands full of snow and shove them down our trousers. I have very fond memories of that.'

When Ben had told Katy Abby's reaction to 'Eric' she had laughed before agreeing that a catwalk model as a bridesmaid and sister-in-law was probably a bride's worst nightmare.

So now, as she sat at the top table, she had a choice between conversation regarding how many episodes of *Peppa Pig* a wedding lasts for and what were her views on Gucci's latest collection. Neither of which appealed in her sober pregnant state and so she stared mournfully out at the sea of bobbing happy faces, who appeared to be having the time of their lives.

'Stop stealing my food,' cried Millie as Katy idly plucked a French fry off Millie's plate of pizza and chips.

'But I wasn't lucky enough to get chips,' said Katy mournfully. 'I got bland chicken with bland vegetables and a single overcooked roast potato.'

'Why didn't you ask for chips?' asked Millie, smearing ketchup around her plate.

'Because you get treated specially because you are a kid. I had to have the grown-ups' menu.'

'Who says?' asked Millie.

Katy thought for a moment.

'Nobody, really. They don't ask you what you want typically, just the kids.'

'If they had asked, would you have said pizza and chips?'

'God, yeah!' said Katy.

'And me,' added Erica, turning to them with a grin. 'Can I have one of your chips?'

Millie stared at the pretty lady then stared down at her plate. She carefully selected the smallest chip and held it up for her in her tiny fingers.

'Millie,' admonished Katy.

Millie stared at her, wide-eyed.

'Sorry,' she said, blinking. 'Would you like ketchup?' she asked Erica.

Katy hoped the ground would swallow her up.

'No, thank you,' laughed Erica and reached over and grabbed the chip out of Millie's hand and put it in her mouth. 'I tell you what,' she mumbled as she chewed, 'wish I'd been offered the kids' menu. These chips are the best I've ever tasted.' She winked at Millie.

Katy cast a glance down towards Erica's tiny waist encased in teal silk and wondered whether the last time she had tasted chips had been before she started school.

'Don't you reckon much to wedding food then either?' Katy asked, trying to make conversation.

'Depends,' shrugged Erica. 'I have to say that Donatella's wedding feast at Castiglioni della Pescaia in Tuscany was to die for, to be honest.'

'Right,' nodded Katy. 'I'm sure.'

'Then of course Ricardo and Jamie's Moroccan-themed banquet in Bedouin tents on the banks of the Nile would take a bit of beating.'

'Obviously,' agreed Katy.

They fell silent for a moment as Katy struggled to drag up a wedding that might stand up to the two extravaganzas that Erica had described.

'Just kidding,' said Erica, bursting into peals of laughter. 'Your face,' she added, cracking up.

It took Katy a moment to realise that Erica had been winding her up. There was no need for wedding envy, Erica hadn't experienced the ultimate in wedding fayre.

'The Bedouin tents weren't on the banks of the River Nile,' continued Erica. 'How weird would that be? Moroccan food in Egypt? No, they had the tents in Jamie's parents' garden in Malvern on the banks of the River Thames.'

'Right,' nodded Katy. 'Of course. In someone's garden on the Thames. How lovely!'

'Oh, for fuck's sake, I'm still kidding!' said Erica. 'You having a sense of humour failure or what? Posh weddings still have shit food, believe you me. There's just less of it. No-one eats at posh weddings, they just regurgitate kale, like they're a field full of cows or something. This is a massive step up from a society wedding. I get to sit down, there's a plate with food on it, someone has chips, and they gave me one. I love this wedding!'

Katy smiled at Erica. Despite being stunningly beautiful and gorgeous and skinny, Katy thought she might find she could face liking her.

'Now, give me the low-down on Abby,' Erica said. 'I have to say, she wasn't what I expected my little brother to shack up with but she seems to love him, right? She's an utter nightmare but besotted by my weirdo brother, am I right?'

'Pretty much,' agreed Katy. 'Where Braindead is concerned, her heart is totally in the right place.'

'Well then, she'll do for me,' said Erica. 'I'm glad he's happy. And I'd just like to thank you, for you know, standing in for Mum. It's really good of you and I can tell Craig thinks a lot of you.'

Katy felt a small tear start to nudge at the corner of her eye.

'It's an honour. I'm very fond of Braindead – sorry, Craig.'

'I think it's a good job he's got you around to keep him on the straight and narrow. I dread to think what he would get up to if he was left to his own devices.'

'I think, despite appearances and actions, that he has his head screwed on,' said Katy.

Erica nodded. 'I just hope he remembers to mention Mum in his speech. She would have liked that.'

Katy thought she saw a tear threatening to hover at the corner of Erica's eye too.

'He said he wasn't preparing a speech,' she admitted. 'He said he wanted to say whatever he was feeling in the moment.'

'Right,' nodded Erica. 'Not reassuring in the slightest.'

'I know,' said Katy. 'I tried to encourage him to have something prepared, just in case, but he wasn't having it.'

Erica took a deep breath just as someone tapped a fork on the side of a champagne glass, heralding the start of the speeches.

'I'm sure he'll do you and your mum proud,' said Katy.

'Let's hope so,' muttered Erica. 'I'll see you on the other side.'

Chapter Seven

Ben

'...and then of course there was the time when Braindead lost his virginity at the bus stop...'

Ben paused. He was good at this best man speech malarkey, he decided. It was a piece of cake... literally. He'd started with the cake joke: 'Well, ladies and gentlemen, it's been an emotional day... even the cake is in tiers...' which had gone down well with the older generation, then he'd moved on to introducing himself. 'So, I'm Ben, Craig's best man, who I've had the pleasure of knowing since we were four years old. Now, he's asked me not to mention any embarrassing stories or mistakes or mishaps he may have had in the past so thanks for listening, everyone, that's it from me.' Then he'd actually sat down; God he was hilarious. He had the whole audience in the palm of his hand.

So he'd rolled out a few palatable stories of Braindead's numerous escapades over the years Ben had known him, but really he had been spoilt for choice. He probably could have written a book about Braindead, never mind a speech. To Millie's delight, he had raised the infamous story of Braindead putting himself through the Christmas tree wrapping machine at the garden centre then lining himself up alongside all the other trees and frightening a poor couple half to death. He'd had to mention Gloria of course. His first love. A stuffed puffin that resided in a pub in Otley that Braindead would buy a packet of prawn cocktail crisps for whenever they went in. Ben conceded that Abby was certainly a step up from a stuffed puffin, though a fair bit more high maintenance, given that she preferred piña coladas to prawn cocktail crisps.

It was going so well he'd thought he'd risk a 'Braindead's previous sex life' story. However, as he looked around the room and as Abby gave him a vicious stare, he decided that he should quit whilst he was ahead. He laughed before telling the crowd that of course Braindead wasn't at a bus stop when he lost his virginity. He'd just wanted to be as he'd heard that thing about buses: 'That if you wait long enough three will come at once!'

There was a pause then uproarious laughter from the drunken friends' table and Abby's cousins' table. He'd got away with it despite the fact that Braindead had actually lost his virginity at the bus stop, the joke being that he reckoned he couldn't take his eyes off the LED screen telling him when his bus was due and so had timed everything accordingly.

Ben glanced over at Braindead, who was beaming at him. He also looked pleased that he hadn't let this story slip. But then Braindead had been doing a lot of beaming lately. He was happy and that made Ben happy. Ben loved Braindead and couldn't imagine his life without him.

He cleared his throat and looked up from his notes, which had been carefully written out for him on prompt cards by Katy. He took a deep breath.

'Finally, ladies and gentlemen, I cannot let this opportunity go by without telling you really who Braindead is. I need to call him Braindead now because that's how I know him. I may be the best man here today but I want to tell you that Braindead is the best man I have ever met in my entire life. The best mate anyone could wish for. I call him Braindead to stop him realising that he is the funniest, wisest, most honest and brilliant and modest human being I know. I am so happy that he has found Abby, who makes him the happiest I have ever seen him. But can I ask you, please, Abby, if you would occasionally let me borrow him because he's my best mate and I cannot imagine my life without him. He's got me through so many things I can't even begin to tell you.'

Ben felt his voice start to crack and tears spring to his eyes. This wasn't supposed to happen; he had to gather himself.

'And I'm so happy that you've found someone, Braindead, because you… well, you…' Ben glanced over towards Katy. 'If it wasn't for you then… Well, let's just say that you have helped me through some sticky patches when it comes to relationships.'

He glanced over again at Katy, who was smiling back, knowing exactly what he meant. Braindead had been instrumental in persuading Ben to attend the birth of Millie despite the fact that Ben had just found out about Katy's one-night stand and there was a chance that Millie wasn't even his daughter. And thank God he had. He couldn't imagine how much he would have kicked himself not to have witnessed Millie's arrival with a full shock of ginger hair, leaving everyone in no doubt whatsoever that she was Ben's.

Ben turned to face Abby. 'Look after him, Abby. You have got yourself the best man there is. He's lucky to have found you and you are lucky to have found him. Braindead, you are a rock star and I love you.'

The crowd *aahed* in unison.

'May I propose a toast to the happy couple,' said Ben, raising his glass, his voice cracking.

'I love you too, mate,' said Braindead, getting up to engulf Ben in a hug as everyone around them rose to their feet and toasted the bride and groom.

Nailed it, thought Ben, hugging Braindead back. He'd not let his friend down. *Now* he could relax.

Chapter Eight

Matthew

Wow, thought Matthew. He'd never seen that before at a wedding. A declaration of love not between the bride and groom, but the groom and best man. Maybe it was because Braindead's mother had died young; he supposed that would have pushed them together. Made them closer. Matthew shook his head. Why on earth was he thinking about this? Who cared why Braindead and Ben were so in love? All they had to do was get through the groom's speech and apparently he was on a promise in a hotel bedroom upstairs. Happy days!

He reached over and squeezed Alison's hand. It had been a bearable two hours. They had been allocated a table with Abby's aunties and uncles so it was clear that Braindead, despite his gratitude, didn't like him enough to plunge him onto a table of his mates. Ah well. He was about to have sex, so who cared?

He leaned over to whisper in Alison's ear.

'So it must just be the groom's speech now,' he said. 'I can't imagine Braindead will have that much to say, can you? Shall we make a run for it as soon as he's finished? Excuse ourselves to use the bathroom or something?'

Alison nodded, a small smile at her lips.

Wow, thought Matthew. Who would have thought that this could be the best wedding he had ever been to? He'd never had sex at a wedding. Never. Not even his own, as Alison had reminded him earlier.

So finally he could pretend this was his wedding night and have the sex he should have had then. Tremendous!

He looked up, hoping to see Braindead ready to embark on his speech, but instead he was sitting back in his chair, sobbing.

'What's wrong with him?' Matthew asked Alison.

'Overcome with emotion, I think,' she replied.

For fuck's sake, thought Matthew. Why now? Totally unnecessary. He had things to do. He had an appointment in a bed upstairs to keep.

'Oh, he's getting up,' announced Alison.

Matthew watched as Ben helped him stand and then they embraced again before pulling apart. Ben patted him on the shoulder and went to take his seat. A spontaneous round of applause rippled around the room. It looked like Braindead was going to let his emotions get the better of him again but he rallied, took a handkerchief out of his pocket, blew his nose then took a deep breath.

'Oh, mate,' he said, shaking his head from side to side and staring at Ben.

'Look at your new wife,' muttered Alison. 'He should be looking at Abby, not Ben.'

'Oh, mate,' repeated Braindead. 'I… I… can't tell you how much that meant to me. I mean, you're my best mate. You've always been there. When my mum died, you were there. You stuck by me despite the fact I was a miserable bastard for a while. You've always stuck by me. And then Katy came along, clearly the love of your life, but you didn't leave me behind. No, I was right there with you. Both of you, and I will never forget that. Never.'

'Talk about Abby,' Alison urged again under her breath, so only Matthew could hear.

Matthew looked over at her sympathetically. She was right, of course. It was borderline obscene the amount of love Braindead was throwing Ben's way. He couldn't imagine that any bride would be happy with such a distraction away from her.

'And I tell you something,' Braindead continued. 'You are an amazing husband, Ben, and if I can be half the husband you are, I'll have done well.' Braindead looked over at Ben and they shared a look that acknowledged a thousand memories.

'I will never forget that day we sat on the train coming back from Edinburgh to see Millie being born,' continued Braindead, shaking his head. 'I was in awe of you, mate. In awe that your love meant more than the fact that she'd had a one-night stand with her ex-boyfriend at a school reunion.'

There was an audible gasp from some of the members of the audience and some confused glances, but Braindead seemed to have got so caught up in what he was trying to express to his buddy that he appeared to have forgotten he was in a room full of people making his bridegroom's speech. Possibly the most important speech of his life.

Whispers started to circulate as people tried to work out what he was saying. This seemed to wake Braindead up from his trance-like state as he stared into the eyes of a now horrified-looking Ben. He looked up as he heard the shocked murmurs and finally addressed his audience.

'I know! Can you believe it?' he asked them. 'What a guy! What a man!' He turned back to look at Ben. 'You are my role model. You know that, don't you?' he said. 'You epitomise what it is to be a truly great husband. You told me earlier that you have to learn to forgive and forget in order for a marriage to survive. It's essential to any marriage, isn't it?'

He looked back out to the crowd. Some looked awkwardly away, clearly having spent their entire married lives harbouring the resentments that are waiting to trip up every couple.

'So let's raise a glass, shall we?' said Braindead. 'I'd like to toast Ben Chapman. The best man and the best husband I have ever known.'

Braindead cheerily raised his glass in the air to stunned silence before a few of the audience managed to gather themselves and stand to join him in his unconventional toast.

Chapter Nine

Matthew

Alison had raised her eyebrows at Matthew when Braindead had indicated in his ramble that Katy had been unfaithful to Ben. She'd raised them in a way that said she wasn't surprised, whilst Matthew's insides felt like they were about to drop out of his backside. A terror gripped him like he'd never experienced. What was Braindead thinking? What was he doing, declaring his own stand-in mother a bit of a slapper at his wedding… in his speech? Only the utter idiot who was Braindead could even begin to think that this was appropriate. Everything within Matthew's body remained clenched as Braindead continued. He fought the urge to get up and wrestle him to the ground in a spectacular James-Bond-style rugby tackle and stuff peach linen napkins in his mouth. Anything to stop him talking.

He also fought the urge to put his hands over Alison's ears as Braindead stumbled on. Or distract her away from potential catastrophe. Perhaps he should get up and fling her over his shoulder in a Tarzan-like fashion and take her up to the bedroom right now before Braindead could spill any more contaminated beans.

Through his mist of terror Matthew kept hearing Braindead's dastardly disclosure '…she'd had a one-night stand with her ex-boyfriend at a school reunion'. The clenching was at metal vice force now. He looked over to Alison to see what she was doing. She was looking around in amusement at those gasping at Braindead's terrible indiscretion, then turned to see Katy's reaction, who had turned bright red in mortification. Don't look at me, Katy, willed Matthew. Whatever you do, don't look at me.

He turned back to look at Alison. It's all right, he reassured himself, Braindead didn't mention my name. Alison won't make the connection. She can't. Sure, she knows we were at school together, but as far as she's concerned, we barely knew each other. She never knew he and Katy were inseparable throughout sixth form until he went to uni. Alison didn't know any of that. And she wouldn't remember that he'd gone to that reunion. No way. They'd just started yet another round of IVF at the time. She'd been obsessed with getting pregnant. There was no way she would remember he went to the reunion whilst up in Leeds at a meeting. In fact, he might not have even mentioned it. For all she knew, he'd stayed the night with his friend and colleague Ian. They'd gone out for a few beers after work; he probably never even mentioned the school reunion. No, there was no way she would remember it. After all, it was over five years ago.

Alison didn't look at him for the rest of Braindead's speech as the groom finally got round to talking about his new wife and how beautiful she was, blah, blah, blah. Unfortunately, after his impassioned speech about Ben and the fact that much of the audience were now in gossipy whispering mode, his toast to his new wife was rather a damp squib.

Everyone settled back in their chairs and awkwardly resumed their chatter, the speeches over and everyone wondering how soon would be acceptable to get up and go to the bar.

Alison turned and gave him a quizzical look and Matthew knew. He knew instantly that the words 'school reunion' had rung some kind of distant bell.

'Different!' said Matthew as jovially as he could muster. 'Trust Braindead to give the weirdest groom's speech of all time. You ready?' he asked. Perhaps if he distracted the wheels of her mind quick enough then they wouldn't lock into a destructive conclusion.

'Didn't you go to a school reunion?' she asked. Her brow was furrowed, the cogs were still turning.

'Oh yeah, I did, didn't I? I'd forgotten about that. Christ, that was a while ago!'

'It was five-and-a-half years ago on 8 December. I'd had the eggs planted that turned into Rebecca and George a week before. I was home alone, petrified it was all going to go wrong again, and you chose to stay up in Leeds and go for a night out rather than come home.' She said all this in a blank tone as though reading it from someone else's diary.

'Really?' replied Matthew. 'Christ, you've got a good memory!' He stood up and held out his hand to her. 'Come on, let's go upstairs,' he said.

She looked up at him, not moving, staring into his eyes.

'I don't think you ever mentioned that Katy was there,' she said slowly and deliberately. 'You told me you were at school together but you never said when we met her again that you'd seen her at the school reunion.'

Matthew felt his jaw go slack whilst everything else tensed. He shook his head, hoping that would buy him time to think of a plausible excuse.

'Er, I don't remember seeing her there. It was kind of busy – I stood at the bar most of the time, to be honest. And I barely knew her. We didn't hang around in the same crowd. Perhaps she spent the night on the dance floor?'

'Or shagging her ex-boyfriend by the sounds of it,' said Alison, the quizzical look still firmly on her face. 'Did you know him?'

Matthew unclenched ever so slightly. Maybe this was the safe path they could go down. Well away from him.

'Oh yes. I remember now. Barney Richardson. They were thick as thieves, quite the couple. I bet it was him.' Alison didn't look convinced. 'I remember she used to come and tell me how much she loved him and wanted to have his babies,' Matthew ploughed on.

Alison screwed her eyes up really tight as though trying to look deep inside his soul. He felt terrified… and naked.

'You just said you barely knew her and yet she used to come and confide her innermost feelings to you?' Alison said slowly.

'Er, well maybe she didn't say that to me… maybe she said that to one of my mates… No, I bet it was Paula, she used to hang around with us at the time. I bet she said it to her. They were big pals. Paula must have told me.'

He was sweating. All over. The lies had made him perspire at an alarming rate and Alison persisted in keeping him under her laser-strength stare.

She got up suddenly.

'I'm going to see if Katy's all right,' she said. 'Must have been so humiliating to have been outed as a slapper in front of an entire wedding. Perhaps she needs a shoulder to cry on.'

'No…' said Matthew, too quickly. Way too quickly. He realised his mistake as Alison's eyes screwed up even further. 'I bet she would prefer to be left alone,' he said. 'As you say, she must feel humiliated. Perhaps you would only rub it in.'

They stared at each other for a few seconds. Matthew could feel his heart thumping. He was surprised that the whole room couldn't hear it.

Alison folded her arms and made no move to find Katy.

'But what if she still has feelings for Barney?' she asked. 'You said he was the love of her life…'

'No… no…' said Matthew. 'She's over him, I swear. She loves Ben. And Barney, well, he's got no feelings for her either… It was just a stupid… stupid one-night stand. They both really regret it, I know they do. It's the worst thing they have ever done and if they could turn back time then they would and stop it happening.'

Alison said nothing.

Matthew knew he had said too much.

She turned and walked away.

'Where are you going?' he asked, pulling up alongside her as she strode purposefully through the dining room.

'To find your ex-girlfriend,' she grimaced.

Chapter Ten

Katy

For the second time during the wedding Katy found herself hiding in the ladies' loos. But this time her heart was beating at a scary pace. She sat on the toilet, stroking her belly.

'It's all right,' she soothed. 'It's all going to be all right.' She didn't know whether she was talking to her unborn baby or to herself.

What was Braindead thinking? Total and utter humiliation along with getting far too close to revealing the secret that had kept them all on the brink of a nervous breakdown for a long time. Had he totally forgotten that he had invited Matthew and Alison to the wedding? Braindead so deserved his nickname. Today of all days… his wedding day. And yet she was supposed to be looking out for him today. Making sure he didn't make any cock-ups. Well, she'd certainly failed there, hadn't she?

She heard the door to the ladies' swing open and she automatically raised her feet off the ground so that should someone look underneath the door, it would be as if she wasn't there. She'd seen it in the films. It always worked.

'I'm really sorry but I'm looking for my wife,' she heard Ben ask a lady, who must be still washing her hands. She'd been at it for what felt like ages.

There was a pause.

'You're the best man, aren't you?' she heard the woman ask. 'The one with the wife who had the one-night stand at the school reunion or something?'

Utter silence.

'The thing is, I was hoping to bump into you to, you know, offer my sympathies and, well, I know this might sound pushy and everything, but they do say that you are most likely to meet your future partner at a wedding and… well, I've been to a lot of weddings, like hundreds of weddings, and I haven't met him yet, but when I saw you get up and do your speech and you were so… well, so adorable, and then Craig said that your wife had cheated on you well… well, I just wanted to say that you know that I've never cheated on anyone in my life and you seem like such a decent man and so if you fancied, you know… swapping numbers and maybe we could go out sometime and…'

'I'm in here!' shouted Katy. She couldn't stand it any longer.

'Katy!' she heard Ben exclaim.

'Oh my God,' the woman had the decency to say. 'Oh God, I am so sorry, so, so sorry, I had no idea you were… you were…'

'Just leave!' Katy shouted back over the toilet door. 'Just please go.'

'Of course,' muttered the woman. 'I'm so sorry… so sorry… I really hope you get back together…'

'We are together,' pointed out Ben.

'Of course, of course you are, I'll go… I'm going…' she shouted loudly, presumably directed at Katy.

'If you ever need to talk,' Katy heard the woman whisper, 'Abby has my number.'

'I can hear you,' shouted Katy.

She heard the door to the ladies' bang shut.

'Are you all right?' asked Ben through the door.

'No,' cried Katy. 'What was Braindead thinking? What am I going to do? I can't go out there now. And everyone will be talking and whispering about me and... and it's all my fault... I've embarrassed you again as well. Oh, Ben, I'm so sorry.'

'Look, come out of there and let's go back in together. Half an hour of the free bar and everyone will have forgotten about it, honestly. We'll kill Braindead later when we can get him alone. Mind you, I think we'll have to line up behind Abby. She's none too impressed with his speech either and the fact that she didn't really feature in it.'

'Everyone's going to think I'm such a slapper,' wailed Katy.

'Thank goodness he didn't mention Matthew by name,' said Ben. 'That would have been a disaster.'

'Oh my God... Oh my God...' Katy thought she was starting to hyperventilate. 'Oh my God, Ben. This is a disaster of epic proportions. Are you sure Braindead didn't say Matthew's name? Are you absolutely sure? Oh my God, I'm so sorry, Ben. I can't believe I'm putting you through this... and on your best friend's wedding day. Are you sure he didn't mention any names?'

'Absolutely sure. All he said was about it happening at a school reunion. No names. Nothing. As long as Matthew keeps his cool there is absolutely nothing to let the cat out of the bag.'

Katy suddenly heard a commotion as the door into the ladies' swept open.

'Alison, don't,' were the words that heralded the doom that was about to fall.

'Alison, please, no,' Katy heard Matthew repeat.

'Is she in there?' she heard Alison ask Ben.

'I am,' said Katy, getting up and opening the door. This wasn't Ben's carnage to deal with.

Katy waddled out into the narrow corridor between the toilets and the sinks. She watched as Alison caught sight of her pregnant bump and sensed her soften slightly. It would be hard to be vile to a pregnant woman, however much she deserved it. She glanced over at Matthew, who had turned a classic Farrow & Ball grey. Had Alison put two and two together and connected Matthew and Katy's pasts together? Their dramatic arrival in the ladies' toilets would indicate that yes, she had. Men in a ladies' toilet would indicate a crisis looming. What else could it indicate? A transgender issue, these days, crossed her mind. There was hope yet!

'I just wanted to clear something up,' said Alison, glancing at Ben this time. 'I'm sorry if this puts you in an awkward position, Ben. I realise this can't be easy for you but I need to ask Katy about Barney.'

'Barney?' said Katy and Ben in unison.

'Yes, Barney,' urged Matthew. 'Barney, the guy you used to go out with at school. The guy I assumed you had the one-night stand with that Braindead so crassly mentioned in his speech.'

A moment's silence.

'Oh yeah, Barney!' shrieked Katy. 'That Barney. My ex Barney.'

'Of course, Barney!' cried Ben. 'Oh yeah, I know all about Barney. Great guy.'

'You see, Alison, Ben and I hadn't been seeing each other for very long and it was just a stupid one-night stand.'

'Braindead made it sound so much worse than it was,' agreed Ben. 'And it was so far in the past that it's all forgotten. Can't believe he was idiotic enough to mention it today. What a numpty!'

Alison stared back at him, blinking.

'You knew,' she whispered.

'What?' said Ben.

'You knew,' she whispered again to him.

Katy stared at her. She couldn't read it. Had Alison cracked it or not? What did she think Ben knew?

'How could you?' said Alison, shaking her head first at Ben, then at Katy and finally, at Matthew.

The door to the ladies' burst open and two fascinator-clad ladies rolled into the narrow room.

'If I don't get these body-shaper pants off there's no way I'm going to be able to drink any more red wine. It's like they're not just squeezing my fat into submission, they're squeezing my liver too,' said one of the ladies before she caught sight of the unlikely gathering at the far end of the toilets.

'Oh right,' she exclaimed, after she had spotted them.

'Leave,' growled Alison, turning to face them.

'Right, shit, okay,' said the lady, grabbing her friend's hand. They started backing out the door as fast as they could. 'Of course, yes, goodbye.'

Alison turned back to the petrified trio but said nothing, confusion and pain written all over her face.

'Alison, it's not what you think,' gasped Matthew, caving first. 'It was a stupid, stupid one-night stand. I, I, was drunk, I lost my head, it was totally meaningless. It meant totally nothing, nothing at all. Did it, Katy?' He turned to face Katy, whose immediate thought was *Don't drag me into it* – until she realised she was in it whether she liked it or not.

'I don't know what to say, Alison,' said Katy, trying to fight off the distraught tears. 'Matthew's right. We… we…'

'Don't… say… we,' spat Alison.

'I mean of course, no, I mean...' spluttered Katy. 'I'm just trying to agree that it was stupid, and thoughtless and reckless and it meant absolutely nothing at all and if I could make it go away I would, but I can't and I wish with all my heart it never happened. I wish every single day that it had never happened.'

'Me too,' nodded Matthew aggressively. 'There is not a day that goes by when I don't feel so ashamed of myself...'

'How did it happen?' demanded Alison.

'What?' cried Matthew. 'What do you mean?'

'I mean, I want to know,' she said in the most scary, menacing tone that Katy had ever heard. 'I want to know *exactly.*'

Matthew swallowed and glanced at Katy, petrified. 'So, er... so I got in a fight with, er... what was his name?'

Katy shook her head, the fear wracking her body making logical thought impossible.

'You remember him?' urged Matthew.

'I don't,' squeaked Katy.

'You do,' Matthew squeaked back.

'I don't,' Katy squeaked back even higher.

Matthew turned back to Alison, terrified. She stared back at him, stony-faced.

'I got in a fight over something with someone I can't remember and then Katy said I could go back to hers because he proper thumped me in the face and so she said I should go back to hers and put some peas on it. So I went back to her flat and she put peas on... on my face and... and... and...'

'And what?' Alison demanded menacingly.

'I can't remember exactly how it... how it started... I think we got talking about old times and...'

'Old times?' barked Alison.

'Yeah, yeah, old times,' replied Matthew. 'W-w-when we used to go out together when we were teenagers.'

The look of anguish on Alison's face was too much for Katy to bear.

'We weren't together long,' she lied. 'Then it all fell apart when we went off to uni and Matthew... well, he...' she trailed off.

'He what?' asked Alison.

'He, er...' She bit her lip.

'He what?' repeated Alison.

'He... I found him... having sex with the Virgin Mary whilst he was dressed as a pantomime donkey.'

Matthew gasped, horrified at Katy's disclosure.

'It was Christmas,' he explained. 'It was a student fancy dress party. I was really drunk... she... she took advantage of me.'

'Seriously!' exclaimed Katy, unable to hide her shock at his version of events.

'You weren't there,' said Matthew. 'You didn't see her when she practically dragged me back to my bedroom.'

'Is that what happened with Katy then?' asked Alison. 'She dragged you back to her place with the lure of frozen peas,' she sneered. 'How could you resist that?'

'She invited me back,' stated Matthew. 'I didn't ask to go back to her flat. She asked me. And she... and she...'

Bloody hell, thought Katy. What is he doing? What is he doing?

'And she jumped on me. She did, Alison, honestly she did. She instigated it, I promise you. Not me... it wasn't me...'

'You utter bastard,' cried Ben before landing a punch on Matthew's face that sent him reeling backwards.

Both Katy and Alison gasped but did nothing to stop him.

Matthew staggered up from the floor, clutching the side of his face, breathing heavily. He looked up at the three of them just as Ben advanced, pulling his arm back to take aim once again. Matthew turned and fled.

Chapter Eleven

Matthew

Well, that went well, thought Matthew as he stumbled out of the ladies' toilets and back into the vast dining room.

What now? He daren't look over his shoulder in case he was met with another blow from Ben. He staggered forward, pushing chairs out of the way as he went. He was vaguely aware of the lights having been lowered and the swirling of fluorescent disco lights around his head but not a lot else. He needed to get to safety and gather his thoughts. He needed to work out how the heck he was going to salvage this situation. This was the greatest disaster he had ever faced. He kept putting one foot in front of the other. He just needed head space so he could work out how to sort this all out.

He suddenly became aware that he did have space. Space all around him. He was in the middle of the dance floor, the lights sporadically blinding him as they swirled. He looked round and just had time to catch sight of most of the guests standing around the edge of the dance floor as if they had been expecting him. But then he realised they weren't gazing at him; they were looking at something behind him. He spun round to find Braindead and Abby in a close embrace, gazing into each other's eyes, clearly not having noticed his rapid entry into the middle of their first dance. He had to get away. He couldn't ruin this moment, despite the fact it was likely that Braindead had ruined his marriage. He spun round to find his exit route, only to see Alison marching towards him, a look of grim determination on her face. He felt himself start to back away. He was afraid, really afraid.

'You all right, mate?' he heard Braindead say as he backed into the happy couple. 'It's not your turn yet. Can you just wait until we've had the first dance and then I'll dance with you if you *really* want to?'

Matthew just had time to give him a look of absolute horror that turned Braindead's grin into a frown before he felt a tap on the shoulder. He froze. That could only be one person.

'I think your wife would like to dance with you first though,' said Braindead helpfully. 'Good to see romance is not dead even when you've been married for as long as you have.'

Matthew turned around slowly, heart in his mouth. His brain was a mush of confusion and denials and apologies and guilt and horror and many things he couldn't make sense of.

Alison's face looked like thunder with a thick veneer of utter disgust. 'Alison... I... I....'

'Don't even try to explain. I've heard enough.'

'Look, just dance with her, mate,' urged Braindead. 'You're stealing our moment. I can't tell you how long it took us to decide on "White Wedding" for our first dance.'

'Please, Alison,' Matthew started to sob. 'Please just listen.'

'Come on, Al,' said Braindead. 'Have a dance with your husband, will you?'

Alison turned her glare to Braindead.

'He's no husband of mine,' she spat. Then she softened. 'Thank you, Braindead,' she said. 'Thank you for being the only one brave enough to tell the truth.'

'What? What do you mean? Truth about what? And what do you mean, he isn't your husband? Of course he is.'

'No,' she said firmly. 'We're done. I never want to see you ever again.'

'No,' cried Matthew. 'Please, Alison, no.'

'Yes,' nodded Alison. Then she pulled her arm back and thumped him in the face, knocking him clean to the ground at Braindead and Abby's feet. She looked down at him for a moment then walked off the dance floor just as Billy Idol sneered and said something about nice days and white weddings.

Chapter Twelve

Ben

'Bloody hell,' muttered Ben under his breath as he watched Alison strut off the dance floor.

He dashed forward, working totally on instinct. He wasn't really sure what he should be doing. When he'd read up on best man etiquette there had been no mention of what to do in the event of the groom revealing in his speech that your wife had a one-night stand a long time ago with one of the other guests. All he could see now was Matthew lying on the floor at the feet of the bride and groom when they should have been sharing an emotional kiss at the end of their first dance.

Braindead looked at him in utter confusion as Ben reached down and dragged Matthew by the shoulders to the edge of the dance floor. The least he could do was somehow get this fiasco billed as a side show rather than taking centre stage as it was now.

'What just happened?' asked Braindead, trotting up behind them.

'I told you not to invite them,' added Abby. 'I knew it would lead to trouble – they look the type.'

Matthew in his boring grey suit and boring side parting looked like the last person to start a fight at a wedding but Ben didn't think that this needed pointing out.

'It's all your fault,' muttered Matthew to Braindead, dabbing at his bloodied lip.

'Not now,' warned Ben. 'Not now,' he added more firmly.

'What does he mean, it's my fault?' asked Braindead. 'I didn't thump him.'

'Ignore him,' said Ben. 'He's confused. You go off and get a drink. I'll get him out of here. Come on, it's your wedding day.'

'If you hadn't have said that stuff in your stupid speech none of this would have happened,' said Matthew miserably.

'What do you mean?' exclaimed Braindead.

'Not *now*,' said Ben even more firmly.

'What's he talking about?' asked Braindead.

'Nothing,' said Ben.

'Tell me,' demanded Braindead.

Ben turned to face his friend on his wedding day. Could he really be this stupid? Had he really no idea that his speech had sparked this catastrophic chain of events?

'You dropped the one-night stand bomb, didn't you?' he pointed out.

'I know, and I will apologise to Katy. I know it was hardly the time or the place but I got carried away and I was just trying to make the point about what a fucking amazing husband you are. I can understand Katy being pissed off but I will make it up to her, I promise I will.'

Ben couldn't believe his ears. 'Have you totally forgotten who she had a one-night stand with?'

'An ex-boyfriend, wasn't it?'

Ben turned to point at Matthew.

Braindead stared at him for a moment and then his body appeared to just collapse in on itself as he began to realise what he had done.

'That was Katy's one-night stand?' gasped Abby. 'She certainly upped her game with you, didn't she?' she said to Ben.

'Oh my God,' Braindead moaned, clutching his stomach. 'I forgot they were here.'

'Alison didn't know anything about it,' Ben thought he should point out.

'Oh bollocks!' gasped Abby.

'She does now,' muttered Matthew sorrowfully.

'Double bollocks!' Abby gasped again.

'What!' gasped Braindead, rearing his head up. 'But… how…? I never meant… I just got carried away and… I never said any names… but how?'

Matthew shrugged. 'She's a smart woman, my wife. Soon to be ex-wife.'

Ben watched as Matthew's head dropped and his shoulders heaved and he began to cry. It hadn't been in any of the etiquette guides either as to what you should do if the groom inadvertently splits up a marriage on his wedding day.

Chapter Thirteen

Katy

Katy arrived on the scene at pretty much the same time as Daniel. However, she waddled whereas he did a knee slide across the dance floor, landing right at Matthew's feet.

'What's happening?' gasped Daniel, somewhat out of breath. 'Gabriel just came and dragged me out of the men's loos, telling me there had been a scrap on the dance floor between a well-dressed prim lady and a slightly scruffy man in a boring suit. Of course I immediately thought of you, Matthew. Tell me the shit hasn't hit the fan after Braindead's appallingly inappropriate and yet curiously touching speech.'

'Thanks, Daniel,' muttered Braindead.

'You're welcome,' replied Daniel. 'So?' he asked Katy. 'Has the shit hit the fan?'

Katy looked down, unable to meet Daniel's eye.

'The shit has hit the fan, the floor, the flowers and the fucking fondue set we bought them as a wedding present,' declared Matthew, struggling to get up from where he had been slumped on the floor. He glared at Braindead.

'I... I don't know what to say,' admitted Braindead.

'Clearly,' spat Matthew. 'Clearly you don't. You never do, do you, until it's out of your stupid mouth.'

'Hey, hey,' said Ben, stepping in between the two of them. 'It's not actually Braindead's fault, is it? You can't blame him.'

Ben looked awkwardly over at Katy. She felt her heart sink to her shoes.

'I can!' said Matthew desperately. 'I can. It was all in the past. We'd buried it. Everyone had moved on. And now he's dug it all up again like the utter idiot he is and wrecked my family in the process.'

'So let me get this straight,' said Abby, her head spinning from side to side in an effort to keep up with what was going on. 'Katy slept with Matthew… whilst Matthew was married.'

No-one said a word.

'And you were with Ben?' she asked Katy.

'Yes,' gasped Katy. 'But… but we hadn't been together long and we certainly weren't married and…'

'Are you trying to say I'm worse than you?' demanded Matthew. 'Because I don't think that's fair.'

'Neither is it fair to say that I came on to you,' retorted Katy.

'Interesting,' mused Daniel. 'Who is more guilty? The married man or the unmarried woman who has a partner and is behaving like a hussy?'

'I am *not* a hussy,' hissed Katy.

Daniel raised one eyebrow.

'Not helping one little bit,' said Katy. She wished that Daniel would just get lost.

'So you all knew,' said Abby. 'You all knew, except that woman… his wife?'

Nobody spoke. She looked slowly at everyone. Braindead, Matthew, Daniel and Katy. Still, nobody spoke.

'But why didn't you tell me?' she asked Braindead. 'I'm your wife. You need to tell me *everything*.'

'It was so long ago,' replied Braindead miserably. 'I'd forgotten all about it until today when Ben and Katy were banging on about how important forgiveness is in a marriage. And I'd totally forgotten who it was she'd slept with!'

'I would just like it to be acknowledged that I was the first one to be told of this indiscretion all those years ago and I have remained totally discreet all along,' added Daniel smugly.

'Still not helping, Daniel,' Katy repeated.

'What can I do?' asked Braindead, looking desperate. 'What can I do? Matthew?'

Matthew looked down at the floor and said nothing.

'I'll go and find Alison,' Braindead said. 'Tell her I made it up just to make Ben look good.'

'What are you talking about?' said Ben. 'You made up a story about my wife cheating on me behind my back to make me look good?'

'Oh, Ben,' said Katy, putting her hand on his arm. 'I'm so sorry.'

'Well, I'll tell her she's got it all wrong. It wasn't Matthew. She's got totally the wrong end of the stick. How about that? I'll tell her it was Daniel or something – anything.'

'Seriously?' said Daniel. 'Like that's plausible! As if I would ever sleep with someone who wears platform shoes to a wedding. I mean, really.'

'But I have to do *something*,' said Braindead. 'I have to put it right. I can't… I can't start married life like this. I can't start married life knowing that I've split up a perfectly happy family.' He dropped to his knees and put his head in his hands.

'We were going to skip the speeches,' announced Matthew, mournfully shaking his head. 'We were going to skip the speeches and sneak back to our room. Alison's idea. It's not often we get a bedroom to ourselves with four kids in the house.' A tear slid down his cheek.

'You were going to have sex during our wedding speeches!' gasped Abby. 'I told you we shouldn't have invited them,' she said to Braindead. 'You made me drop my dentist off the list for these two. There's no way he would have had sex during my wedding. No way!'

'But how can you be sure?' asked Daniel. 'Who knows how many of your guests are planning to take the opportunity to have a quick one during the evening buffet?'

'The buffet?' exclaimed Abby. 'But I ordered profiteroles and asparagus tips and smoked salmon blinis. It's not just *any* old buffet!'

'Well, you never know, the smoked salmon might just keep them interested, but if I were you I'd do a quick headcount during supper time,' replied Daniel.

Abby was looking increasingly distraught. 'Weddings aren't for *other* people to have sex at!' she exclaimed.

'Of course they are,' replied Daniel. 'Who else is going to have sex?'

'Me!' shrieked Abby. 'Me. I want to have sex at my wedding. Not think about *other* people doing it.'

'We're going to have to sort out this mess I've made first,' replied Braindead, who had gone very pale. 'I can't, I don't, I don't think I can... I mean, how can I when I know there's four kids who have just lost their father because I let the cat out of the bag over his one-night stand with my best man's wife? How could anyone have sex, knowing they had caused that?'

'It's all right, mate,' muttered Matthew, getting up. 'It's your wedding day. You carry on and enjoy yourselves. Have a ball. Fill your boots. Have lots of sex. This isn't your fault. I got myself into this mess so I'll just have to find a way out of it.' He shuffled off the dance floor.

'Bloody hell,' muttered Abby. 'Anyone for a Jägerbomb?'

Chapter Fourteen

Katy

'Well that went well,' Katy sighed heavily, finally lowering herself down onto the settee in their lounge with a cup of tea. 'I'm not sure I ever want to go to another wedding ever again after that. Weddings and me are *no more*.'

They'd opted not to stay at the hotel. Not much point as Katy wasn't drinking so she could drive them home, plus the thought of trying to get an overexcited Millie to sleep in the same room as them at the end of a long day had been enough to put them off.

Ben sat down next to her in a daze. He was pretty drunk. Not ridiculous, she'd seen him worse, but still he had that glazed look of someone who couldn't quite focus.

After Matthew had left, Ben, Braindead and Abby had headed straight to the bar and downed a couple of shots each. This didn't appear to cheer Braindead up much until Ben took him to one side, stared him deep in the eyes and put his hands on his shoulders.

'Listen to me. Forget it,' he'd said. 'That's what I've done and so can you. Now you *must* focus on your wedding day. Because if you don't you will regret it for the rest of your life.'

Braindead had swallowed and nodded.

'I'll try,' he said. Then he walked back to the bar and ordered another round of shots. Getting utterly inebriated appeared to be the only way he could forget making the most catastrophic groom's speech of all time. By the time they were all on the dance floor at midnight dancing to 'Angels' by Robbie Williams, Ben was having to physically hold him up as he had about as much strength in his legs as a scarecrow. Fortunately, Abby wasn't much better and it had been left to Ben and Katy to get them up to the honeymoon suite. They'd left Braindead sparked out on the floor whilst Katy tucked Abby into bed, still in her wedding dress. She'd been talking utter gibberish by this point until Katy had used her best mother tone of 'go to sleep' which appeared to do the trick – or possibly Abby just passed out.

They'd driven home in silence, Millie asleep in the back and Ben nodding off in the front as Katy wondered how on earth they were going to face the aftermath of Braindead's thoughtless disclosure.

'Poor Braindead,' muttered Ben now. 'He's come out with some stupid things in his time but… well, he's really done it this time, hasn't he?'

'I'm so sorry, Ben,' Katy spluttered out. 'It must have been horrible for you too. I… I'm so sorry that the damn thing just won't go away.'

'Shhhh,' said Ben, patting her arm. 'I know you're sorry. I know it was a mistake. I've forgiven you.' He leaned over to stroke her bump. 'It's in the past. There are more important things in my life now.'

'But it's not in the past now any more, is it?' said Katy desperately. 'I… I can't imagine how Alison is feeling. I feel so terrible all over again. And her face!' she cried, covering her own face. 'I will never forget the look on her face when she realised.'

'I know,' nodded Ben. 'And when she realised that I'd known all along. Like she was mad at me because I hadn't told her.' He blew his cheeks out.

They sat in silence reliving the horror of the wedding's main event.

'Maybe I should talk to Alison,' suggested Katy.

'Seriously?' said Ben. 'Do you seriously think that Alison will want to listen to you?'

'Probably not,' she admitted. 'But I have to do something.'

Ben didn't answer. She looked over. His eyes were drooping as if he was about to fall asleep. She was overcome with a deep flush of love for him. Apart from decking Matthew, he had shown none of the humiliation or anger he could have displayed today. He'd put Braindead first, which was unbelievable in the circumstances. Sure, they had been to hell and back when he first found out about her one-night stand but they'd got through it and it made her love him even more. His forgiveness was the most miraculous thing he could ever have given her and today made her cherish it even more than ever. He might be eight years younger than her but he was possibly the most mature man she had ever met and her love for him seemed to grow all the time. Today had been yet another display of the kind of man he was. No wonder Braindead had got all emotional and lost control of himself whilst paying tribute to his best man. He was indeed lucky to have Ben as a best friend and Katy was lucky to have him as a husband.

She eased herself up off the sofa and grabbed a rug off the chair and laid it over him. She wouldn't wake him; he looked knackered.

She walked up the stairs and couldn't stop her thoughts moving to Alison, who was also probably sleeping alone tonight. She didn't hold out much hope of Matthew fixing his marriage quickly, if ever. Alison, after all, prided herself on doing everything perfectly. Her husband sleeping with his ex certainly did not fall into that category.

Katy slowly eased her clothes off and fell gratefully into her maternity pyjamas before collapsing on the bed. She stared up at the ceiling for some time, raking over the day. Should she have seen it coming? She was the stand-in mother of the groom, after all. Should she have given Braindead a good talking-to as to what he could and couldn't mention in his speech – the latter including her dodgy one-night stand? But there was no way she could predict what was going to come out of Braindead's mouth at the best of times, let alone when he was under pressure. Perhaps what she should have predicted, however, was that this day was bound to come. Her one-night stand with Matthew had caused so many close shaves with catastrophe that it was inevitable that one day the bell would finally toll. However, it had turned out that this time it wouldn't be her life under threat, but Matthew's, who had so far managed to hide his unfaithfulness.

The baby began to kick and automatically, her hand reached up to feel the ripples cascading over her belly. Tears sprang to her eyes that yet again one stupid decision over five years ago had come back to haunt her. She screwed her eyes up and actually prayed for Matthew and Alison. That somehow Alison would find a way to forgive her husband because, if she didn't, the consequences were too much for Katy to bear.

Katy felt an itch under her arm and reached inside her pyjamas to scratch. She pulled out a piece of pink horseshoe confetti. That hadn't brought much good luck today. She sighed, putting it on the bedside table. She could really do with her wedding days being over. She was nearly forty after all! But she feared the worst was yet to come. How on earth she was going to manage at her mother's wedding to her Spanish toy boy after this, Katy had no idea.

Chapter Fifteen

Matthew

'You see, there was your error,' said Ian as he looked at Matthew across the breakfast table. 'In fact, you are facing a catalogue of errors that led to the situation you are now in.'

Matthew was only too painfully aware of that. He'd hoped that Ian would give him better support in his hour of need. But he should have known better. When had Ian ever been known to be supportive during their long friendship? He generally saw his role in life as taking the mickey out of his friend at each and every opportunity, something Matthew had been only too aware of when he'd knocked on Ian's door last night, having failed to convince Alison to let him into their marital home.

She must have literally jumped straight in their car and driven herself home after she'd stormed off the dance floor, leaving all her belongings in the hotel room. By the time he'd caught up with her in a taxi the door had been double-bolted from the inside and no amount of hammering or calling could raise a response. Eventually he'd admitted defeat, called Ian, then called another cab to collect him from outside his own front door and deposit him at his friend's flat. Ian had been waiting with a bottle of whisky in which Matthew could drown himself.

He now found himself sitting at Ian's breakfast table in his grey suit from the day before, his face matching its colour. Matthew braced himself for Ian's review of the day's events that he had half managed to blurt out the night before.

'As soon as Alison said she fancied some activity under the covers you should have had her out of that wedding and up those stairs pronto,' said Ian, shaking his head.

'I know! Don't you think I haven't gone over and over that moment in my mind? It just would have been rude to leave before the end of the speeches... or that's what we thought. We were being polite!'

'Your next error. You only need to be polite at a wedding if you are a main guest as far as I'm concerned. And you were, what, invited *three* weeks ago? So likely as not you were a stand-in because someone dropped out and they'd already confirmed numbers so had paid for the food anyway.'

'Braindead *really* wanted me to go,' protested Matthew. 'He was really quite emotional when he invited me. Honestly. My tax advice has paid for their honeymoon. That's what he said.'

'And this is how he repays you?' enquired Ian. 'A last-minute wedding invite to make sure there aren't any empty chairs and then tells a room full of people you shagged your ex behind your wife's back. Sure... He's your biggest fan. What a guy!'

'He's not like that,' replied Matthew. 'Honestly, he just got carried away... I can't really blame him.'

'Bad things always happen at weddings,' said Ian, shaking his head. 'I mean, I got married at mine, and look what a poor decision that was.' He grinned. Matthew tried to raise a smile but he wasn't really feeling it.

'Best wedding I ever went to,' Ian continued, 'was a colleague of Carol's. I knew absolutely no-one. Zip. And no-one knew me. It was like the perfect wedding, to be honest. You don't have to be sociable, you don't have to make sure you talk to anyone, you can just be anyone. I nearly gave the bride's uncle a heart attack in the loos. He was trying to make conversation and just said to me, "Bride or groom?" like he wanted to find out who had invited me. Anyway, I looked back at him and giggled and said, "Actually, groom. I'd have him. He's gorgeous!" He went bright red and fled, then proceeded to point me out to all the bride's relatives for the rest of the night! Hysterical. Carol wasn't too impressed when I told her, though.'

'Hilarious,' sighed Matthew, not really in the mood for Ian's top ten wedding stories of all time.

'To be honest, mate,' said Ian, 'I can't believe you got away with it for so long anyway.'

'Got away with what?'

'Alison not finding out you'd slept with your ex.'

'I guess so.'

'It took Carol precisely three weeks to find out I was sleeping with that Marie.'

'Big difference,' said Matthew. 'You wanted her to find out. You practically had sex in front of her.'

'She wasn't due home until later. It's not my fault her night out got cancelled. You're right, though. Our marriage had been dead a long time. Marie did us both a favour.'

'I'm sure Marie saw it that way at the time.'

'Well, if it hadn't have been for Marie then we wouldn't have got divorced and Carol wouldn't have found boring Bob, who makes her happier than I ever could. So I'm sure if Carol saw Marie in the street she would go over and shake her hand and thank her for the years of torture she saved her from, having to stay married to me.'

Matthew scratched his head. Ian and Carol's divorce had been over fifteen years ago. He didn't think Ian quite understood the rawness of the situation Matthew was in.

'I don't want to divorce Alison, I love Alison,' said Matthew. He swallowed. 'I didn't sleep with Katy in order to get rid of Alison.'

'So why did you then?' asked Ian.

Matthew looked up at him, shocked.

'I can't really remember,' he sighed eventually. 'We were going through a bad patch, that's true, but that was because we were struggling so much to have a baby. It had taken us over. And, well, Katy was there and willing and, well, I guess all my teenage emotions got the better of me and it just kind of happened before I had time to think about the fact that doing that would mean one day I would be sat here in your flat listening to your stupid wedding stories and not at home with my wife and children.'

'You're welcome,' said Ian. 'You can stay as long as you like.'

'What am I going to do?' he asked. 'I don't know what to do.'

'Ask for your wedding present back?' said Ian helpfully.

Matthew leaned forward and put his head in his hands.

'Shall I ring Lena?' asked Ian. 'See what the temperature is like in your house this morning?'

'Yes!' gasped Matthew. 'Ring her, ring her now.' That was the first sensible thing Ian had said all morning. Lena was their nanny, employed when Alison fell pregnant unexpectedly for the third time when she already had three-year-old twins and an eighteen-month-old. Lena, a thirty-four-year-old from Lithuania, had saved their sanity. That was until she had decided to fall in love with Ian, which had nearly driven them all mad as Alison didn't approve of him and was frightened that he would break her heart and then she would flee back to Lithuania, leaving Alison and Matthew devasted with four kids under four hanging round their necks. But a curious thing had happened. After all Ian's philandering following his divorce, it was Lena who had brought him to heel, Lena who fairly and squarely captured his heart and turned him into something resembling a besotted partner. Now, six months down the line, Alison and Matthew were left fearful that at some point they would want to progress their relationship, which might again leave them bereft.

Matthew watched as Ian took out his phone and searched for Lena's number. He held the phone to his ear and tried to give his friend a reassuring smile.

'Hello, gorgeous and how are you this fine morning?' Ian said into the phone. 'Yes, yes, he's here. Did you hear what happened?'

Ian nodded whilst Matthew held his breath.

'Well, the reason why she has barely come out of the bedroom at all today and has told you under no circumstances to let Matthew into the house if he turns up is because yesterday at the wedding she discovered that Matthew had slept with his ex.'

Matthew waited for Ian to add the further explanation required to make him sound less bad.

'Yes, they were married at the time,' he added.

Matthew started shaking his head violently.

'No, they didn't have any children then but they were going through IVF. They really struggled to conceive the twins, you know. Firing blanks, I suspect.'

Matthew reached forward and snatched the phone out of Ian's hand.

'Lena,' he gasped. 'It's Matthew. Have you seen Alison? Have you spoken to her? Is she okay?'

There was silence at the end of the phone.

'Lena? Are you there?'

'How could you, Matthew?' she gasped. 'Why? I don't understand. I thought you were different.'

The shock could be heard in her voice. He needed to explain. She needed to be not so shocked. Hang on a minute… This was Lena he was speaking to. Lena the nanny. Matthew had always struggled with how he should interact with a paid employee living in his home. He bounced between awkward over-politeness and utter frustration that, despite the fact she was lovely and much-needed, he couldn't help but dream of the day when once again he could walk around in his bad underwear and go to the toilet with the door open.

And now here he was, being judged by the nanny. What did one say in this situation? He had no idea and yet he suspected he very much needed to keep Lena on side as she might be his only way of infiltrating the house.

'It was a long time ago, Lena. Naturally I'm devastated and I will do anything to put this right. Where is Alison now?'

'In her room. She came down for coffee, told me not to let you in the house, then went back to bed.'

'How did she look?'

Lena said nothing for a moment.

'She looked broken,' she said simply.

Matthew let out a breath. He felt tears rush to his eyes. He had to put this right. Whatever happened, he must fix this.

'Will you tell her I called?' he said, trying to hold back the tears. 'Will you tell her I need to speak to her? I need to explain. I need her to understand.' It was no good, a tear slipped down his cheek.

'I will try,' answered Lena.

'Lena,' he said, his voice breaking. 'Please look after her. And the kids. Until she will talk to me will you please take care of them and please call me if you need anything or you are worried? Will you promise me that?'

Again there was a pause.

'I will,' replied Lena.

'Thank you,' said Matthew before handing the phone back to Ian and dropping his head to his arms and sobbing.

'I'll call you back,' he heard Ian say quickly before he felt his hand on his shoulder, which made him cry even more.

Chapter Sixteen

Katy

For once Katy was relieved to be back at work on Monday. Any distraction from the weekend's events felt like a massive relief and she couldn't wait to get stuck into researching a potential new client that she had been putting off for some time. The morning had passed quickly as she happily lost herself in the information galaxy of the internet until she was interrupted by her desk phone ringing. She expected it to be the receptionist but it wasn't, it was Daniel.

'Come down to reception,' he hissed at her. 'I've got something to show you.'

'Reception? Can't you just bring whatever it is up here?'

'No. You need to see it down here. Just pop downstairs for a minute. You won't regret it.'

The phone clicked off. It's all right for him to say 'pop downstairs', thought Katy, easing herself out of her chair. But 'popping' didn't really happen when you were four months pregnant. Even short journeys needed to be contemplated and eased into, minimising the need for any quick, energetic movements.

She waited for the lift, wondering what on earth was so important that Daniel required her presence in reception. They had worked together at Butler and Calder Advertising Agency for more years than she cared to remember and she couldn't recall the last time she had seen Daniel spend any time in reception. He never went down there, even to greet clients. He was way too important as creative director of the agency. He had minions to fetch his clients for meetings, so this would be a most unusual gathering for the two of them, in a location he tended to believe was reserved for lesser mortals.

Daniel had been very quiet this weekend. She'd hoped he would phone her so they could have chewed over the events of the wedding and she could have got some advice on what she should do. But there had been radio silence and she hadn't wanted to call him as she knew that Gabriel was in town. Given that Daniel only got weekends with Gabriel, she figured it would be only polite to wait until Monday at work when they could have a really good gossip and possibly come up with a plan as to how she was going to solve this mess. She'd deal with whatever he was so desperate to show her and then she would take him for coffee. She needed him and his way of delivering a blunt summary of her misdemeanours. He added a certain clarity to her actions that were useful in helping her work out what to do next.

The lift opened up onto the ground-floor reception and she stepped out. Daniel was lounging on the quirky designer sofa, which was essential to reassure all clients when they came for meetings that they were in a 'creative space'. He was not alone. He was laughing hysterically at a woman sitting on the other end wearing a leopard-print fur coat, a bright red beret and towering rainbow platform shoes. A look on Katy that would have had her guided to the local mental hospital but, on this woman, looked supremely stylish and elegant.

'Katy!' exclaimed Daniel, getting up and dashing towards her. 'You remember Erica, don't you? From the wedding? Braindead's sister?'

'Of course,' replied Katy. 'Don't you remember I sat next to her? I told you I'd lost the wedding seating plan lottery when I found out I was sitting next to a supermodel when I'm four months pregnant.' Katy smiled warmly at Erica.

'Sorry about that,' apologised Erica. 'I thought you looked lovely, by the way. Way sexier than me. There is nothing sexier than a pregnant woman.'

Katy stared at Erica as she rose gracefully off the sofa. Clearly, she had never been pregnant! Who was this woman? Absolutely stunning and lovely too.

'Well, we literally had a ball since Saturday,' announced Daniel overexcitedly. 'We bonded, you see, over the quality of the napkins.' He looked back at Erica fondly. 'We both agreed that typically the quality of the food in an establishment is directly related to the quality of the napkins. You might as well dispense with all these food guides and just rate a restaurant based on its table linen.'

'Right,' nodded Katy. Daniel was almost giddy with excitement at this gastronomic insight. She'd not seen him this way since he discovered he'd got front-row tickets to see Helen Mirren in the West End.

'Apart from Gio's,' interrupted Erica. 'There is always an exception.'

'Of course!' exclaimed Daniel, slapping his forehead. 'Apart from Gio's!' he laughed hysterically, clutching at Erica's arm. 'Have you been to Gio's, Katy? What am I saying, of course you haven't, you're married, how would you have come across Gio's? Erica took us last night. Oh my God, the best night ever! It's in a railway carriage, Katy, can you imagine? On a piece of disused railway. And the gnocchi, oh my, the gnocchi was to absolutely die for and then Gio came out and took a mandolin off the wall and started to serenade the three of us. Can you imagine?'

'Being serenaded in an old railway carriage, in a disused railway track… No, I can't… thankfully.'

'She has no imagination,' Daniel said turning to Erica. 'Didn't I tell you she has no imagination?' He turned back to Katy. 'The napkins were vintage kitchen roll,' he told her.

'Are you serious?' said Katy. She knew now he had totally lost the plot.

'Vintage,' he nodded. 'Proper seventies prints on them and everything. To be honest, I stole some. Thought I might frame them. You know, like a domestic installation.'

'Is that what you brought me downstairs to see?' asked Katy. 'Some vintage kitchen roll?'

'No!' gasped Daniel, laughing hysterically again. What was with him? Was he on drugs? Katy glanced over at Erica, who seemed serenely calm and not high in any way. What on earth was going on?

'Erica wanted to say hello. She stayed at ours last night because we were celebrating,' he clamped his hand over his mouth as if he'd let the cat out of some kind of bag. 'No!' he cried. 'I didn't want to tell you like that… I'm so excited, I'm getting it all wrong.'

'Just spit it out,' demanded Katy, getting slightly cross. Her legs were aching, she needed a sit-down and her nose was a little out of joint that, in the space of under forty-eight hours, Daniel and Erica had clearly bonded in a dramatic fashion to the extent that they shared an admiration for vintage kitchen roll, Erica had been allowed to bed down in Daniel's immaculate flat (something Katy had never been invited to do) and, to top it all, they'd been out celebrating. Celebrating what, and why hadn't she been invited? Okay, so she'd had one of the worst nights of her life on Saturday but that didn't mean that she should be excluded from any form of happiness.

Daniel clasped his hands together under his nose as if in some kind of manic prayer. He still didn't speak but Katy noticed signs of his eyes welling up and he was having trouble breathing. Had he taken something? She looked over at Erica accusingly this time. Had she and her supermodel lifestyle led him astray?

'I don't know how to say it,' he gasped suddenly.

'Would you like me to tell her?' Erica asked.

'Yes,' cried Daniel. 'Yes. Then I can watch her reaction properly and you will tell her so much better than me,' he added admiringly. This friendship thing with Erica was already wearing very thin.

'He's getting married,' said Erica with a huge smile.

Katy took a sharp intake of breath as Daniel gazed at her, clearly beside himself. She glanced, confused, between Daniel and Erica. How had this happened? How had this happened like this?

Katy shook her head in bewilderment for a second as a million thoughts rattled through her mind. Daniel was *her* friend. Her closest friend. Okay, so he could be a complete and utter nightmare but he was her best friend. How could she not have been involved in this? How come she was standing in the reception of Butler and Calder being told by a virtual stranger that her best friend was getting married? And, to top it all, if it hadn't been for her, Daniel would never have met Gabriel. If her mother hadn't got the forty-five-year itch then she would never have come to stay for Christmas to show off her new Spanish boyfriend, who invited his son Gabriel to join them. And if Katy hadn't invited Daniel for Christmas lunch because he was in deep trauma over his last boyfriend leaving him then he would never have met Gabriel, let alone got engaged to him! She was in the thick of it. Right there in amongst it sorting out Daniel's love life, and then he had the audacity to turn up with a woman he had barely met and let her announce to Katy that he was in fact engaged. Katy couldn't help it. She was beside herself. And then it dawned on her, the worst thing of all: the hideous prospect of yet another wedding. She had no idea if she could face the stress.

'Katy?' asked Daniel, a look of confusion smothering his face. 'Aren't you pleased for me? We'll be practically related!'

Katy was speechless. She was pleased. Of course she was, but this was all wrong.

'When did he propose?' she managed to ask.

'Last night,' said Daniel. 'At Gio's. Gabriel asked him to play "Lady in Red" on his mandolin. I was wearing that red cashmere sweater. You should have been there, Katy. It was so romantic.'

Katy looked at Daniel. He was clearly beside himself with happiness. She looked away. She wanted to cry at the bitter disappointment that she hadn't been there to witness the moment herself. That she'd been at home, wedged into a chair.

'Why didn't you call me straight away?' she found herself asking.

Daniel looked wounded.

'It all went a bit crazy, to be honest,' said Erica. 'Gio got out the grappa so no-one can really remember much about the rest of the night. And Gabriel spent a long time on the phone crying with his father and then Daniel had to cry with his father too… It was quite exhausting to watch.'

'You spoke to Carlos?' asked Katy in wonder.

'Yes,' nodded Daniel. 'He's so happy for us. Truly over the moon. Ridiculously happy. I mean, like, weeping-with-joy happy. Can you believe it? A father-in-law who loves me! It's truly a dream come true.'

'Did you speak to my mother?' Katy barely dared ask.

'Well, yes,' nodded Daniel. 'She's happy too. She said she was going straight out to get herself a T-shirt that reads, "I introduced my boyfriend's son to his future husband, hashtag howcoolamI!" She's hysterical, your mum.'

'She didn't introduce you, *I* introduced you,' said Katy. This conversation was going in completely the wrong direction.

'Katy, what is wrong with you?' asked Daniel. 'Why can't you just be happy for me?'

'Of course I'm happy for you,' cried Katy. 'I'm just not happy about all this,' she said, swirling her hand around in front of her.

'What do you mean, this?' said Daniel, doing the same. 'What "this" are you referring to on the day which will go down in history as one of the happiest in my life? I can tell already that "this" has the potential to make me feel bad, which quite frankly is really quite selfish of you.'

Katy stared back at him. He was right. Of course he was right. The fact she wasn't happy about the way she had found out was irrelevant. It wasn't about her. How she felt didn't matter. All that mattered was that Daniel was probably the happiest man alive at this moment and she should be over the moon for him.

'Forget it,' she said, lunging forward to embrace him over her belly. 'You're right. The "this" doesn't matter. It's the most amazing news. Utterly brilliant, Daniel. I couldn't be happier for you. You getting married... it's... it's... a miracle and Gabriel is going to make you a wonderful husband and you are going to be a wonderful husband and I couldn't be happier if I was going to marry Gabriel myself.'

'Okay, so you were doing really well until you went a bit weird on the last bit,' said Daniel.

'I know,' she replied. 'I got a bit carried away. I just want you to know that I'm so happy for you. You must bring Gabriel over really soon so we can celebrate. Well, you can celebrate and I'll suck on a lemon or something. But you must come over with him so I can hear all about when you are thinking and where and all that exciting stuff.'

Katy grinned happily. Yes, she was over her immediate reaction and back in the game. Daniel getting married was going to be a welcome distraction from the trauma of her mother's wedding. Knowing him, it would be a theatrical and flamboyant masterpiece of the likes that had never been seen before, which would be huge fun to attend. And by the time they set a date she would have had the baby so would be able to enjoy it as most weddings should be enjoyed: with a glass in one's hand.

'Well, we were talking about that sometime last night, weren't we?' Daniel said to Erica. 'I can't remember whether it was before the honeymoon argument, which went from Argentina because I have always wanted to learn the tango, or New Orleans, because it's Gabriel's dream to play the saxophone on stage there, or after the heated debate on hog roast or dim sum. I bet you can guess which one I was gunning for?'

'Dim sum?' offered Katy.

'Of course. Who wants dead pig as their wedding breakfast? Anyway, I sat there, didn't I, Erica, sometime in the middle of last night, and said, "Do you know who we are missing?"'

'He did,' nodded Erica. 'He got a bit teary actually.'

'I said that the person we really need now is Katy,' continued Daniel.

'Ahhhh, did you?' said Katy, starting to well up herself at the thought that she had actually been missed during this most important evening in Daniel's life.

'Yes, I said we are really missing Katy,' continued Daniel, 'because she is the most organised person I know and if anyone can moderate an argument over hog roast or dim sum then Katy can. And of course

I know that you will always come down on my side so that's another reason why we decided right there and then to give you the role of wedding co-ordinator for this whole shebang, with me as creative director, of course. I can't think of anyone better able to deliver my vision. And then of course we must give Gabriel a role. But I'll think of one to keep him happy and Erica is more than happy to be involved, aren't you, as she has the best contacts book you can imagine. She said she'd give you anything you need, Katy. Isn't that kind of her? What a massively fortuitous thing to meet her the day before I got engaged. What would we do without her?'

Katy stared at Daniel. How insulting that the only reason she had been missed during the previous night's events was because of her organisational skills. Not because of their friendship or the fact he would have liked her there to share his joy. Oh no! He wanted her there to make sure Gabriel agreed to whatever elaborate plans Daniel had already started to cook up for his wedding. And it was becoming very clear that Daniel was expecting her to do all the donkey work to make his dream wedding happen whilst Erica presumably took all the glory as the one providing the cool contacts that Daniel so craved. There was something about weddings that brought out your true role in someone's life. Clearly Daniel saw her as the friend who kept his shit together. Not the friend who made him look cool or who he liked to spend nights out on the town with.

'So we thought we'd all come round to yours next Saturday night if that's okay and have our first planning meeting. Erica says she's sticking around in Leeds for a while because… well, you tell her why, Erica.'

'Because I'm vastly overpaid for what I do,' she said with a smile. 'I thought I'd take a bit of a break and spend some time in my hometown.'

'What she's not telling you is that she's got a two-day shoot in Prague for Valentino in a month's time that pays her enough to rough it with us until then. What a gem, eh?'

Katy nodded silently.

'So, Erica can join us. I'll bring the flipchart and pens. I'm hoping to get around to doing a mood board by then. Well, several mood boards actually. I have a few ideas floating around in my head so I need to do some serious thinking.'

'I could meet you for a Martini one night before then?' said Erica. 'I could take a look at what you are thinking.'

'Would you?' gasped Daniel. 'Wow, that would be so helpful!'

Who says 'meet you for a Martini', thought Katy. She was so conflicted. She so wanted to hate the gorgeous supermodel that was Erica, what with her epic contacts book and her inside knowledge of what was in, but Erica somehow still managed to come across as a genuinely nice person – which was even more annoying.

'Well, if you think I could add anything,' said Erica.

'I'd be honoured, truly,' gushed Daniel. He turned back to Katy.

'So, shall we meet at yours at, say, seven?' asked Daniel. 'And I'll tell you what, don't worry about feeding us. I'll bring some street food.'

Street food, thought Katy. Does he mean takeaway? Is that what we are calling it now? She pulled a face.

'I bet Gio would do us a takeaway,' said Erica. 'I'll ask him, if you like.'

'Really!' exclaimed Daniel. 'Oh my God! Did I mention the gnocchi?' he said to Katy.

'Yes,' she said through gritted teeth.

'Oh, please ask him if you wouldn't mind, Erica. I think I might die if I don't get to eat Gio's gnocchi again sometime soon.'

Erica laughed. She looked at Katy. 'It's good,' she said. 'But not that good.'

Katy couldn't help but smile back. Yes, Erica really was very nice.

'So, we are all set then,' declared Daniel. 'The working party for the wedding of Daniel and Gabriel will have its first meeting this Saturday at seven sharp at the kitchen table of Katy. Dress code smart casual.' He grinned.

Katy tried to grin back, already knowing which member of the working party would be doing most of the working.

Chapter Seventeen

Ben

Ben sat staring blankly at the *Tweenies*. Normally he restricted Millie's TV time on a weekday and in particular he restricted the *Tweenies* because – well, they all wanted locking up, quite frankly. But today he needed thinking time, he needed space. So Millie could watch what the hell she liked as far as he was concerned as long as she kept quiet long enough for him to apply some thought.

He looked down again at his phone and the text he had just received from Braindead, who by rights should have been having the time of his life on the beaches and in the clubs of Ibiza with his new bride. He should not have been sending the type of text Ben had just read.

Hi, mate – sorry to text but having a shit time. Can't stop thinking about my speech and what I did. Can you find out if Alison and Matthew are okay… please. I need to know I haven't broken up a marriage.

Of course Ben didn't know what the aftermath of the speech had been, but he doubted very much if all had been forgiven and forgotten already. He suspected that Alison would take a very long time to recover from the shock and when she did, he doubted even more her ability to forgive.

He scrolled down for Alison's number. He still had it from the time she had helped him out when Katy had gone back to work and Ben had taken on all childcare duties. She had been an utter godsend to him when he was too embarrassed to admit to Katy he had no clue what he was doing. He wondered whether Alison would have been quite so helpful had she known the mammoth secret he had kept from her all these years. He suspected not. The look she'd given him when she'd realised that Ben had known all along about Katy and Matthew's one-night stand still made him shudder. He'd gladly accepted her help when all along he'd known that her husband had cheated on her. He felt ashamed of himself.

He looked back down at his phone and found Alison's number.

How are you doing? Ben

He thought he'd better put his name on it in case she had deleted his number, which was more than likely. He sighed and glanced up at the TV. It was a riot of garish colours and adults dressed in ridiculous costumes. Millie was transfixed. Ben winced. His mobile pinged.

I never want to see you, your wife or my husband ever again. That is how I am doing.

Ben groaned. Not what he wanted to hear. That was bleak. What should he tell Braindead?

Can't get hold of either of them. Worry about it when you get back.
But for now, enjoy your honeymoon because you won't ever have
another one… hopefully

Ben put his phone face down on the coffee table. He didn't want to
have to deal with what Braindead's response might be. He was crying out
for help and Ben had no idea what he could do for him. He leant back
on the sofa, covering his face with his hands. Why did Braindead have
to get himself in these kinds of scrapes? It always seemed to happen to
him. Even on his wedding day he couldn't keep himself out of trouble.

Ben was suddenly aware of a buzzing and looked back down at
his phone. There was a glow coming from the underside that was
demanding his attention. Surely Braindead wasn't calling him from his
actual honeymoon. No-one rang their mates from their honeymoon,
did they, however desperate they were?

He grabbed the phone and looked at the screen, letting out a sigh of
relief. An unusual reaction for when his mother-in-law was calling him.
In fact, it was unusual all round. Rita never called him direct. And it
looked like she wanted to FaceTime him at that. He automatically felt his
hand reach up to smooth his hair down. What was he doing? It was his
mother-in-law. She knew he was a scruffy bugger and yet she still thought
the sun shone out of his backside, much to Katy's disgruntlement. Ben
couldn't do any wrong in the eyes of Rita. In fact, she had been known to
imply that Katy's greatest achievement had been bagging Ben as a husband.
This did not go down well with Katy and so Ben was careful to try and
keep his mother-in-law at arm's length, doing his best to ignore her often
inappropriate comments about his sportsmanlike physique and how lucky
Katy was to have found a much younger man to take care of her needs.

'Hello, Rita,' he said, holding his phone out in front of him. 'Katy's still at work if you are trying to get hold of her.'

'No, Ben. It's not her I wanted to talk to,' said Rita's lips.

Ben felt himself pull away in slight revulsion. His mother-in-law was a trooper when it came to trying to embrace new technology but sometimes her use of it was somewhat disturbing. She was holding the screen too close and all he could see was Rita's red-lipstick-smeared lips rolling around the screen. Unfortunately she also had something stuck in her teeth, making the effect very disturbing.

'It's you I wanted,' her lips continued in what was feeling like some kind of weird 0800 phone call experience. He decided to look up away from the screen and hope that she didn't notice.

'I wanted to see your reaction when I ask you a very important question,' said Rita's lips. 'It's something deeply personal to me and I've thought about it for a very long time. I even had a long chat with Carlos last night and he agreed that he couldn't see me doing it with anyone else. You are the man for the job, he said.'

Ben felt his heart start to beat a little bit faster. What on earth were Rita's lips talking about? He knew she had a soft spot for him but surely this was going a bit far. And what on earth was Carlos thinking, encouraging her? He was about to be her husband, for goodness' sake.

'Carlos even said how good we would look together,' continued the lips. 'He said he would enjoy seeing you playing the role. Right by my side. If you are willing, of course? To play the role?'

'Willing to play which role?' Ben barely dared to ask. 'And please could you pull the screen away from your face? I can only see your lips at the moment.'

'Oh,' said Rita and the screen went blank for a minute as she adjusted her grip. Then he heard a bang, which was probably her dropping her phone, before she reappeared, this time at an appropriate distance.

'Carlos is holding it for me now,' said Rita. 'Is that better?'

'Yes,' Ben nodded, although now he could see that she was wearing a low-cut bikini top which barely encased her ample breasts. He found himself looking at her lips again as that was better than staring at her cleavage.

'So will you do it?' she asked eagerly.

'Do what?' replied Ben.

'You've not asked him yet,' he heard a muffled voice – presumably Carlos – saying.

'I did, didn't I?' said Rita, looking up and away from the screen.

'No, you didn't. Start again,' he heard Carlos urge.

'Right-o,' said Rita, staring back at Ben. 'Right. So, Ben, I wanted to ask you if you would be kind enough to give me away at our wedding?'

'Really, I mean really?' replied Ben, adjusting his tone between 'really's'. He went from dismay to surprise in a matter of seconds.

'Yes, really,' nodded Rita. 'I know you must be wondering why I'm putting this huge responsibility on you but I want you by my side as we walk down the aisle. I can't think of anyone I'd rather have, quite frankly.'

Ben was dumbfounded. He hadn't been expecting that. Given the stress of Braindead's nuptials, he'd been quite looking forward to having a non-role in their wedding. Merging into the background and being just a 'normal guest' sounded really appealing right now.

'Hiya,' he heard a voice ring out from the kitchen. Katy had just arrived back from work.

'Katy's back,' he told Rita.

'Brilliant!' said Rita, clapping her hands. 'We can tell her the good news together. And I need to talk to her about Daniel's engagement. She must be so excited.'

'Daniel's what?'

'Daniel's engagement, hasn't she told you? He's getting married to Gabriel. They rang us from the restaurant last night even though it was two in the morning. Carlos is so happy and I'm over the moon to have Daniel as a son-in-law. I've been tweeking about it all day. Graham Norton liked one of my tweeks. It's so exciting.'

'Everything all right?' he heard Katy say behind him. 'Sorry I'm a bit late, I've got some brilliant news.'

'You didn't tell me that Daniel had got engaged,' said Ben, turning round.

He watched as Katy's face fell. Oh shit, he thought. He wasn't supposed to know.

'How do you know?' she asked.

'Hi, darling,' he heard Rita shout from behind him. 'Isn't it marvellous? I've been dying to talk to you about it but I promised I wouldn't say anything until Daniel told you himself. I can't tell you how excited I am to have Daniel as a son-in-law. I've just been telling Ben that I've been tweeking all day and Graham Norton liked one of my tweeks. How amazing is that?'

Katy slumped down on the sofa next to Ben looking utterly deflated. Ben knew her well enough to know that she wouldn't be happy that Rita got to share Daniel's news with him before she did. Katy and her mum had never been close, with Rita seeming to resent her daughter for all the freedoms her generation had been able to take for granted and hers hadn't. This wasn't going to go down well.

'It suits him, don't you think?' continued Rita. 'He makes a radiant fiancé. They were both positively glowing on the phone last night. Have you been in touch with Gabriel, by the way, to say congratulations?'

'Not yet,' muttered Katy.

'Well, you really must. You are about to be practically related and you must make sure he understands he is welcome in the family. You know, despite the fact he is… well, gay.'

'Mother!' exclaimed Katy. 'You can't say that.'

'Say what? Oh, you know what I mean. There are some people of my generation who wouldn't welcome this type of thing at all, you know,' continued Rita. 'You are very lucky that I have such an open mind and am ecstatic that I have a gay stepson and stepson-in-law. I'm proud, Katy. Do you hear me? Proud to be a gay parent.'

'You're not a gay parent, are you, Mother?' sighed Katy. 'You're just a parent. Well, when you want to be. When you can be bothered.'

Ben put his arm around her.

'What was that?' asked Rita. 'I didn't quite catch that.'

'Nothing,' said Katy. 'It's great news, it really is. I'm really happy for them.'

'And another wedding!' exclaimed Rita. 'How exciting is that? Of course I'm sure they will wait a decent length of time before they plan theirs. I mean, there is another very important wedding coming up in the very near future, isn't there?'

'Yes, Mum,' nodded Katy.

'Speaking of which, do you want to tell Katy your news?' Rita asked Ben.

Ben gulped. Not really, he thought. Not after Katy had looked so crestfallen that her mother had taken the glory of sharing Daniel's engagement away from her. He wasn't sure him standing in as father of the bride was going to cheer her up any.

'Shall I talk to her about it later?' he said hopefully.

'No, tell her now. I want to see her face,' replied Rita.

Katy turned to look at him in confusion. He'd take confusion. That was probably better than the next emotion she was about to go through. He put his hand on her bump and gave it a stroke.

'Your mother,' he said slowly, 'has asked me if I will give her away at her wedding.'

Katy's expression didn't change for a moment. Didn't flicker. Then she looked down at her hands before looking back.

'How lovely,' she said through gritted teeth. 'Perfect, just perfect,' she said in a way that meant it was far from perfect. He took her hand and squeezed it sympathetically.

'I knew you'd be over the moon,' rang out Rita's voice. 'I had the idea when I was watching the end of *An Officer and a Gentleman*. You know, when Richard Gere walks into the factory in his US Navy uniform and sweeps Debra Winger off her feet, literally. I immediately thought of Ben. I knew he would be perfect to give me away.'

Katy stared the phone, waiting for her mother to clarify her inspiration but nothing came.

'It's going to be amazing,' said Rita. 'I'm so excited. Do you think Daniel and Gabriel would be pageboys – how cool would that be? What do you think, Katy?'

'I've no idea,' said Katy flatly.

'And have you got anything to wear yet? Not white, I hope. You can't wear white at someone else's wedding, you know.'

'I know, Mum, and no, I haven't got anything yet because I don't know what size I'm going to be so I'm trying to wait until the last minute.'

'Very wise. Such a shame you're going to be fat on the photos.'

Ben glanced over at Katy in horror.

'Still, I suppose we can put you at the back or stand you behind Uncle Vernon.'

'I'll do my best to be invisible, Mum,' said Katy.

'Well, yes, of course I would have had you take me down the aisle but you're so big so I thought Ben would be the next best thing.'

'Good thinking, Mum.'

'Well, we'd better go. Give my babies a huge hug, won't you?' Rita said, waving manically.

'Babies?' questioned Katy. 'You've only got one grandchild so far.'

'No, I meant Daniel and Gabriel, silly.'

'Oh yeah – of course, silly me,' replied Katy. 'Bye then, Mum.'

'Bye,' replied Rita, throwing kisses from her blood-red lips like confetti.

Suddenly the room was quiet apart from the Tweenies singing an inane song in the background. Ben stared ahead in mini shock.

'What just happened there?' he finally asked.

'My mother just… well, my mother was just being my mother,' replied Katy.

'Are you okay?' asked Ben.

Katy shrugged. 'I shouldn't be surprised, should I? She's been doing it all my life, why should she be any different now? Putting me firmly in my place. Out of sight, if possible.'

'I'm sure she didn't mean it,' said Ben.

'You know she did,' replied Katy.

They fell silent again.

'Good news about Daniel and Gabriel,' offered Ben, trying to lighten the mood.

'Yeah,' shrugged Katy. 'It's brilliant.'

'You okay?' he asked.

'Of course I am,' laughed Katy manically. 'All my nearest and dearest are getting married. They're happy. It's amazing. I'm over the moon.'

'Yeah, right,' replied Ben.

'Just wish we didn't have to go through all this crap just for the sake of seeing them go up the aisle. Why does their happiness have to cause so much hassle?' she demanded. 'And just when we should be concentrating on this one coming along,' she added, stroking her belly.

Ben didn't know what to say. He reached out and put his hand over hers and their soon-to-arrive baby. Wedding season was a major distraction and certainly wasn't going to plan.

His phone beeped in his hand and he prayed it wasn't Rita coming back to cause more offence. He glanced down at the screen to see that Braindead had texted him and his heart sank.

You heard from Matthew or Alison yet? Please let me know. Can't do the business until I know they are OK. Still not sure if that means I'm not married yet?

He hadn't realised that Katy was looking over his shoulder as he read the message.

'Jesus!' said Katy, falling back on the sofa. 'I'd forgotten for a moment the wedding we'd already been to that I wish I hadn't. I don't think I should be let within a mile of a wedding, to be quite honest. I'm a disaster zone. I may have ruined Matthew and Alison's marriage, Braindead is incapable of consummating his because of me, I'm ruining the photos of my mother's wedding because I'm enormous and my best friend… well… my best friend wants me there as a general dogsbody, not as his best bloody friend because he's found a new best friend to play with. So I'm really thinking that I shouldn't be going to any weddings ever again. Weddings and me do not mix… at all… in the slightest. Not any more.'

'I think you're exaggerating,' sighed Ben, easing himself up off the sofa. 'Fancy a beer?'

He'd had enough of all this wedding talk. Weddings were supposed to be something to look forward to and yet at the moment they seemed to be causing way too much angst in their lives.

Katy stared back at him in wonder then pointed to her baby bump.

'Sorry,' he shrugged. 'Forgot for a minute.'

'Well, that's exactly it, isn't it? This is what we should be focusing on. Not multiple weddings from hell,' said Katy.

'You're right,' replied Ben. 'This kid is going to end up with a complex if we're not careful and it's not even born yet.'

He walked out into the kitchen and grabbed a beer from the fridge and a can of some fancy-flavoured mineral water that poor Katy was trying to convince herself was as good as wine.

'I'm going to see Alison,' she announced as he walked back into the lounge.

'What! Are you insane?'

'No,' she replied, shaking her head. 'It's the only way I can keep my sanity. If I can mend Alison and Matthew then Braindead can do what he needs to do and then I might just about be able to deal with the wedding from hell of my mother and Daniel becoming Bridezilla for the next six months.'

'But, Alison?' protested Ben.

'What choice do I have, Ben? I have to put this right so that this baby stands half a chance of coming out to a sane mother. I cannot face another wedding until at least their marriage is mended.'

Chapter Eighteen

Katy

Katy looked up at the highly polished brass door knocker and felt sick as she remembered when she had first visited Matthew and Alison's very smart five-bedroom executive new build on a highly sought-after estate. Alison had unwittingly invited her and Ben to dinner when they met at antenatal classes. It was clear that Alison wanted to be Katy's friend as she was new to the area but had no idea that Katy was the last person she should be latching onto. It had been uncomfortable and awkward, especially as Matthew had also been trying his damnedest to put Ben down; he clearly had written him off as too young and unsuitable for Katy. What a weird night that had been.

Katy glanced down at her hand as she knocked on the door. She'd sat for a good hour at work writing down what to say and how to say it. She'd thought as hard about this conversation as she had for many a new client presentation. In fact, she'd thought harder as it seemed that if she couldn't put right her enormous error from over five years ago then the future looked bleak. She didn't think she'd ever be able to feel comfortable in her own happiness when she had destroyed someone else's.

For a millisecond she'd considered putting together a PowerPoint presentation. After all, Alison was known to be the most anally organised person on the planet. She might like the careful planning and thought that had gone into attempting to unravel and make sense of Katy and Matthew's appalling behaviour. But Katy decided that perhaps that was going too far. Perhaps that would come across a little too efficient even for Alison. So Katy had put prompt words on the back of her hand to make sure she hit all of her key messages. She wanted to make sure that Alison understood exactly what she was saying. The words included: *mistake*, *stupid*, *meaningless* and *catastrophic lapse in judgement* (abbreviated to *CLinJ*).

Katy pulled down her maternity dress, which she had carefully selected as the one that made her look the most maternal. She figured being pregnant had to be her secret weapon. No-one could be that mad at a pregnant woman, could they?

'Oh,' said a woman who opened the door and who wasn't Alison. Katy knew this must be Lena the nanny. She was thrown for a minute, having expected to confront Alison on the doorstep.

'Erm, could I see Alison, just for a minute?' she asked. 'My name is Katy. I really need to talk to her.'

'Well, er,' faltered Lena. 'I shall ask her,' she said, shutting the door in her face.

Katy took a step back and glanced at her hand again. Not a good start. Fifty-fifty on whether Alison would let her in given she had warning of her arrival.

The door opened and Lena reappeared.

'You've got five minutes in the kitchen,' she said, nodding her head towards one of the five doors that led off the double-height hallway.

'Oh, thank you, thank you,' gushed Katy. She was past the first hurdle.

She pushed down on the handle and peered cautiously round the door. Alison was sitting in a large comfy chair in the bay window with a cat on her lap. Katy would have half expected her to say 'I've been expecting you' had she not looked so terrible.

Whenever Katy had previously seen Alison she had been immaculately turned out, even wearing make-up to antenatal classes. Alison normally set a lot of store in keeping up appearances and yet here she was with her hair scraped back in a messy ponytail, not a scrap of make-up and a curious grey pallor to her face that indicated a lack of any real sleep. Katy fought the urge to dash up to her and put her arms around her. She also did her best to quell the tears that sprang to her eyes.

'Well?' said Alison, not looking up but concentrating on stroking her cat.

Katy gulped and glanced down at her hand but none of the words she had so carefully crafted seemed to have the ability to soothe this poor broken woman.

'I just wanted to come and say… well, to say to you that… well, that I'm sorry, so very, very sorry.'

Alison looked up sharply, anger flooding her face.

'Sorry!' she shrieked. 'Sorry! Is that it? Is that all you have to say, having destroyed my life? Sorry!'

'No, I… er… I… er…' Katy glanced down at her hand. 'It was a catastrophic lapse in judgement… yes, that's what it was. It was a mistake, it was stupid, meaningless, utterly meaningless.'

Alison stared back at her.

'It meant nothing,' Katy said more firmly.

'You already said that,' pointed out Alison.

'I know,' whimpered Katy. 'But it's true. It didn't.'

Alison was shaking her head now in firm denial of everything Katy had said.

'It wasn't, was it?' she spat. 'Look at me,' she said. 'You may think it was meaningless, but I don't. You slept with my husband whilst we were *trying* for a baby. How am I supposed to think that is meaningless? If it meant nothing then why the hell did you do it? What was the point? It doesn't make sense.'

'I... I... did it for... for revenge,' Katy found herself saying. 'I was still mad at Matthew for dumping me when he went to uni. I... I thought if I slept with him then walked away, then he would get a taste of his own medicine. Feel how I felt when we broke up. I didn't want him or anything, I promise. I didn't want him back. I wanted to teach him a lesson, that's all.'

'And did it ever enter your tiny little mind what your pathetically little screwed-up revenge plot could do to me?'

'No,' sobbed Katy. 'Of course not. If I'd thought of that, I never would have done it.'

Tears were sliding down her face now. She couldn't hold them back. She'd come prepared, or so she'd thought, but now she was totally exposed. Alison could literally see right through her.

'So did he want you?' demanded Alison.

'What?'

'Did he want you? For your nasty little plan to work, I'm assuming that you must have thought he wanted you?'

Katy looked up at her and tried to hide the shock at her question. She wasn't sure if Matthew had wanted her but then the memory of him visiting her in the labour ward came flooding back. When he'd offered to leave Alison and make a new life with Katy. He had wanted her then but she had rejected him. She shook her head to block it out of her mind.

'No... no... that's not what I meant, not at all... Like I said, it was meaningless.'

'That's the third time you've said that.'

Katy let out a sob and bowed her head.

'It's not just the fact that you slept together,' began Alison, 'it's the lengths you both went to, to lie about it. You lied to me, Katy. You've always been lying to me and you've turned my husband into a liar. For all these years you shared this massive secret and I was oblivious. Did you laugh at me behind my back? Is that what you did? For being so stupid as to not pick up on it. Were you laughing at me?'

'No! Of course not,' said Katy. 'We did everything we could to back out of each other's lives but then somehow... somehow circumstances kept putting us back together. It was awful. I never wanted to live this lie.'

'Oh, poor Katy,' said Alison scornfully. 'Must have been terrible for you.'

'I know,' said Katy. 'Nowhere near as terrible as for you. I know that.'

'I bet you couldn't believe it, could you, when we turned up at the same antenatal classes. What are the chances of that? I can remember sitting in the car after our first class and asking Matthew why he'd run out midway through. He told me he'd felt sick but was that the shock of seeing you again? You see, I can't stop thinking of all these times we've spent together or run into each other and all I've wanted is to be friends and all you've been thinking about is the time you shagged my husband.'

'No... no... it's not like that. It's in the past, Alison. I don't think about it. It's not significant any more. Not to me.' Katy's voice faded as she sensed that wasn't the right thing to say. Alison's nostrils flared.

'I mean,' faltered Katy. 'I mean, I realise it's significant to you, I'm just trying to say that... that I don't think it's significant enough to affect the rest of our lives. It was stupid but it was a long time ago and all I really want is to see you and Matthew together and your family happy and this to be in the past, where it belongs.'

Alison did not respond.

'There's not a day goes by when I don't regret it,' continued Katy. 'Ever since that day we walked into the antenatal class and I saw you sat there next to Matthew, I realised what I'd done, what we'd done, and how stupid and pointless it had been.'

'Had you been trying for a baby too?' Alison suddenly asked.

'No,' said Katy automatically. 'No. Millie was an accident but a very happy one.'

Alison was studying her carefully. She was thinking, processing, and to Katy's horror, she realised what she must be thinking about. She froze; words would not come out of her mouth. She had to speak. Stop Alison thinking. Anything to stop her thinking.

'A mistake,' said Alison nodding, then her hand flew up to her mouth in shock as the realisation dawned on her.

'No, no!' exclaimed Katy. 'No, it's not what you think.'

'Millie could be Matthew's?' she said, her mouth wide open in horror.

'No, no!' wailed Katy. 'No, she's Ben's. Hair, Alison, hair. She has Ben's ginger hair. You've seen her, she's Ben all over.'

Alison stared back at her. Processing the latest piece of the puzzle that she had just handed her.

'We did a paternity test,' Katy admitted. 'Ben wasn't bothered but I wanted to make sure that he was in no doubt. That we never had to question it ever again. I can show you the paperwork if you want... whatever you need, but I can promise you Millie is Ben's.'

Alison didn't speak for what felt like hours. Then she finally spoke in a low growl.

'But she could have been. You didn't deny it. She could have been Matthew's or you wouldn't have taken the test. Oh my God,' she said, her hand flying to her mouth. 'Imagine.'

'I'm so sorry,' sobbed Katy again.

'Get out,' shouted Alison, her eyes blazing. 'Get – out – now.'

Chapter Nineteen

Katy

You had better come. Come now. Daniel devastated at the news.
We're at Gio's. I'll send a car. Erica

Katy stared down at the text message she'd just received. Daniel devastated… What on earth had happened? She was sending a car… who does that? No-one sends a car because someone is upset! Where was Erica sending the car? What was Katy supposed to do? Go down into reception and wait for it there? None of it made any sense.

Katy logged into her computer and glanced at her diary. Fortunately it was lunchtime and she didn't have another meeting until two o'clock or else Erica could send as many cars as she wanted, Katy wouldn't be going anywhere.

And what was Daniel doing with Erica at Gio's in the middle of the day on a work day anyway? Okay, so he was totally obsessed with this damn wedding but the working party wasn't due to meet until Saturday night. They'd agreed. Not that Katy was in any kind of mood to discuss wedding plans after her catastrophic meeting with Alison. Quite frankly, she wanted to crawl into a hole and never be seen again.

Alison's anger and anguish had sent Katy down into such deep dark gloom and despair that she had no idea how she was going to drag herself out of it, let alone throw herself into the planning of not one but two glorious weddings.

Katy sighed and reached for her coat from the back of her chair. She'd better at least go down into reception and see if the car had been sent. Better go and find out what the latest was in terms of devastation that had descended on those around her.

*

'Are you sure this is it?' she asked the driver when he pulled up in a derelict car park.

'Yes,' he nodded. 'I know it doesn't look much, does it, but whatever is in that carriage over there must be pretty special because I'm always dropping her off here.'

'Right,' nodded Katy. 'So, do you work for Erica then?'

'Only when she's in the country.'

'Right,' said Katy, still looking dubiously out of the window.

'Let me help you out,' said the driver, leaping out of the car and opening the door. 'Now, be careful going across this car park in your condition,' he told her, grabbing her arm and helping her to ease herself up. 'There are some horrendous potholes. We don't want you falling down one.'

'Thank you,' she said, pulling herself up straight.

She took a deep breath and started to walk towards the extremely unwelcoming-looking carriage.

'Good luck,' called the man behind her. She turned. 'I think you might need it, given the state of the two in there.' He smiled and waved, got back in his car before starting it and pulling out of the car park.

She suddenly felt like she was in a crime show, being sent to some dodgy part of Leeds to meet a criminal. What if it hadn't been Erica who texted her? What if she was being set up? What if it was Alison and she'd masqueraded as Erica and got her down here under false pretences and was about to bludgeon her to death? She had every right to, after all. Katy had slept with her husband. Why wouldn't she want her dead?

She took her phone out and checked the text from Erica again. They had swapped numbers at the wedding... before Braindead's speech. It was unlikely that Alison had first kidnapped Erica and taken her phone in order to lure her here. Wasn't it? Of course it was. She was being ridiculous. The folic acid she was taking must be sending her brain wappy. That or the stress of multiple weddings and a breakup.

She walked towards the carriage and noticed a small set of steps leading up to a side door. On closer inspection there was a very discreet sign that read 'Gio's' on the door in navy and brushed silver. So discreet that if you happened to wander by, you would never in a million years think that this was apparently one of Leeds' most sought-after dining establishments. You would definitely think it was a disused railway carriage.

Katy walked up the steps, pushed on the handle and felt it give. She peered inside. Inside it looked like... well, a railway carriage really. The lighting was lower perhaps, but there were tables topped with Formica, seats upholstered with gaudy patterned fabric and an aisle running down the middle. At the far end it looked like a space had been cleared for a small bar, where she could see Erica and Daniel perching on bar stools, Daniel's head resting on Erica's shoulder.

Erica looked up then nudged Daniel to make him aware Katy had arrived. She noticed his face was ashen as he leapt off his stool, ran down the narrow corridor and engulfed her in a hug.

'Oh, Katy, what am I going to do? Tell me what to do. It's all a disaster!'

'What? What's happened?' she asked as Erica joined them and placed a reassuring hand on Daniel's shoulder, shaking her head from side to side slowly.

Katy's heart immediately started to beat too fast. She'd seen that type of headshake before. On the TV. The sad headshake was the code that someone had just died.

'Who died?' she gasped. 'Not Gabriel? Tell me it's not Gabriel,' she said, pushing Daniel away so she could look at him. His eyes were red raw and laden with bags. He looked terrible. She gasped again. 'It is, isn't it? Oh no, poor you!' she said, pulling him towards her again. 'Poor you! How can this have happened?'

Erica was shaking her head again but this time in a different way. More urgent and with a frown.

'He's not dead,' said Daniel, pulling back. 'Of course he's not dead.'

'Oh my God – thank goodness,' gasped Katy, feeling her knees go weak. She needed to sit down but there was nowhere because all the carriage seats appeared too small for her pregnant body.

She clutched her heart and tried to slow her breathing, holding onto Daniel's shoulder.

'But the worst thing has happened,' declared Daniel.

'What could be worse than your fiancé dying?' asked Katy.

'Carlos and Rita have suggested we have a… a… joint wedding and… and… Gabriel said yes!'

Katy stared at Daniel as she tried to process what he was saying.

'Joint wedding,' reiterated Daniel. 'And with your mother… and in a dodgy bar in Spain. It's… it's… just not what I dreamed of, Katy.

Not at all. You know me. My wedding… well, it's all about me, isn't it? It's got to be all about me. I can't share a wedding. I *can't* do it!'

Katy didn't know what to say. She didn't know whether to laugh or cry. She couldn't quite decide if this was utterly hilarious or indeed tragic.

'How did it happen?' she asked. 'Whose idea was it?'

'Carlos's apparently. Gabriel said that he called him to run some dates by him – you know, before our working party meeting on Saturday – and apparently, he just came out with it. Just said, why don't you come here and get married and, whilst you're about it, why don't you just get married with us?'

'And what does Gabriel think?'

'He thinks it's a great idea. He wanted to get married in Spain anyway, which I wasn't averse to, but I had this idea of a beautiful hilltop hotel with a spa, not a tourists' bar on the strip surrounded by sunburned lager louts.'

'It might not be like that,' said Katy.

'Whatever it's like, it won't be something out of the Mr and Mrs Smith book, will it?'

'Unlikely,' she agreed.

'What do I do, Katy? This is all of my hopes and dreams in tatters. I just don't know what to do.'

Katy looked over his shoulder at Erica. How come she was the one he ran to when it all went pear-shaped?

'What did you tell him to do?' she asked Erica.

'Call you?' she shrugged.

'Will you talk to Rita?' Daniel urged Katy. 'Talk to your mum and convince her it's a bad idea. I'm sure she doesn't really want to get married with me, does she? Rita strikes me as just like me, wants all the attention on her. Surely she thinks this is a terrible idea, don't you think?'

Katy thought about it. In normal circumstances she would agree. The last thing her mother would want would to be upstaged by another bride. The thought of sharing her big day with another couple would horrify her. But, given their conversation the other night, Katy suspected actually on this occasion, Rita might not agree. Her mother was already excited about the kudos she felt she was getting by having a gay stepson and there was no end to the bragging rights she would have if she shared her wedding with the happy gay couple. Rita would be the coolest pensioner on the block. Katy could imagine her now practically with a rainbow flag as a wedding dress, so proud would she be of her progressive family.

'I'd like to agree with you, Daniel, for all our sakes,' said Katy. 'But I think the problem is that she loves Gabriel, she adores you and the prospect of being able to tell all her cronies that she is the most modern of brides because she is sharing her wedding day with her gay stepson will be an opportunity my mother would not want to miss. You and Gabriel are the ultimate wedding accessory that she would want to embrace with both hands.'

'Pleeeease talk to her, pleeease,' begged Daniel.

Katy couldn't bear the thought of yet another difficult conversation this week.

'What about what Gabriel wants?' she asked.

Erica suddenly appeared behind Daniel, a full Martini glass in hand.

'Oh, cheers, darling,' he gushed, grabbing hold of it and taking a huge slug. 'You are a life-saver.'

'What about Gabriel?' repeated Katy, trying not to be perturbed that Erica was seen as the life-saver just for arriving with a cocktail.

'Oh, Gabriel. You know what he's like. Too relaxed for words. He thinks it's a great idea. He said it cuts down on the number of weddings—'

'Good point,' interrupted Katy. That indeed was a major upside.

'Irrelevant,' said Daniel. 'Anyway, I think he's just overwhelmed that his dad wants to be so involved. Apparently they had a bit of a rocky patch when Gabriel first came out so the fact that Carlos wants to be such a big part of our day is quite the revelation.'

Katy looked at Daniel. 'Well then, don't you think that you should respect Gabriel's view on that? If Gabriel wants to share his wedding with his dad, shouldn't you just go with it if that makes him happy?'

Daniel stared back at Katy.

'But sharing my wedding day,' he gasped. 'My *wedding* day. My *big gay wedding day!*' He shook his head. 'It's the ultimate in discrimination.'

'Why is it?' exclaimed Katy. 'Surely this is all about acceptance and inclusion. All the things you want, surely?'

'No, it's not,' said Daniel, taking another glug of his cocktail. 'If I were a bride, if I were a woman, then no-one would even dream of asking me to share my wedding, would they? Not a chance in hell. No, it's just because I'm gay that this is even being considered. Oh, let's show how cool we are by having the gay couple get married at our wedding. I am *not* a performing monkey. I am *not* the entertainment. I am *not* the sideshow.'

'I don't think that's how Carlos sees it, do you?'

'Maybe not,' replied Daniel, 'but your mother will. Think about it. How will your mother and I agree on anything in regards to the wedding? Flowers? I don't even want flowers, I want miniature spruces imported from Norway and your mother will want something dreadful, like pink carnations or, heaven forbid, roses! And food? Don't get me started on food. I intend to fly Gio to our wedding, where we will build him a kitchen in the centre of the room and we will gather round and eat gnocchi straight from the pan. What will your mother want? Chicken in mushroom sauce, guaranteed, with dauphinoise potatoes and green beans. I can almost taste it, it's so predictable.'

'Surely in Spain it will be tapas?' said Katy.

'Tapas!' exclaimed Daniel. 'So last year.'

'Right,' nodded Katy. 'I had no idea.'

'And don't get me started on the guest list. I'm going to get married surrounded by leather-faced pensioners who insist on calling me Dan because they think that means they're my mate and who will get drunk and get the karaoke machine out, which will interfere with the opera singer that Erica has put me in touch with, who does the most heartbreaking version of "Ave Maria" you have ever heard. Imagine that overlaid with "Hi Ho Silver Lining". Face it, Katy. It's just not going to work, is it?'

Katy stared back at Daniel. She didn't know what she was supposed to do or say. Indeed, she couldn't imagine her mum and Daniel agreeing on anything and the result being a dog's dinner of a wedding, but what was she supposed to do about it?

'I need to sit down,' she said pleadingly, suddenly feeling a little woozy.

'Come up here,' said Erica, stepping in and leading her to the top of the carriage to a larger seat. 'Would you like some gnocchi?' she asked gently.

'Oh yes,' replied Katy, suddenly realising how hungry she was. 'Yes, please.'

'Believe me,' said Daniel. 'You'll taste Gio's gnocchi and you'll realise there can be nothing else that can pass our lips at my wedding. You'll taste it and then you will understand that whatever happens, I cannot get married with your mother.'

Chapter Twenty

Ben

Forty minutes' delay, thank the Lord, thought Ben, getting to arrivals with a squeal of burnt rubber on the soles of his sneakers. He'd somehow got snarled up with a parent at the school where he was currently doing teacher training. It was a posh school in a posh area and he was struggling with the demands of the parents, who clearly had very high expectations.

He'd known he was in trouble when a very serious-looking woman approached him at the school gate.

'Are you Mr Chapman?' she asked.

'I might be,' he replied with a grin.

She looked back at him, confused. Clearly she didn't understand the concept of humour.

'How can I help you?' he asked.

'Jacob came home yesterday and said he had had the best day ever at school,' she replied.

'Excellent news,' replied Ben, thinking surely any parent would be delighted to learn their child had had the best day ever at school.

'But when I asked him what he had been doing, he said he had been sticking pins into Mr Chapman.'

'Ah, yes,' laughed Ben. 'Well, you see, they're not real pins, just paper pins, and for some reason the kids are much more willing to learn their spellings if they get to stick a pin in me when they get them right. Go figure, heh? We had nearly a hundred per cent correct yesterday. That's a vast improvement, I can tell you.'

'But Jacob gets them all right every week. We practise them together every morning. He does not need to stick pins into anybody in order to get his spellings correct.'

'Well, he's a very lucky man to have such a supportive mother,' replied Ben. 'Unfortunately, some of the other children do require the incentive of doing me harm in order to get them all right.'

'Well, I'd ask if in future you could not include Jacob in these pointless violence-inducing games. It's clearly unnecessary for him.'

'Apart from the fact he came home and said he'd really enjoyed school. So it can't have been totally pointless for him, can it?'

'*Do not* encourage him to stick pins in you again or I shall be asking to see Mrs Pendleton,' replied the mother before turning away and flouncing off.

'For fuck's sake!' Ben had muttered before turning round and realising the altercation had caused him to be much later than planned picking up Braindead and Abby.

Now at the airport, he found himself a chair facing the arrivals gate and settled himself down on it to watch the incoming hordes of holidaymakers.

He smiled to himself as he watched what was clearly a stag do arriving back from a huge weekend. Not a hint of a suntan between them. He doubted if they had got out their beds before the middle of the afternoon, choosing to enjoy the nightlife rather than the sunshine. They looked pale and listless, actually terrible. One guy had stitches on his forehead and another had a black eye. Ben hoped that neither was the groom. Thank goodness Braindead hadn't wanted a weekend away for the stag do. Ben knew he'd got past the age when the thought of a few days completely hammered appealed. He'd breathed a sigh of relief when Braindead said he wanted a night down his local microbrewery and he wanted to try every single ale at least once. This had of course led to a pretty dramatic hangover but no injuries were incurred and they had gotten into a pretty interesting conversation with a man who restored furniture for a living. Christ, they were getting old!

You could also tell the couples who had perhaps not had the holiday they expected. Every few minutes a man would come out pushing a trolley with a miserable look on his face and then a few seconds later a woman would trot up behind, scowling. Clearly a week of nothing but each other had not been the tonic that these couples required to revive their flagging relationships. Ben prayed that was not how Braindead would emerge – but given their last text conversation, he had no idea whether or not the honeymoon had been a success in the end.

He heard Abby's cackle before he saw her. He had been watching a bunch of OAPs cluster through, shrieking happily as they spotted their offspring waiting to take them home. No doubt they were thinking that now was payback time after the years of taxiing they had done for them, back in the day. As the automatic door opened again, in came Abby, tottering on high heels and in a short skirt and an enormous-brimmed sun hat and sunglasses. She looked beach-ready, not grey-wet-Leeds-Bradford-airport-ready, but at least she was smiling – grinning from ear to ear, in fact – as she embraced Ben, engulfing him in a heady mix of perfume and suntan cream.

'Good time then?' he asked as she pulled away.

'Oh my God,' she shrieked, 'the best! You should have seen our room, Ben. Huge. Just huge, bigger than the Co-op at the corner of our road, I reckon. Braindead really splashed out. I felt like an actual celebrity, honestly. I kept expecting to see long lenses pointed at our balcony. We were on the top floor and everything. They didn't call it the penthouse but it was the penthouse, seriously amazing.'

'Great, good,' said Ben. 'And have you left Braindead there?' he asked, looking around.

'I'm here, mate,' said Braindead approaching them, his trolley stacked high with leopard-skin-patterned luggage. Clearly Abby's, not his.

'How's it going, mate?' Ben asked, stepping forward to embrace him. He'd missed his friend, although he knew he was going to have to start getting used to seeing him less now that he was married maybe? Although Braindead was usually a law unto himself when it came to conventions. Ben wasn't sure what his view would be of how much time one should spend with one's new wife.

'Great, mate,' replied Braindead. 'Great,' he nodded.

Ben scrutinised him but could not glean how he really was and whether he had managed to enjoy his honeymoon.

'Er... shall you and I go get the car?' said Braindead. 'Save Abby having to walk miles in those shoes. We could pick you up outside arrivals,' he told her. 'Just over there, look, outside that shop.'

Abby looked over to where he was pointing and nodded. 'Yes,' she said. 'I'll be sitting on that bench.'

They watched as she tottered off towards the bench, clearly ready to take the weight off those towering heels.

'So, I'm up in the multi-storey,' Ben told Braindead. 'You can wait here too if you like with Abby.'

'No,' said Braindead, shaking his head and already heading towards the lifts. 'I'll come with you. I need to know if it's all sorted. Why didn't you text me? I've been waiting to hear from you.'

Ben jogged to catch up with him. 'You haven't, have you? I told you to forget about it. Enjoy your honeymoon.'

'And I told you I couldn't. So what's happened then? Have you heard from Alison?'

Ben bit his lip. What should he tell him? He figured he didn't have much choice but to tell him the truth.

'Alison did text me back,' he said. 'I'm afraid it's not good news. She's chucked Matthew out.'

'What!' exclaimed Braindead. 'No! But that's temporary, right? Got to be. She'll forgive him, won't she? She's got to.'

Ben wondered if he should tell him about Katy's visit to Alison.

'I'll go and see her,' said Braindead. 'Make her see sense. Make her see that it shouldn't destroy their family.'

'Braindead, no,' said Ben. 'Katy's tried that. She went to see Alison and, well, let's just say it didn't help.'

'Why? What did she say?' asked Braindead.

Ben swallowed. This wasn't easy for him to say. 'Well, Alison clocked there was a tiny possibility that Matthew could have been Millie's father. Of course Katy was clear that he wasn't, but Alison was understandably shocked at the possibility. Especially as they had been going through IVF at the time.'

Braindead stopped in his tracks, clearly trying to process what Ben was saying.

'I'm sorry,' said Ben, laying a hand on his shoulder. 'I know it's not what you wanted to hear.'

'We're screwed,' said Braindead, looking up at him wide-eyed. 'She's never going to let him back, is she?'

'Possibly not,' agreed Ben. 'But it's still not your fault.' Ben felt a curious twist of anger that, despite having forgiven Katy long ago for her one-night stand with Matthew, the consequences were now hurting his best mate and he didn't know what to do about it.

Braindead shook his head. 'We've got to sort it out,' he said. 'We have to. I can't... I can't... I still haven't...'

'What!' exclaimed Ben. 'You mean...?'

Braindead nodded. 'Every time I try, I just picture Alison and, well...'

'A libido crusher if ever there was one,' agreed Ben.

'It's a nightmare,' said Braindead.

'But... but what about Abby? She looks like she's had a great honeymoon?' pointed out Ben.

'Oh, she has.' Braindead nodded vigorously. 'I've... shall we say I've made sure that I have looked after her in that department.'

Ben stared at his friend. Was he saying what he thought he was saying?

Braindead stared back.

'It's been really hard work,' he admitted eventually.

'But, but hasn't she noticed, you know, that...?' asked Ben.

'I said it was my wedding present,' said Braindead. 'That it was all about her and not to worry about me. It was a honeymoon present. That seemed to suffice as an explanation.'

'Right,' nodded Ben, still not quite believing that he was having this conversation.

'In fact, in some ways it could all work out well. She's already said that it's my turn on our first anniversary,' said Braindead.

'Right,' said Ben again.

'Mmmm,' agreed Braindead.

'Shall we pretend we never had this conversation?' asked Ben.

'Better had,' agreed Braindead. 'Best not mention it to Abby.'

'Of course not, no way, never,' replied Ben.

'Unless perhaps she forgets about it on our anniversary and she needs a nudge from someone.'

'No way,' said Ben. 'Not ever.'

'Fair enough,' sighed Braindead. 'Hopefully, it won't matter though of course by then. Hopefully… you know…'

'You'll have got past the Alison image thing and been able to perform?'

'Yes,' said Braindead. 'Or else I could have one of those annulment things on my hands, couldn't I?'

Chapter Twenty-One

Katy

The situation has progressed – help!

Katy sat in the impossibly small toilet at Gio's and sent a text to Ben. Of course they had thought it was ironically cool to use the existing carriage toilet as the one for the restaurant. She had no idea how she had wedged her pregnant body in there but somehow, by backing herself in, she had managed it. How she was going to get out, she had no idea. But she knew she had to take a breather from Daniel's desperate face and call in reinforcements.

Which situation? replied Ben.

Katy sighed and began to text back.

The Wedding situation. Carlos wants Gabriel and Daniel to have a joint wedding with them. Can you imagine? My mum and Daniel – two Bridezillas on a scale never before seen. This is not going to work. In full-on panic mode. X

Katy looked up and tried to control her breathing. She did feel on the verge of a total panic attack, if she was honest. She could see a lifetime spent hiding in toilets away from wedding traumas stretching out in front of her.

Holy Shit! came the reply.

My *thoughts exactly!* replied Katy.

Is now a good time to tell you that Braindead still hasn't had sex because he pictures Alison crying every time he goes to do the deed?

Katy stared down at her phone. This was very bad news indeed. She couldn't decide what was worse. The prospect of mediating between her mother and Daniel on their wedding, or the fact that her actions had now possibly ruined not just one marriage but potentially another before it had even got off the ground. Right now it felt like the safest place to be was locked in a toilet in a disused railway carriage.

Chapter Twenty-Two

Matthew

'Ow,' he howled, pulling the flimsy clingfilm off his microwave dinner. He shuffled it towards the plate gingerly, then tipped over the gooey mass that apparently was lasagne. It slipped and slid all over the plate like an unwelcome oil slick on a beach. Was it really lasagne? He studied the packaging and saw that the picture on the front bore no resemblance whatsoever to what was now puddled on his plate. The picture implied there was actual beef in the dish whereas as far as he could see there were perhaps grains of meat lurking somewhere under the pinkish swirl of white sauce mixed unattractively with tepid tomatoes.

He sighed and picked the dish up and carried it into the sitting room, where he had an opened bottle of beer waiting as well as the TV turned onto a sports channel. If his world hadn't collapsed around him then this scenario could actually have made him happy. He wasn't allowed to eat in front of the TV at home, particularly not in front of the sport. Alison said he wouldn't enjoy his food and he would spill something on the carpet if he got overexcited about a result. Instead, they aimed to all eat as a family round the dinner table at night, which could be chaotic and loud and noisy and most certainly didn't lead to enjoyment of food, but he loved it and it made his heart hurt to know he was missing it every night. Missing those moments when he stared round the table at his wife and four children and wondered how on earth that had happened and how nothing on the planet could make him happier.

He felt a sting of tears in his eyes as he dug his fork into the mush. He felt sick with worry that he would never sit there with his family around a table again. He took a slug of his beer and sniffed, diverting his attention to the match on the telly. Maybe his visitor tonight would have some bright ideas as to how to put everything back together again.

It was one–all in a very boring match when Ian burst in. Matthew had only managed half of his lasagne and the dirty plate sat on the coffee table, congealing in a very unattractive manner.

'Quick!' Ian said, gathering up a discarded pizza box and two dirty glasses left from the night before on the table. 'Lena is only five minutes behind me. Come on, you need to tidy up quick!'

Matthew looked up, startled.

'Why? Has she got Alison with her?' He felt his heart soar with anticipation.

'No!' said Ian. 'I just know from bitter experience that traces of the bachelor lifestyle, i.e. everywhere in a right state, are inconducive to a romantic evening with one's girlfriend. I once got a woman back here one night and she insisted that I mop the floor in the kitchen before we went to bed. She said she needed to get the disgusting image out of her head. I mean, what is it with women and the need to be tidy?'

Matthew couldn't help but think about Alison and her somewhat OCD approach to tidiness. Living in Ian's hovel, he had never missed it more.

'You don't mind making yourself scarce, do you?' Ian said as he switched the TV off in front of him.

'I was watching that,' Matthew protested.

'Sport on the telly, mate. Another big turn-off. Huge. Never put the sport on the telly if you think she's in the mood for romance. On another occasion I went back to a girl's house and it was all systems go, if you know what I mean. I just flicked Sky on to check the final scores and well… she'd ordered me an Uber before I even got to the bottom of the Premiership table. Anyway, why don't you take yourself down to the Anchor at the end of the road for a couple of hours? The beer's good, but don't get talking to the landlord unless you want to have the tits bored off you about his sciatica.'

'But I've got someone coming round,' said Matthew. 'I'm sorry, I didn't realise you had a night in with Lena planned.'

'Someone coming round? Who? A woman? Jesus, Matthew! I thought you wanted to get back with Alison?'

'No, of course not a woman. No, Braindead is coming over. You know, the guy who let the cat out of the bag at his wedding? He's just back from honeymoon and wants to see what he can do to try and make amends.'

Ian paused his sweeping of crumbs off the coffee table.

'But it's not really his fault, is it? I mean, he was an idiot and all that. Utter cretin by the sounds of it, but it wasn't him who slept with his ex, was it? It was you.'

'I know. You don't have to tell me that. You can't shoot the messenger but he sounded desperate. I think he feels really bad about it, like really bad. He was nearly crying on the phone when I said I haven't seen the kids since his wedding. He just wants to help. You never know, maybe he might think of something.'

'With a name like Braindead?'

'He's surprisingly smart in an odd sort of way.'

'Well, he can be surprisingly smart with you down the pub. Your misdemeanour and your presence here is in danger of jeopardising my relationship if I don't spend some quality time with Lena.'

'Can I just talk to her for a minute when she gets here though?' asked Matthew. 'Ask her how the kids are.'

'I suppose,' shrugged Ian. 'If you must. I'm just going to go and make the bed quick. You know, just in case. Another top tip for you if it doesn't work out with Alison: always make sure your bed is made. I've had women walk away from an unmade bed before. Epic fail!'

Matthew picked up his dirty plate and walked through to the kitchen, mentally preparing questions to ask Lena when she arrived. He doubted that she would be very forthcoming, however, as it appeared she was understandably very much on Alison's side. The doorbell rang and he shouted to Ian that he would answer it. He pulled open the front door and there stood the unlikely pair of Braindead and Lena.

'I mean, I couldn't be sorrier for what I've done,' Braindead was saying seriously to Lena. 'I'm such an idiot.'

Lena glanced over at Matthew before putting her hand on Braindead's arm.

'You are not the stupid one,' she said. 'He is,' she continued, giving Matthew a cursory nod and then pushing past him.

'Lena,' said Matthew, ignoring Braindead and chasing after her into the kitchen. 'Lena,' he said. 'I'm so glad to see you. Please tell me how the kids are. I can't tell you how much I am missing them. Are they OK? Have they asked after me?'

Lena ignored Matthew as she busied herself taking her coat off. Making him wait for his answer. When she was happy that her coat was hung up correctly, she turned to face him.

'Alison said to tell you that you may visit the children at the house on Saturday. You may come at 10 a.m. and must be gone by 2 p.m. Alison will not be there but I have been asked to be present.' She nodded curtly.

'Well, that's good news, isn't it, mate?' asked Braindead, standing in the kitchen door. 'A good sign, Alison letting you see the kids. It's an opportunity. Got to be.'

Matthew sat down heavily on a chair. The thought of being able to see his children made him feel dizzy. It was progress, it was something.

'Thank you,' he said to Lena. 'Tell Alison, thank you. I... er... I, er, appreciate it.'

'She's a very good mother,' replied Lena, nodding.

'Hello, you,' said Ian, bustling in and engulfing his girlfriend in a hug. She lost her rather frosty demeanour and embraced him warmly, the smile coming back to her lips. They pulled apart and Ian looked around awkwardly for a moment, spotting Matthew with his head in his hands and a stranger standing by the doorway.

'You must be Brainless,' he said, stepping forward and thrusting his hand towards Braindead. 'The mastermind behind all this chaos?'

Braindead shook Ian's hand mutely, the colour draining from his face. 'I'm so sorry,' he spluttered. 'I can't tell you how sorry I am that I said what I said. I forgot where I was for a minute, and I don't know what I was thinking and I was so happy because, you know, it was my wedding day and then I saw Matthew coming for me across the dance floor and I didn't know what I'd done, but then I realised and ever since I've not been able to forgive myself. I'm here to put it right. We have to put it right, do you understand?'

Ian's mouth had fallen open at Braindead's passion.

'We do,' he eventually nodded. 'We do, because quite frankly, this epic error Matthew made all those years ago is getting in the way of all of our lives.' He put his arm around Lena. 'Quite frankly, I did not envisage at the age of forty-seven I'd be shacking up with my best mate in a glorified bedsit because we had both screwed up our marriages. Now, fortunately for me, I can see a bright path ahead, but Matthew moving in has caused me to take a bit of a wrong turn, the lights are dimming fast and so the sooner we get him back in that house, the better, don't you think?'

'Of course,' nodded Braindead vigorously. 'I keep thinking of the children. Oh my God, the children!' he said, close to tears.

'Fine, you worry about the children if that's what motivates you. What motivates me is getting time alone with this young lady.'

Lena blushed.

'So,' continued Ian, 'you'd both better go down the pub and work out what's going to fix this because I cannot stand to look at his miserable face any longer.'

*

'You been mates long?' Braindead asked Matthew as he took the first sip of his pint.

'Me and Ian?' said Matthew. 'We've been colleagues for about fifteen years. I did start off down in the London office but I moved up here when we started the family.'

'Seems like a nice bloke,' said Braindead.

'He reminds me a bit of you,' said Matthew.

'Really?'

'Yeah. Says what he thinks. Lack of filter. Engages mouth before brain quite often.'

'I'm so sorry, Matthew,' said Braindead. 'I still can't believe what I did.'

Matthew shook his head. 'As Ian has pointed out to me on many occasions recently, it's not your fault I slept with Katy. It's my massive bloody huge error and quite frankly, it's a miracle it hasn't all come out sooner. I can't blame you, can I?'

'I know, but I still need to help you fix it – I just have to.'

Matthew sighed. 'But I have no idea what to do. It was a massive mistake, but it's all in the past. I don't want to let it ruin my family's future. I can't let it.'

They sat in silence.

'I'm thinking of calling Katy,' admitted Matthew. 'See if she will go and see Alison…'

'And tell her sex with you was the worst experience of her life,' nodded Braindead.

'No… no… not that exactly… That it just meant nothing, you know. Maybe she would be more willing to listen to me if she heard that from Katy.'

'Too late,' said Braindead.

'What do you mean, too late?'

'She's already been to see her.'

'Seriously? When?'

'Not sure. Ben told me. I don't think it went to plan. In fact, it sounded like she made it worse, to be honest.'

'How? What happened?'

Braindead took another large slug of his drink before he spoke.

'Well, I think Alison clocked, given the timing and everything, it was possible that you could be Millie's dad.'

'What!' said Matthew. 'No way! No, not that. No, she didn't need to know that, did she? Oh no, no, no… this is bad, really bad. Why on earth did Katy mention anything about that?'

'I'm sure she didn't mean to. I think that Alison just worked it out.'

Matthew stared at Braindead and could feel his eyes start to itch again. He felt like his heart was truly in his boots as he cast his mind back to the months before Alison finally got pregnant. How much the IVF had taken over their lives, transforming her into a gibbering, obsessive wreck. She had been a nightmare to live with, not allowing anything else to bring light into their relationship. Every single conversation, every single act of love, every single moment was weighed down by the desperation to conceive. He knew it was inexcusable but it had been a contributing factor to his kamikaze decision to sleep with Katy. She had reminded him of his carefree days of teenage dating when the huge subject of starting a family was nowhere on the horizon. The alcohol had fuzzed his brain and lulled him into thinking that just one night wouldn't matter. He'd wanted to taste freedom of body and mind away from the pain he saw in his wife's eyes every single day. But he had been so naïve. So stupid. That was nothing compared to the pain Alison must be feeling right now.

'That's it,' he said to Braindead. 'It's over.' He felt the tears start to creep out the corners of his eyes. 'She'll never forgive me that. She'll just be thinking about how she would have felt if Millie had been mine. Me creating a baby with someone else at the very point we were so desperately trying to conceive our own. It's like… it would have been like the ultimate in sheer cruelty.' He buried his head in his hands.

Matthew sat there for what felt like ages, unable to lift his face away from his hands for fear of what he might release. He kept picturing Alison's face had fate intervened and Millie turned out to be his and Alison hadn't conceived the twins. What an evil trick that would have been.

He felt Braindead's hand on his shoulder and that was it – he had to let it out. He fell sideways onto the bench they were sharing, into

Braindead's shoulder. As he let out the first sob he felt himself shudder. He couldn't control it. His life was over. He had no idea how he could pull it back. How could he ever apologise enough for dicing with the possibility of putting Alison through the ultimate cruelty?

Braindead's other arm circled his shoulders as he shuddered again, sobs coming out silently but energetically.

He raised his head, reaching in his pocket for a handkerchief before remembering he didn't have one because he wasn't living at home any more with his endless supply of beautifully ironed handkerchiefs.

'I'll get you a tissue,' said Braindead, getting up abruptly and disappearing. Matthew gazed down at his hands, too worried to meet anyone else's stare.

Braindead arrived back with an entire toilet roll. In pink.

'I had to go in the ladies',' he said. 'There was none in the gents' so I crept in the ladies' and stole one as quick as I could. My heart was going like a train because I thought someone was going to catch me.'

'Thanks,' sniffed Matthew, unrolling a length of the paper then blowing his nose. 'Sorry you had to do that.'

'I'll live,' he replied. 'And I'm sorry, you know… about it all.'

'I just don't know if she can ever forgive me for possibly fathering another woman's baby,' muttered Matthew.

'But I guess men do it all the time… You know, whenever you have sex I suppose you could possibly father a child. Fucking hell, that's deep for a Tuesday night!'

'I know, but my timing… well, it was my timing that might make what is unforgiveable, totally unforgiveable.'

Chapter Twenty-Three

Katy

When Daniel called Katy was standing in the middle of the Co-op, wondering what crisps would be most acceptable to accompany the wedding working party meeting (or wedding disaster meeting, as Daniel now liked to call it).

'Nachos or Doritos?' she asked as she picked up the phone.

'Well, I'm bringing a very delicate Riesling so I think actually I'd go with a plain cracker if I were you. Maybe with a hint of rosemary?'

'You are such a knob sometimes,' said Katy, throwing the Doritos in the basket and marching towards the counter to pay.

'I know,' replied Daniel. 'But I'm your knob.'

'So are you on your way?' asked Katy.

'Not quite,' replied Daniel. 'I'm just hiding on the balcony so Gabriel doesn't hear.'

'I didn't know he was coming up this weekend?'

'Well, he wasn't but then I had this brilliant idea. I thought I'd bring him to the wedding crisis meeting and you can convince him that having a joint wedding is the catastrophic idea that it truly is.'

'What!' exclaimed Katy. 'What do you mean, *I* can convince him?'

'Well, it's got to be you, hasn't it? I've been thinking about it really hard and I can't be the one to be seen to get in the way of Gabriel's misguided idea that getting married alongside his dad and stepmum is a good idea. But *you* can.'

'No, Daniel. No,' said Katy, trying to pay for her shopping whilst smiling apologetically at the cashier. 'Why do I have to be the bearer of bad news?'

'Because you are the daughter of a bride, best friend of a groom and pregnant. Therefore no-one can get mad at you.'

Katy swallowed. 'What about Erica, can't she do it? She doesn't really know anyone so it doesn't matter if people get mad with her.'

'She's a model, Katy. People are mean to her all the time. Give her a break.'

Katy felt herself gasp. Wrong on so many levels, surely.

'So, we'll see you in about half an hour then,' said Daniel. 'Bye.'

Katy gaped at her phone. She'd thought tonight was going to be bad enough without the extra duties of shattering people's dreams so that Daniel could fulfill his own.

*

'Hi, I'm back,' said Katy, pushing the back door open. Before she'd gone out Ben had been putting Millie to bed, so she wasn't surprised that she didn't get an answer. However, as she took her coat off, she heard voices, adult voices, coming from the lounge.

'Oh hello, Braindead,' she said as she walked into the lounge and found Ben and his friend nursing two cans of beer. 'Good honeymoon? No, of course not, not really,' she said, slumping down onto the chair. 'Sorry, Ben told me about... about, well, I'm so sorry to hear that.'

'The buffet breakfast was good,' replied Braindead. 'So, you know, it wasn't all bad. They did pancakes.'

'Well, that's great,' replied Katy. 'Really glad that the pancakes are the best thing you have to say about your honeymoon.'

'Braindead has been to see Matthew,' said Ben gravely.

'Have you?' replied Katy. 'How is he? Is he okay?'

'He's not okay, Katy. Not at all. He cried. Right here,' he explained, pointing to his right shoulder. 'I had to go and get him bog roll from the ladies'. It was a total car crash.'

'Has he spoken to Alison since the wedding?' asked Katy.

'I don't think so. She won't speak to him but she's letting him see the kids this weekend but she said she wouldn't be there. The nanny is going to supervise.'

Katy felt her heart sink further.

'He doesn't think she is ever going to forgive him, Katy,' said Braindead desperately. 'Like, ever. He thinks it's over. He's given up.'

Katy sat back in her chair, deflated. She wasn't surprised but it didn't make it feel any easier.

'And he's not very happy that you went to see her,' added Braindead. 'In fact, he said it was you making her realise the whole timing thing that means she'll never let him back. He kept banging on and on about timing. Said it couldn't have been worse.'

Katy looked across uncomfortably at Ben. This had to be so painful for him. Having to drag up the whole timing thing again that had led to this problem in the first place. Why had she had sex that night with Matthew? Why? Why? Why?

They fell into silence. Katy contemplated her role in the downfall of Matthew and Alison's marriage. She had never made a bigger mistake in her life, she realised, and she had no idea any more how she could put it right. Ben reached over and squeezed her hand and she wanted to cry at her incredible good fortune that at this very moment he was more concerned for how bad she was feeling than for what she'd done to get herself in this situation in the first place. She looked at him with tears in her eyes, wanting to throw herself on him and thank him from the bottom of her heart for being the most amazing husband in the history of the universe, but she wasn't sure how Braindead would cope with such a display of marital affection at this point. He looked just as troubled as her, which only served to make her feel worse.

She heard the ring of the front doorbell and felt her heart sink even further – if that were possible. The thought of how on earth she was going to navigate the next hour or so of conversation was beyond her.

'It's Daniel, Gabriel and Erica,' said Katy, getting up. 'Here to talk about the next wedding disaster on our calendar.'

'Erica?' said Braindead. 'As in Eric?'

'Yeah, your sister,' replied Katy.

'What's she doing with Daniel?'

'Didn't you know they are, like, best buddies these days? Practically inseparable.'

'Really?' said Braindead, looking confused. 'But she has, like, loads of gay friends. Why did she have to have mine? That's just typical of her. Anything I have, she wants.'

Katy and Ben stared at Braindead, who actually had his bottom lip stuck out.

'Sibling rivalry over… Daniel!' exclaimed Katy, shaking her head. 'I no longer understand this world.'

*

It took some time to settle everyone around their kitchen table. Largely because there was a minor dispute as to who would sit next to Daniel. Of course, Gabriel wanted to as he was his fiancé but he was soon barged out of the way by Braindead, who stood so close to Daniel that their shoulders were touching. He glared at his sister when she tried to take the seat on the other side of Daniel. She glared back before sticking two fingers up at him. He stuck two fingers back. She slapped his fingers down and then he slapped her hand back and before anyone could dive into the crisps in the middle of the table they were slapping each other like five-year-olds.

'Children, children!' said Daniel, grabbing both of their hands and forcing them down. 'Shall we elevate this meeting to the status that it deserves rather than indulging in petty school playground antics?'

'Sorry, Daniel,' said Braindead, sitting down with a thud, still glaring at his sister. Somehow he had assumed he was to be included in the night's activity despite the fact he hadn't been invited. Katy hadn't had the heart to ask him to leave; however, she did have reservations about what contribution he might make to the subject at hand.

Finally, they were all settled and Ben had organised everyone a drink. Katy looked at the large glasses of wine lining the table and had never wanted alcohol more. She knew this whole scenario would look rosier through the filter of several glasses of Chardonnay.

'So, over to you then, Katy,' said Daniel when there was a decent lull in conversation. 'Let's get started, shall we, and then we can all decamp to Gio's? Well, those without babysitting issues obviously.' He grimaced at Katy. 'Take it away, Katy,' he said, beaming at her.

'Bastard,' she mouthed at him. She couldn't believe the situation he had put her in as she contemplated how to mastermind a conversation that would lead to Daniel's wedding wishes being fulfilled.

'Thank you so much for helping us with this,' said Gabriel before Katy could get her thoughts in order. 'So kind of you. So thoughtful. I am so busy that I'm not sure I could do our wedding justice but I know you will be superb and of course you know Daniel so well that you will make sure that it is everything he ever dreamed of.'

Katy nodded and reached over and took a tiny sip of Ben's wine.

'And of course it's just perfect,' continued Gabriel as if he had just made a major revelation. 'You know Rita so well too and so you are the perfect person to make everyone's dreams come true. Cheers to you!' he grinned, holding his wine glass up to her in a toast. Everyone else picked their glasses up to join him.

Katy didn't pick up her glass of water. She caught sight of Ben, who was trying not to laugh as he recognised the horrendous position she was in. She grimaced back, thinking perhaps he wasn't such a perfect husband.

'So, about the whole joint wedding thing?' she said, wanting to get it over as quickly as possible so they would all decamp to Gio's and she could go and bury her head in the sand somewhere.

'Oh my God,' interrupted Gabriel, 'I know exactly what it is you are going to say. I couldn't believe it when my father made such a generous offer. Unbelievable! To want to share his wedding day… and with me and my gorgeous fiancé. I mean, when I came out to him he didn't speak to me for six months. Did you know that? Six months and then he called. He called me to say my mother was very ill and I must go to see her immediately.' He stopped, the emotion causing him to pause his story. Katy watched as Daniel reached over and took his hand.

'It's okay,' Daniel said quietly.

'I went to see her,' continued Gabriel. 'And she said, the last time I ever saw her, that she was so proud of me and it was her dying wish to see my father proud of me too.' He paused again, pushing his fists into his eye sockets. 'Oh my!' he muttered. He lowered his hands. 'My father came in and he looked at my mother and he put his arms around me and he hugged me sooo tight and we cried. We cried together for so long. But do you know what? My mother couldn't stop smiling. She looked so happy. So content to see us in each other's arms. That's how I remember her. Smiling that day at me and my father holding each other. She died the very next day.'

No-one said anything until Braindead got up, walked around Daniel and put his arms around his sister.

Everyone turned to stare as they both hid their faces in each other's shoulders. When Braindead finally raised his head his eyes were wet with tears. He silently moved back to his seat whilst Erica dabbed her eyes with a tissue.

'Our mum made us promise to look after each other the day before she died,' said Erica. She looked down at her damp tissue. 'Sometimes we forget that,' she added.

'I'm glad you got to see her smile,' said Braindead, looking up at Gabriel. 'It matters.'

Gabriel nodded. He gazed around at the concerned faces looking at him. He raised a weak smile.

'And now we will stop with the stories of the dead mothers, shall we?' he said. 'We will be happy now and talk of the best wedding ever. Please continue, Katy.'

Katy blinked at him. How did you follow that? She looked over to Daniel, who looked stricken, conflicted, confused. He was still holding Gabriel's hands across the table, clearly trying to process what it all meant to his dream wedding. Daniel was such a perfectionist. His entire career was based around him creating the best possible images for the brands they worked on. Image was important to him and his wedding was perhaps the most important display of his own personal image that he had ever had the opportunity to orchestrate. For Daniel his wedding was the ultimate branding opportunity. A chance to shout from the rooftops who he was and what his very special marriage meant. She wasn't sure if he could let this opportunity go, even if it meant so much to Gabriel.

Daniel looked completely lost. Which was unusual. Normally he was absolutely in control of every situation he found himself in. It was clear he was grappling with his own desires and wishes and those of Gabriel, which did not match his own. What was he thinking? Who should he put first? If he put Gabriel first, how would he stop himself resenting him? If he put himself first, how would he stop himself feeling bad about it?

Welcome to marriage, thought Katy.

Chapter Twenty-Four

Ben

What was all that about, thought Ben, grabbing his glass and taking a massive swig. Gabriel in tears? Braindead and Erica hugging, Daniel virtually in tears. Ben had lost track of what the hell was going on. Why did weddings do this to people? Random crying and hugging? What was all that for?

Surely it was all quite straightforward? Daniel needed to suck it up and agree to get married in Spain with Rita and Carlos. No biggie. Then they'd just need to make a list of all the other stuff that you had to have an opinion on but wasn't worth falling out over, like flowers and invites and presents list and all that. And then he and Braindead could slide off to the pub.

Job done. Pain over.

No-one was talking now. Katy was staring at Daniel, waiting for him to give the all-clear that he had listened to Gabriel's story of heartbreak and so the Spanish wedding was on. But Daniel wasn't saying anything. He was just sitting there, still grasping Gabriel's hands. But Ben had had enough: he wasn't going to sit there all night wasting valuable time while they waited for Daniel to give the green light.

'So,' said Ben, sitting up in his chair. 'Sounds like what we need to do is put together a list of ideally how you would like this wedding to pan out so that you can talk to Carlos and Rita to make sure it's the wedding of everyone's dreams. Does that sound like a plan, Daniel?'

Daniel looked over at him sharply, like a rabbit in the headlights. He was on the spot now. He had to run or face the glare full-on.

'Daniel?' prompted Ben. 'Is that a good idea?'

The room was silent. Daniel stared back at him.

'Yes,' he finally whispered.

'Yes,' repeated Katy. Ben thought he saw her do a fist pump out the corner of his eye.

'I'll write it all down for you,' she added, grabbing a notepad from the bench behind her and a pen. 'I'll write it down and then you can do a FaceTime or something and talk it through. Agree together. Between the four of you. Right, off you go, Daniel. What are your must-haves?'

Katy reached over and gave Ben a grateful squeeze on his arm. Ben breathed out. Maybe this wouldn't take too long after all. But then he noticed Daniel reaching down and dragging an iPad out of his bag and laying it on the table so everyone could see. He tapped a few times on the screen until some words appeared.

*

The essence of a wedding comes from the union of two hearts and minds and their collective dreams merged into one beautiful tableau.

*

Ben read it twice before he made any sense of it.

'Who wrote that?' he asked.

'I did,' replied Daniel.

'Bloody hell, Daniel!' said Braindead. 'What in the name of rose petal confetti is that?'

'It's a vision statement,' said Daniel. 'For our wedding.'

'I didn't have a vision statement,' said Braindead. 'Should we have had a vision statement? Nobody ever mentioned a vision statement to me. Katy?'

'Calm down, buddy,' said Ben. 'It's wanky advertising speak.'

'It is not wanky advertising speak!' said Daniel. 'It's… it's…'

'Wanky advertising speak,' agreed Katy.

'Katy!' said Daniel. 'You are supposed to be my friend. And might I point out to you that "wanky advertising speak", as you call it, pays your wages.'

'I know, but seriously, Daniel? Is this going to help at all? Come on, get your mood boards out. I know you have them. Let's see the pretty pictures and then maybe we can get somewhere.'

Daniel skimmed his finger across the screen and it was lit up by an array of turquoise blues and emerald greens with flashes of bronze. Pictures of shrubbery and ribbons and candlesticks and chandeliers and fireplaces and scenery appeared to randomly litter the page, linked by a strict palette of colours.

'This is it,' said Daniel. 'This is our wedding. The green of Gabe's eyes and the blue of mine mixed with the bronze of Gabriel's arms. I want to walk down the aisle and feel like I'm swimming in his eyes and sinking into his arms.'

'Wow!' said Braindead. 'Is that what an essence does for you?'

'Wow!' said Katy. 'I have to admit it's beautiful.'

It looked like a page from a fashion magazine or a very stylish interiors magazine. This had taken Daniel a lot of pain and effort. Ben looked over to Gabriel to see his reaction. His eyes were wide and he was smiling, clearly impressed by his future husband's efforts.

'Is that a Louis Vuitton?' asked Erica, pointing at a suitcase.

'Of course,' replied Daniel. 'Vintage, actually. I'd love to track one down and have it as the cake stand. Especially if we could track down someone who could build a luggage rack for it.'

'Great idea,' she agreed.

'Well, this is a great start, Daniel,' said Katy. 'Brilliant, just lovely. You and Gabriel all over.'

'So, shall I email it to you and you can send it to your mother?' said Daniel, skimming the screen again. 'There you go,' he said. 'See what she says.'

'*I'm* emailing it to my mother?' questioned Katy.

'Yes,' nodded Daniel.

She grimaced.

'Why don't we email it now,' suggested Ben, 'and then maybe Daniel and Gabriel can call them tomorrow and have a lovely chat about it all?'

'Oh yes,' said Katy, flashing him a grateful smile. 'That's a great idea.' She picked up her phone from the table and tapped it until she looked up at everyone smiling. 'There we go,' she said. 'I've sent it to Mum and said you'll call her tomorrow to discuss.'

'Perfect,' said Ben. He stood up, hoping this would signal the end of all wedding talk for the rest of the evening. 'Can I get anyone another drink? I'll go and grab the wine, shall I?'

He practically ran out of the lounge and into the kitchen. He was just reaching into the fridge when he sensed someone behind him.

'Tremendous effort there, Ben,' said Erica, leaning against the worktop.

He grinned. 'I don't know what you mean,' he said, straightening up.

'Excellent deflection of all responsibility away from poor Katy back into the hands of the two reluctant brides.'

'Well,' said Ben. 'They have to sort it out, don't they? I mean, it's not fair on Katy, is it, having to be the go-between. She's got enough on already, what with being pregnant and all that.'

Erica gave him a slow smile. 'You always did put others first,' she said, nodding at him. 'Despite the whole "bit of a lad" thing you have going on here, you always were the kind one.'

'No, I wasn't!' denied Ben, feeling himself start to blush.

'You were. My brother would have been in a right mess now if it wasn't for you. It was you who dragged him through after Mum died. Made him carry on with footie and hanging around on street corners when all he wanted to do was stay at home in bed. I can remember you coming round every Saturday morning and literally heaving him out of bed. I remember you throwing cold water over him one day just to make him get up.'

Ben shrugged. 'I didn't do anything special,' he said.

Erica shook her head. 'Most mates would have given up. Most of mine did. In fact, all of mine did. They didn't know what to say to me and when I stopped going out, they were only too happy not to have the depressed, motherless girl in the crowd, who no-one knew how to talk to.'

'I'm sorry to hear that,' said Ben, nervously starting to peel a label off a bottle of beer.

'I was jealous of my brother, you know. Because he had you.' Erica looked at the floor. Her cheeks were pink. Ben hoped she wouldn't cry – she looked like she could. There had been enough of that already this evening. 'And he still has you,' she said, looking up again straight at Ben. 'Lucky bastard.'

Ben swallowed. He tried to tear his eyes away from her face but she was staring at him so intensely.

'Do you remember that New Year's Eve party we had at ours, after Dad left for New Zealand?' she asked.

Ben laughed, relieved the tension appeared to have been released.

'How could I forget that night?' he said. 'What a car crash! Braindead forgot to buy in any booze other than Newcastle Brown and he bought a job lot of out-of-date pork pies cheap, thinking he'd get away with it. Everyone was either complaining or puking up.'

'The cleaning-up was insane, do you remember?' said Erica. 'Took two days. There was puke everywhere.'

'I feel sick just to think about it.'

'I think about it a lot,' said Erica, giving him that intense stare again.

'Why?' he exclaimed. 'Worst party ever.'

She hesitated for a moment before nodding her head. 'You're right,' she agreed. 'Nothing went to plan at all.'

'Well, that's Braindead for you.'

'I only came back for you,' she said, holding his gaze.

'What do you mean?' he muttered.

'In fact, I gave my bro the idea,' she continued. '"Have a New Year's Eve party," I said, "before the house gets sold. Before our family home is gone forever. Let's say goodbye to it properly."'

'I know. I remember that was the idea before Braindead got hold of it.'

'I lied,' said Erica, shaking her head before glancing over at the door furtively, then looking back. 'I didn't care about that, I just wanted an excuse to come back and see you.' She bit her lip and looked down. 'The plan wasn't to say goodbye to the house, it was to see you and... and be with you on New Year's Eve because then we might kiss and that would have been my New Year's resolution come true already. But instead at midnight I was throwing up out-of-date pork pies, thanks to my wonderful brother.'

Ben was aware that his mouth was moving but nothing was coming out.

'I… I don't know what to say,' he stuttered. He stared at Erica in her sleek outfit that was probably 'on trend' – not that he had any idea about those types of things; he couldn't have spotted 'on trend' if it hit him over the head with a baseball bat. He glanced down at his bright yellow Minion slippers poking out the bottom of his dad jeans and wondered what parallel universe he had landed in now.

'I think about that New Year's Eve all the time,' she said, looking back up at him.

Bloody hell, thought Ben, his head was about to explode. This was Erica, his best friend's sister – or 'Eric', as he used to call her due to her tomboy antics. Eric, who he'd chased and teased and wound up as if she were his own sister. Eric, who not long after that New Year's Eve party left Leeds for London and began her road to modelling success. Eric the model, who travelled the world at the top of her game, courted by the great and good of the fashion industry, the world quite literally at her feet, and she still thought not snogging him over fifteen years ago was the biggest regret of her life?

This was not a reasonable thing for him to be able to understand.

He needed to extract himself asap and return to normality.

'I'm sorry, I've unsettled you,' she said, reaching out and touching his arm. She was as white as a sheet. Clearly it had taken a lot to make her confession. 'I wouldn't have said anything only… only,' she swallowed, 'well, in for a penny, in for a pound. I just thought, fuck this sounds terrible now, but I just thought that you should know, given my brother's revelation at his wedding – you know, about Katy and her ex – well, I just wanted you to know the full facts, I guess. Whilst we appear to be in a period of full disclosure I just wanted to put it out there.'

She held his gaze for a moment longer but then cast her eyes down when he made no response.

'And now I'm going to make my excuses and leave because I can see that you are in shock or horror or something and I may have made a huge enormous fuck-up yet again. So if you don't mind, I'll just go out this door at the back and you can tell everyone that I had to go because I had an urgent modelling call or felt sick or something.'

She turned and grabbed the handle of the door and walked out, closing it behind her. Ben gripped onto the end of the counter. He felt a bit dizzy – it was all too much to take in.

'You are such a life-saver,' said Katy, coming in. 'What would I do without you?' She walked over and put her arms around his neck.

He tried to look her in the eye but his thoughts were elsewhere, trying to make sense of what Erica had said. He was aware of Katy talking to him and of her protruding bump pressing up against his belly but he couldn't listen to her, he was too confused.

'Ben?' she finally cut through.

'What? Sorry, I was miles away.'

'I said, when everyone is gone can we just put our pyjamas on and drink hot chocolate and watch a movie?'

He looked down at her. He really fancied going out for a beer with Braindead, but she looked at him so pleadingly.

'You always put other people first,' he heard Erica's words again.

'Is it all right if I go out for a drink with Braindead?' he asked.

She looked momentarily wounded but nodded. 'Of course you can. Good idea. I'll, er… you don't mind if I watch *Bridesmaids* though, do you?'

Mind, thought Ben. He'd be only too happy not to sit through a wedding-based movie. It was the last thing he needed and he was surprised that Katy could stomach it after this evening. 'Of course,' he said. 'You go for it.'

'Erica?' said Daniel as he walked into the kitchen. 'Oh, get a room, you two!' he added, catching sight of Ben and Katy with their arms around each other. 'Where's Erica?'

'Oh, er, she had to go. Some modelling emergency or something?' Ben said.

'A modelling emergency!' said Daniel. 'What, like a broken nail or a dropped false eyelash? Don't ever tell her I said that, will you? She hates the modelling stereotype, she's so down-to-earth. Can you believe she's even a model? I mean, she cooks her own food and everything... and she even eats it!'

'I'm not sure exactly but she got a text and had to shoot off,' said Ben, quickly turning to pick up the wine bottle. 'I'm sure she'll be in touch.'

'Did she say she was still going to Gio's?' asked Daniel. 'Because we are testing canapés tonight and knowing Erica, she will have had the finest canapés there are on the planet and so her advice will be invaluable. Her taste is excellent. Have you noticed?' he asked Ben. 'Has she always been like that? From when she was younger, I mean.'

'Erm, well... I...' stumbled Ben. 'I didn't really spend that much time with her. I just used to hang out with Braindead.'

'More fool you!' said Daniel. 'I think you and Braindead could have benefitted greatly from taking more notice of that sister of his. She is really quite extraordinary.'

'All hail Queen Erica,' interrupted Katy sarcastically. 'Looks like you've been dumped for the night though, Daniel, so I'm afraid you'll have to suffer our lower-quality company rather than swanning round with your new best mate.'

'Jealousy really doesn't suit you,' said Daniel.

'I'm not jealous!' exclaimed Katy.

'You so are,' he replied. 'But then who wouldn't be? I think she might quite possibly be the perfect woman. Don't you think so, Ben?'

'What?' replied Ben, startled. He hadn't been listening – he'd drifted off, trying to make sense of anything Erica had said to him.

'Erica is possibly the perfect woman,' repeated Daniel.

Ben glanced at Katy, horrified. What had he missed?

'If you like that sort of thing,' he muttered, then turned away to get the wine out of the fridge and to hide his discomfort.

'I just need the bathroom,' he said, turning back around when he'd had a moment to gather himself, having already forgotten what he'd been looking for in the fridge. He tried not to make a run for the door – he just needed to sit down and contemplate before he could tackle any kind of conversation.

Chapter Twenty-Five

Katy

Katy was feeling almost light-headed. Tonight had gone so much better than expected, thanks to Ben guiding them all through the various landmines that existed in the build-up to the Wedding of the Year. She felt at least one weight had been lifted off her shoulders. Hopefully now the two happy couples would talk tomorrow and they would sort it out between them, whilst she planned a day of rest and relaxation and caring for her family. Maybe they would have a Sunday roast. She hadn't done that in a while. Yes, tomorrow would be all about family time. Her family. She might even go and do some shopping for the new baby. Yes, that was exactly what she would do. Spend some time planning for their new arrival rather than having to think about the planning of other people's weddings.

She leaned forward, turning the volume down on the TV, as her phone rang. She was hoping it would be an unknown number that she could just cut off. But it wasn't. It was her mother. Worse than that, it was her mother on FaceTime. Katy had clearly stated in her email that Rita should call Gabriel and Daniel tomorrow to discuss the wedding plans. So hopefully this was just a social call and she hadn't picked up her email yet. Yes, that must be it. It was too quick to be responding. Her mother was just ringing for a chat. She'd say hello and then explain that she was researching weddings by watching *Bridesmaids* so she couldn't talk.

'Hi, Mum,' she said, clicking on the accept call button. Rita sprang to life in front of her. There was a lot of background noise. Perhaps she was in Carlos's bar?

'Katy?' said Rita, peering into the screen. 'Katy? Is that you?'

'Of course it's me, Mother. You rang me,' she replied.

'Well, you can never be too sure, can you? Where these calls go. I thought I was ringing your father once and got the Water Board instead. I'd told them all about Doreen next door having to go into hospital to have her bunions done before they got a word in edgeways and asked me if I had a problem with my water supply.'

'Oh dear,' said Katy, trying to look like she was looking at her mother when really she was watching the telly.

'Anyway, I haven't called to talk to you about Doreen's bunions. Although I do believe she is still having problems with them despite three very expensive consultations on Harley Street, so she tells me – although she is partial to a touch of fantasy, is our Doreen. She once told me that her daughter had been invited to a garden party by the Queen. I mean, as if. Do you remember Melanie? She had buck teeth and one leg shorter than the other. As if they would allow her into Buckingham Palace. I think she married a policeman, you know. Poor thing.'

Katy really couldn't be bothered with correcting her mother's political incorrectness just now. Really she just wanted to disappear and watch the telly and not have to talk to anyone.

'I'm afraid it's well past Millie's bedtime,' she told her mum, thinking she might want to talk to her granddaughter. Rita did have a habit of calling at the most inappropriate times to speak to her, like teatime when they were just in the middle of a vegetable stand-off with Katy demanding that Millie couldn't leave the table until she had eaten all of her broccoli.

'Of course I know she must be in bed,' said Rita. 'I've called you about this thing you sent me.'

'What thing?'

'This picture thing from Gabriel and Daniel.'

'It's not a picture thing. It's how they want their wedding to look.'

'But it's so dark and gloomy and… and dull. Why would anyone want their wedding to look like that? That green. Oh my God, it's like slimy moss or something.'

'Apparently it's the colour of Gabriel's eyes,' said Katy.

'His eyes are sludgy green? Why on earth would you want to make a point of that?'

'Because they do, Mother. Green is the colour they want to base the look of their wedding on.'

'Can't they pick another shade of green? It's just so depressing.'

Katy thought about some of the arguments she had witnessed at work when clients suggested altering colours within a campaign. Daniel could talk for twenty minutes about why a particular shade of off-white was perfect and why no other shade of off-white would come anywhere close.

'Why don't you talk to Daniel about it as I suggested?' said Katy. 'You have his number, don't you? Give him a call.'

'Oh no, I couldn't do that.'

'Why not?'

'Well, he might be upset with me.'

'You never know,' replied Katy, crossing her fingers. 'He might agree with you.' She knew this wouldn't happen even if hell froze over.

'No, no, you tell him, dear. Tell him I love his picture, it's very pretty, but I really think that some brighter, fresher colours would be more suitable for such a happy occasion. Tell him Carlos thinks so too. To be honest, I showed Carlos and he just shrugged. I don't think he would care if we got married naked and had Hula Hoops for rings, he's just so happy to be marrying me and that his son is finally settling down and wanting to be happy.'

'You need to tell him, Mum. It's your wedding, not mine,' said Katy firmly.

'But you're his friend. He'll take it better from you and it doesn't matter if he falls out with you whereas if we fall out before the big day it could all be a disaster, couldn't it? And you wouldn't want that, would you?'

Katy just stared at her.

'Anyway, it's not too much to ask, is it? A few pinks and yellows – that's all I'm asking. Pastel shades, I was thinking. Subtle. That's what I'm after.'

Katy thought about the last time the word 'pastel' had been mentioned in a meeting with Daniel as a suggestion for branding colours for a new restaurant chain they were working on. He'd pretended to shoot himself in the head and lain down on the floor and refused to get up until everyone agreed that pastel colours belonged on grandmas' knickers, not a high-end restaurant logo.

'Anyway, I'll leave it with you, darling. I'm sure you know what I like as well as Daniel so you can come up with something that will keep us all happy. Better go. You look tired, you should go to bed. Carlos has just made me a margarita, so bye for now.'

Katy watched as her mother raised a very large cocktail glass in front of her face as if to taunt her further.

'Bottoms up!' she said before the screen went blank.

Katy picked up a cushion and threw it across the room.

Chapter Twenty-Six

Matthew

It was a strange thing being a guest at your own house. Matthew drew up in front of the executive five-bedroom detached house that he'd worked very long hours to put himself in a position to be able to purchase and that he was no longer allowed to live in.

He stared up at it. It was exactly the same. You wouldn't know that there had been a seismic shift in the daily lives of its inhabitants. It still looked like his house. But of course it wasn't any more. It was his estranged wife's house and the home of their four children. He'd looked that word up on Google – 'estranged'. What a weird word it was. The official meaning was 'no longer close or affectionate to someone'. He figured that was pretty accurate. Affection was not a word that could be used to describe his and Alison's marriage at the moment. He figured it came from 'stranger'. To become a stranger perhaps. But this didn't feel right. They were not strangers. They could never be strangers. They knew each other backwards and yet at the moment Matthew had no way of reaching Alison. The person he knew best in the world was out of his reach and he had no idea what bridge he could build to get back to her.

He sighed and pulled himself out of the car. He was so excited to see his children but at the same time he knew it was going to break his heart. That spending time with them was only going to remind him of how much he had screwed up his life. That he had done something so stupid before any of these little people, who he now loved more than life itself, had arrived in his life. He had done something before they were even born that meant he had lost the life he planned with them. Four lives he wouldn't get to live and breathe every day. He hastily brushed a tear from his eye. He couldn't let them see him upset. Today had to be about fun and not regrets.

He fumbled for his key as he approached the front door then wondered if actually he should knock. Seeing as he was estranged from his house as well then maybe it would be presumptuous to use his key? Alison would not be there though, or so Lena had said, and it would feel more than weird to stand there and wait for the nanny to come and open the door to him in his own house. Wouldn't it? He didn't know. Who knew what the protocol was in this strange new world he was living in?

He put the key in the lock and felt it turn and open. Well, at least she hadn't changed the locks.

There was a clatter as he saw three little people sitting on contraptions hurtle towards him across the cavernous hall.

'Daddy!' shouted Rebecca. 'Daddy's back,' she said, causing Matthew to bite his lip yet again and force down the tears.

He watched as she leapt off a bright blue bear with wheels and threw herself at him. He hoisted her up in his arms and squeezed her so tight to his chest and breathed in the smell of toast and baby shampoo.

He couldn't move. He just kept breathing and holding and breathing and holding, not wanting the moment to end, until she wriggled backwards so she could look at him.

'What's this?' she said, reaching out to touch the fuzz that he'd allowed to take root on his chin.

'It's a beard,' he said.

'It's prickly. Like a hedgehog.'

'Have you touched a hedgehog?'

'No, silly Daddy! How would I touch a hedgehog, they only live in France.'

'Do they? I never knew that.'

'Yes. Bertie at school told me. He saw one there last summer. They fed it croissants. They only eat croissants, that's why they live in France.'

'Well, you would, wouldn't you? They do have the best croissants in France.'

'And Balados.'

'Balados? Where's that?'

'It's where Eloise went on holiday in the summer and it was very hot and they had breakfast every morning and she said there was a mountain of bread and they even cooked pancakes for you. The big ones. With Nutella.'

'Wow, sounds like heaven!'

'Can we go, Daddy? Eloise said it was the best and they got to stay up until nine o clock. Please can we go, Daddy? All of us, with Mummy. We can leave Eva behind if you think she's too small. Lena will look after her, won't you, Lena?'

'We'll see,' said Matthew. He put her down, having spotted Lena lurking by the door, obviously unclear on what her role was on this unusual day.

'I need to see how these chaps are doing first,' he said, striding over to where George and Harry were currently chasing each other in a police car and on a wooden horse respectively. 'Come here, you pair,' he said, scooping them up. 'Have you got a hug for me?'

They laughed and giggled as he tickled them both before he had to let go.

'Where have you been, Daddy?' asked George. 'Mum took me to football practice and she shouted all the wrong things from the sidelines. She's never played football, can you believe it? But she kept shouting. Why can't you take me to football practice?'

'I'll ask Mummy if I can take you next week,' said Matthew, feeling a lump form in his throat.

'She'll say yes,' said George. 'She didn't like it very much. Why aren't you here, Daddy?' he asked. 'Why don't you go to bed here? I asked Mummy and she said you were busy at work and couldn't stay at home but if you were busy at work, why would you go and sleep somewhere else? Are you sleeping at work, Daddy?'

Matthew glanced over at Lena. She looked away. He didn't pay her enough to come up with a palatable explanation as to why George's mum and dad were 'estranged'.

What should he say? To be honest, he was surprised that Alison hadn't been in touch to at least discuss what they should tell the children. In this situation he would have imagined her HR background kicking in and her wanting to agree a consistent message for explaining the current breakdown of their relationship. But he had heard nothing. No conversation had been held about what had happened or the practicalities of how they would live their lives going forward. He could only assume that she was as clueless about what to say to four children under five as he was.

'You're right, buddy,' said Matthew, crouching down to look George in the eye. 'Work is really tough at the moment so I'm staying there.'

'How long for?'

'I don't know.'

'Do they pay you extra?'

'Er, yes, they do. That's right.'

'So can we go to Balados, where they cook you pancakes every day?'

'Maybe,' said Matthew, getting up again. He needed to terminate this conversation. 'Where's Eva?' he asked, turning to Lena.

'She's in the kitchen in the playpen,' she said. 'Come through. Should I get you a coffee?'

'I don't know,' Matthew said. 'Should you?'

They stared at each other for a moment, both confused as to what they should be doing. Lena concluded first.

'Yes, I should,' she said, turning and walking back into the kitchen.

He followed her into the familiar room as he had so many times and yet when he walked in, he somehow expected it to look different. Like Alison would want to have changed things to show him she was moving on. But it looked exactly the same. There was no indication of the transformation the household had been through. No indication at all.

He walked over to the playpen taking pride of place in the window and bent to scoop Eva up in his arms. He sniffed again. The unmistakable smell of baby, it had never smelt sweeter. He cradled her in his arms and she looked up at him with her big blue eyes and smiled as if she knew exactly who he was and she had been waiting for him. All was well. Daddy was back, she appeared to be saying.

'She's grown,' he said to Lena, feeling a hint of joy tickle his heart. How could holding your baby daughter in your arms not make you feel joy in your heart even if you knew it was going to be fleeting? She was perfect. Soft and smooth and sweet. He held her close to his heart and screwed his eyes tight shut, wanting the moment to last forever.

He had four hours. Ten till two had been his allotted time and he was determined to make the most of it. To a certain extent it made him realise what he had been missing out on. Four uninterrupted hours just messing about with your kids. He couldn't remember the last time he had done that. Life got in the way usually. DIY, shopping, attending other children's parties, visiting relatives, paying bills, cooking, homework supervision, work calls and emails, all the mundane things cluttering out spending time with loved ones, just hanging out. Just chatting, just playing. He couldn't remember if he had ever spent four hours just hanging out with his kids. What had he been doing? Spending too much time on all the other stuff.

After lunch, the three older kids persuaded him to bake cookies with them whilst Eva had her afternoon nap. Although, as Matthew discovered, they didn't mean 'bake', they meant 'get the ingredients out, make a massive mess weighing them out and stirring them up and then eating most of the mixture before it even got to the baking stage'. That was their definition of baking. But it was bliss, helping, guiding, watching and eating the by now grubby dough. Cookies had never tasted so good.

At 1.45 p.m. exactly Lena came into the kitchen and gasped at the state they were all in.

'Wow!' she said. 'Those cookies had better be good, given the mess you have made.'

Matthew peered into the oven before telling her that there were maybe four edible cookies being baked. The rest were residing in their tummies.

Lena looked horrified, her eyes darting from the kids covered in flour and sugar to Matthew.

'It's all right,' he said. 'I'll clean them up and the kitchen.'

Lena looked at the large clock on the wall then back at Matthew.

'I promised I'd make sure you were gone by two,' she said, clearly mortified at the position she was in.

'It's okay,' said Matthew, who had no wish to embarrass her even further. 'How about the biggest foam bath ever, kids?' he said to them. 'Get you shipshape sharpish.'

Lena was shaking her head, still very anxious.

'They always have a bath after dinner. You know how Alison is about routines.'

Of course he did. He'd been married to her for nearly ten years. Of course he knew that a bath in the middle of the day was totally off-piste and unacceptable. What was he thinking?

'Right, I'll get them upstairs and get them cleaned up and then come down here and sort the kitchen. It won't take a minute. You sit down, Lena. Make yourself a cup of tea or something. I'll be back down shortly.'

He had a race up the stairs with Rebecca, George and Harry, who of course scattered floury hand marks all over the bannister. He managed to herd them all into the family bathroom but cleaning up and re-dressing three small children was never going to be the quick in-and-out activity he'd thought. First, Harry wandered off and he couldn't find him. It took the three of them some time before they discovered him asleep inside his walk-in wardrobe in just his pants. Then Rebecca in a strop worthy of a teenager ordered them all out of the bathroom whilst she went to the toilet, which took so long that Harry had practically fallen back to sleep again. Then George had a complete meltdown because Matthew couldn't find his favourite Tractor Ted T-shirt to wear. He knew he should go and ask Lena but he didn't want to leave the three of them unsupervised and the thought of corralling them all downstairs again and then back up filled him with horror.

He glanced at his watch. It was twenty past two already. How had that happened? He should really have known better than to think that he would be able to clean and change three children in fifteen minutes.

After five more minutes he managed to persuade George into a Power Rangers pyjama top, after they had debated that Power Rangers were much more grown-up than Tractor Ted and were aimed at least at seven-year-olds so it would be way cooler to wear that.

He glanced at his watch again, his heart beating way too fast. He was desperate to see Alison but he knew that if she came back and found him still there it would hardly be the right environment for their first meeting since Braindead's wedding.

Matthew was just putting the last of the floury clothes in the laundry when he heard the front door open. He found himself looking round for an escape route, maybe a hidden emergency exit somewhere. Then he had a word with himself and told himself just to walk down the stairs like an adult, apologise for his lateness in leaving, before politely requesting a mutually agreeable time when they could have a decent talk. Then he would leave.

He cleared his throat, tucked his shirt in, brushed flour off his shoulder and took a deep breath.

'Come on, kids,' he said. 'I think that's your mum back. Shall we go see?'

'Yay!' shrieked Rebecca. 'She can try our cookies now,' she added, tearing out the bedroom and down the stairs.

All three children were in the kitchen by the time Matthew caught up with them. They crowded round their mum, who was at the kitchen table unloading shopping bags. Matthew's heart leapt in his mouth the minute he saw her: she looked different and yet so familiar. Like she was a clone – same body, but different person.

'I'm so sorry,' he gushed. 'We made cookies and there was an awful mess and I couldn't just leave Lena to clear up and then Harry hid in the wardrobe and I couldn't find him...'

Alison held his gaze the whole time he was coming out with this tumbling apology until he was forced to tail off.

'He sleeps in his wardrobe now,' she said simply. 'Since you've been away.'

Matthew felt himself sag. What did you say to that? He swallowed. His throat was completely dry with the sheer panic of wanting to say the right thing. The magic words that would make this all right, that would make this thing disappear. There must have been some sentences somewhere that would have that power but he was exhausted with the effort of trying to work out what they were because in truth that was all he thought about day and night.

'Lena, would you like to take the children into the playroom?' said Alison, without taking her eyes off Matthew.

'Of course,' gasped Lena. She had been standing there motionless, again unsure of what her role was in this tangled situation. 'Come on, everyone. Let's get the Lego out. Come on, this way.'

'You won't leave, will you?' asked Harry, taking Matthew's hand.

Matthew looked down at him and then at Alison. She didn't flinch.

'I'll say bye before I go, okay? Now, go and build me a spaceship with a hamburger on top of it, will you? The best one yet.'

Harry looked at him accusingly and then at his mother before he sloped after his siblings away from the tension.

'I know you wanted me gone,' Matthew said to Alison. 'I'm sorry.'

She didn't reply. The room was silent. All that could be heard was the faint chatter of children in the playroom across the hall.

'I'm so sorry,' he said. 'Not for still being here, I mean for everything.'

Still she didn't respond.

'I would do anything to turn the clock back. Anything. I can't believe I did such a stupid thing. It was madness... I...'

He stopped as he watched Alison drop in a chair and put her face in her hands. He didn't know what to do. She clearly needed comforting but he figured not from him. He kept his post awkwardly by the door until she raised her head.

'Millie could have been yours,' she stated matter-of-factly. She didn't look at him, just gazed into the distance.

'I know,' said Matthew. 'I had no idea... I wouldn't have... I... I... She said she was on the pill... Not that that makes it any better, of course.'

'I keep going over and over it in my head,' Alison said, turning to him, her face white as a sheet. 'I can see it as real as if it actually happened. I can picture you coming home and sitting me down. Holding my hands and telling me, despite us trying everything to get a child, going through years of disappointment and stress, that you had a one-night stand with an ex-girlfriend and now you are a daddy. Just like that, as if by magic. One crack of the whip with someone else and, hey presto, a baby.'

'But that didn't happen, did it, Alison?' said Matthew, stepping forward and taking a chair next to her. 'It *didn't* happen.'

'But it could have,' spat Alison. 'That's what I can't stop thinking about. You could have put me in that situation. Me, absolutely desperate for a child, and you coming home and telling me you'd made someone else pregnant.'

'But it *didn't* happen, did it?' pleaded Matthew. 'Millie is Ben's. And now we have not one but four amazing children. Who would have thought it? We hit the jackpot, Alison, as far as children are concerned.'

He took her hands in his but she gazed back at him, looking bewildered.

'Why?' she asked. 'Why did you do it?'

He looked away for a moment. He'd had plenty of time to think about this over the last few weeks. There was a confused jumble of reasons why. He didn't know where to start.

'I wish I knew exactly why,' he said slowly. 'That there was a reason big enough to justify what I did. But there isn't one. I was just very stupid and I was also very sad... I... I...' he faltered, not knowing how to go on. She looked back at him expectantly and he knew he had no choice.

'I was sad because, well... I thought I'd lost my wife.'

'What on earth does that mean?'

'You were so obsessed with getting pregnant it was like that was all that mattered. We talked about nothing else. Our whole lives were wrapped around having a baby and... and we kind of lost ourselves for a bit, I think.'

Matthew had never chosen his words so carefully. He felt like he was balancing on a high wire, about fall off at any second.

'We stopped being Matthew and Alison,' he continued. 'We were just two people on this hopeless trail of disappointment. It was miserable, Alison. Wasn't it? Admit it. Both of us were miserable for a moment there. It was like we were trapped in this massive hole and I couldn't save us. The only thing that could drag us out was having a baby and given it was looking increasingly unlikely, then it felt like we were going to be trapped in that hole forever.'

Alison was watching him intently as a single tear fell down her cheek. He fought the urge to brush it away – he didn't think he was allowed to do that. Not yet.

He swallowed. She said nothing. He had to carry on.

'I guess Katy reminded me of who I used to be. She reminded me of a time when I didn't have a care in the world. I stopped thinking about our struggle just for a while and it felt like such a relief.'

Alison looked away.

'Do you remember how hard it was?' he asked her. 'We never really talked about how sad it was making us at the time. Do you remember how miserable we were?'

'Of course I do!' she gasped, more tears flowing now. 'Of course I remember,' she said, scrabbling for breath. She looked up at him, her eyes red raw. She was breathing fast and rocking as if she was about to take off. 'I was on anti-depressants, that's how miserable I was,' she said, the rocking getting faster.

'Anti-depressants? What do you mean, anti-depressants?'

'I was on anti-depressants. I went to the doctor because I felt so low.'

'But... but you never said?' said Matthew, reeling.

The rocking slowed down; she made an attempt to control her breathing.

'Why didn't you tell me?' he asked, taking her hand again.

She snatched it away. 'Admit I'd failed there too? Admit that I couldn't control my emotions as well as not being able to give you a baby?'

'You weren't failing. None of it was your fault.'

'It felt like it,' she said. 'You never said anything but the fact that it was me who was the problem with our fertility and not you... Well, how do you think that made me feel?'

'It wasn't your fault,' repeated Matthew.

Alison looked away, her face suddenly hardening.

'Don't talk to me about feeling sad,' she added. 'Because I can guarantee you have no idea what sad feels like.' The rocking started again. 'But at least I chose medication and not fucking my ex-girlfriend.' She stood up, the chair clattering to the floor behind her, and walked out of the room.

Chapter Twenty-Seven

Ben

'So the good news is that we've had sex,' said Braindead, sitting down and putting a pint in front of Ben.

'Wow, brilliant!' said Ben, raising his glass. 'Cheers to you! Well done on having sex with your wife! I tell you, there are not that many married men who can make such a boast.'

'Give over,' said Braindead, taking a swig.

Ben looked at him and thought how much his friend had to learn about marriage.

'So was it all right then, once you'd got round to it?' he asked.

'Not really,' admitted Braindead. 'I kept picturing Alison crying but I decided that for the sake of my own marriage I had to grin and bear it.'

'What, the image of Alison whilst you are having sex with your wife?'

'Yes,' said Braindead, nodding.

'It'll be better next time,' said Ben, trying to reassure him.

'Oh, it was. I discovered that if I picture Alison with her back to me it's not so off-putting. The minute she pops up, I have to tell her to turn around and that seems to do the trick.'

'If you can tell her to turn around, can't you tell her to go away?' asked Ben.

Braindead scrutinised him for a moment. 'I don't think so,' he said eventually. 'I don't think she'll listen to that. She'll only listen to that when she's back with her husband, I reckon.'

'So it's like she's haunting you. But she might stop if she has Matthew back.'

'Yes!' exclaimed Braindead. 'That's exactly what it feels like. Haunting me whilst I have sex.'

Ben decided that Braindead made his brain hurt sometimes.

'Well, at least you're having sex again. That's good, isn't it?'

'Oh, it is indeed. It was Erica, actually – she told me to stop being such a wuss and get on with it. Sisters, hey?'

Ben instantly felt his insides somersault at the mention of Erica's name.

'She sticking around for long then?' he asked tentatively.

Braindead shrugged. 'Seems like it. Daniel's letting her stay in his spare room. Not sure why she wants to stick around here, though – I mean, she hasn't before, has she? Felt like she's avoided it since Mum died.'

'Perhaps she wants to spend time with you?' said Ben.

'Maybe. Whenever I see her though all she wants to talk about is the past. Bit weird that, don't you think?'

'You know what she told me?' said Ben, finding himself mock laughing. He felt the need to get it out there. Their conversation. He'd been going over and over it in his head, trying to make any sense of the revelation that not only had his best friend's sister fancied him but also that a supermodel was suddenly within his grasp. It was just the most ridiculous thing that he could be thinking and he needed it out of his brain and into safe open waters where it could be mocked and laughed about and then disappear before it did any harm to him or anyone else.

'Did she tell you that I once let her put curlers in my hair and shave my armpits? Did she tell you that?' Braindead said accusingly. 'She promised me that she would never, ever, ever tell anyone that. I can't believe she waited all this time and let that secret out. Why? Why would she do that?'

'She didn't,' said Ben.

'She didn't tell you that I let her curl my hair and shave my armpits?'

'No. Why did you let her do that?'

'Because she said if I didn't, she would tell Amy Bagshaw that I fancied her and I did, but I didn't want Amy to know that I did. That would have been embarrassing.'

'More embarrassing than shaved armpits?'

'No, as it turns out. You have no idea how painful it was. Why women do it, I have no idea. Tickling is bad enough, imagine scraping a blade across them. Ridiculous!'

'I can imagine,' agreed Ben.

'So what did she tell you then?'

'Well, remember that New Year's Eve party you had in your dad's house before it got sold?'

'The one where I gave everyone food poisoning?'

'That's the one.' Ben swallowed and could feel his cheeks starting to burn just at the thought of what he was about to say. 'Well, she reckons she suggested that party only because she wanted to see me and she planned to kiss me but then she got sick with everyone else and the moment passed.'

Braindead had been about to take a sip of his pint but he halted as Ben unwound Erica's story in front of him.

'She wanted to kiss *you*?' said Braindead incredulously.

'So she said,' replied Ben.

'No,' said Braindead, shaking his head. 'No way! Not Erica and you. Not happening.'

'Of course it's not happening, I'm just telling you what she told me. That when we were younger she apparently fancied me. I had no idea, mate. Honestly, it came as big a shock to me as clearly it has to you.'

Braindead was twisting his mouth as though about to throw up.

'But that's all wrong,' he said, shaking his head. 'You're like a brother to me – in fact, you are my brother and she's my sister and so she can't fancy you. It's not allowed.'

'Look, like I said, I had no idea. None at all, I promise you. I just thought you might find it funny, that's all.'

'Funny!' exclaimed Braindead. 'Funny finding out that my sister wanted to have sex with my best-friend-slash-brother? What's funny about that?'

Ben didn't know what to say. When he put it like that it didn't sound funny at all. It sounded weird and a bit sordid and ridiculous.

'I'm sorry,' he said eventually. 'I shouldn't have mentioned it.'

'No, you shouldn't,' said Braindead, slamming his pint down. 'As if I haven't enough problems with my sex life without now having to get rid of the image of you and my sister having sex. Why is having sex so complicated once you've married?'

Chapter Twenty-Eight

Katy

I know I'm not talking to you but will you come and look at suits with me at lunch? Dx

Katy looked at the text and sighed. She wasn't quite sure if it was in relief or despair. She suspected that Daniel was having a major sulk with her since she had informed him of Rita's dislike of his colour scheme but it hadn't been confirmed until this text. He'd been cordial in meetings, professional even, but there had been none of their typical banter and certainly none of the usual open character assassination that their relationship thrived on.

Don't you want to take fashion icon Erica? Kx

Don't be so childish and… jealous. I'll see you downstairs in ten minutes. Dx

She wasn't having that. Her, childish and jealous? He was the one throwing his toys out of the cot because Rita didn't share his view on colour themes for the wedding.

She gathered her things and went to the toilet. At the moment she did seem to spend half her life in there and consequently was thinking of asking at the next directors' meeting whether an extra-wide toilet should be put in for pregnant ladies. She knew, however, this would be shouted down through fear of discriminating against other sectors of society. Workplace toilet assignment was such a touchy subject these days. Male, female, unisex? Add pregnant to that and they could soon have more toilets than offices!

*

Daniel didn't even smile at her when she arrived in reception, just got up and walked to the door, clearly assuming she would simply fall into step with him.

'I don't need you to make small talk,' he said. 'I'm not interested. Just come along and have the small talk to the shop guy, who will no doubt want to ask me how excited I am about my upcoming nuptials and you can inform him why I am not excited about the most important day in my life.'

'Explaining that it is all my fault presumably?' said Katy.

'Precisely,' agreed Daniel.

'You only want me there to deflect any wedding-related questions.'

'I do.'

'What if they think we are getting married?' she asked.

He deigned to look at her with his eyebrows raised.

'You are pregnant.'

'A good reason to be getting married.'

'You are so not my type.'

'Have you told them you are marrying a guy?'

'No. I am long past going round wearing my sexuality on my sleeve. That's so nineties.'

'Right. Of course,' said Katy. They fell into silence for a while until they pushed open the doors of Harvey Nichols, where the first thing they saw was an enormous poster of Erica promoting a handbag brand.

'So, where is your new best accessory today then?' asked Katy, nodding at the sign.

'I take it you mean Erica? That's very mean, you know. She hates being treated like she has no personality and is just being used for her looks.'

Katy glanced back at the poster. Erica was topless with the handbag protecting her modesty. She looked absolutely flawless.

'I'd like to be used for my looks, just once,' sighed Katy as she ran her hand over her baby bump.

Daniel looked down at her. 'It's a good job you've got a good personality,' he said.

She looked back up at him sharply. He smiled. Just a small one.

'I'll take that as a compliment,' she said.

'It was meant as one,' he replied.

Katy felt a small piece of relief flow through her body. Perhaps they could be friends again.

'She's gone a bit weird,' said Daniel.

'Who has?'

'Erica.'

'In what way?'

'Well, she doesn't want to go out any more. All she does is stay in my flat and mope about. I think she's either sick or possibly she's *in love*!'

'In love?'

'Yeah. She's showing all the symptoms. Total lack of concentration even when I'm talking to her.'

'Heaven forbid anyone should lose concentration whilst you are talking to them!' exclaimed Katy.

'I know. I'm interesting, it's a fact. Other people have told me.'

'Of course they have, Daniel.'

'In fact, she reminds me of what I was like when I was seventeen and hankering after Toby Mitchell in the Upper Sixth. I couldn't concentrate, couldn't do anything. All I did all day was dream about him with this dopey look on my face. My mum kept asking me if I was constipated. She kept trying to sneak figs into my food. I've never been able to touch a fig since. Figs in quiche is a memory that is very difficult to shake off.'

'Have you asked her if she is constipated?'

'No! Katy, seriously, what do you take me for? She doesn't eat enough to be constipated. It would take her a year to get a blockage with the amount she consumes.'

'Well, it must be love then if it isn't constipation,' said Katy. 'How exciting! Have you asked her who it is? Have you met anyone she seems keen on whilst you have been out and about?'

'No, not a soul. I've been wracking my brains but we haven't met anyone of her calibre. I mean, she has excellent taste, Katy. I can't imagine anyone in Leeds quite coming up to scratch.'

'What do you mean?' she replied indignantly. 'There are a lot of tasteful people in Leeds. Leeds is cool.'

'The mere fact that you described it as "cool" shows you know nothing about it. I imagine Erica to be attracted by someone enormously creative but very understated. You know, someone who hides their light under a bushel. Someone who has no idea how cool they are.'

'Someone like you, you mean?'

'Exactly,' replied Daniel. 'A non-gay me would suit her perfectly.'

'But if you weren't gay, you wouldn't be you.'

'That is a very good point. Poor Erica. She's never going to find someone, is she?'

'Perhaps she's sick of the types she meets in the modelling world. Have you ever thought of that? Perhaps she wants a normal guy. An unpretentious guy who treats her like a normal person. You know, like a plumber or a builder or an accountant.'

Daniel looked at her in astonishment. 'An accountant!' he exclaimed.

'I'm just trying to point out that often it's good to marry outside your profession. Gives you a new outlook on life. I love the fact that Ben has nothing to do with advertising. Can't think of anything more depressing than going home every night and talking about washing powder branding.'

'Instead, you get to hear about other people's kids,' pointed out Daniel. 'What a joy!'

Katy looked at him. 'It's a joy to have a husband who comes home having enjoyed his day at work and done something worthwhile. I couldn't be prouder of Ben being a teacher.'

'My husband is an architect,' said Daniel as if he had said it for the first time.

'You like the idea of that, don't you?' said Katy.

Daniel nodded.

'I bet you can't wait to go somewhere fancy and have to introduce Gabriel and tell them your husband is an architect.'

He nodded even harder.

'You are so shallow,' she told him.

Daniel kept nodding.

'So you don't think that Erica would like to introduce her husband as an accountant?' she asked.

Daniel thought for a minute.

'Maybe,' he said. 'She keeps saying how much she loves being back amongst people from her past. Real people, she keeps calling them. Perhaps she's after a real person, although accountants aren't real, are they? Accountants have been developed by robots and are run by drones.'

Katy shook her head. She'd missed these random chats with Daniel.

'Come on, let's get you a suit you can miserably get married in,' she said, taking his arm and dragging him towards the elevator.

*

'My fiancé?' she heard Daniel saying as he walked out of the fitting area with the sales assistant. 'Oh, he's an accountant, I mean architect. He's a very successful architect for a practice in London but he's moving up here to join their Leeds office as soon as we are married.'

'An architect?' said the impossibly good-looking sales assistant whose jaw looked like it was cut from pure granite. 'They build houses, right?'

Daniel looked at him, horrified.

'Gabriel is currently working on the design of a new office block in the City.'

'Oh, they build offices too? I didn't realise that.'

'No, they design them. Builders build them.'

'Right,' the assistant replied, looking not in the slightest bit interested. 'You look amazing in that suit, by the way. Like, stellar. Suits you better than anyone I have seen try it on.'

'Really?' asked Daniel, suddenly looking at him like he was the cleverest man on earth. 'Do you really think so?'

'Sure,' he shrugged. 'Not many guys can carry off a green suit. It can look kind of old-fashioned unless you've got the rest of the package that makes it look good.'

'And you think I have the package?' asked Daniel.

'Sure,' the guy shrugged again. 'The right colouring, the right shoes, the right haircut makes such a difference.'

'Didn't I say this was my best ever haircut?' said Daniel, turning to Katy, who was slumped on a dreadfully uncomfortable leather sofa. 'I told you, didn't I, that the guy in Greek Street was an absolute genius.'

Katy watched as Daniel turned to face the mirror and smoothed down the back of his head.

'How do I look?' he asked, turning to face her.

She gave him a once-over. He looked, as always, perfect. The suit was in emerald green linen, which he wore with a crisp white shirt and navy tie. He was so stylish, almost as if he could have just walked off the catwalk. For all his faults, Daniel did have exquisite taste and he had never looked better.

'Perfect,' she said. 'Utterly perfect.'

Daniel nodded. He looked sad – she knew why.

'Pity the rest of the wedding won't be perfect,' he muttered at the floor.

She swallowed and shifted her bump to a more comfortable position. She watched as he turned to look into the mirror again and admired his reflection.

'It is perfect, isn't it?' he said, biting his lip. 'I saw this suit in *Esquire* last year and when I saw it, I thought if I ever get married I want to get married in that suit because I knew it was perfect. And I hadn't even met Gabriel then but I dared to dream that I might meet someone and marry them in a little rundown church on a hilltop in Italy and I would arrive and a single bell would be ringing and it would be the most beautiful day with all of my closest friends around me and I would know it was the best day of my life, wearing this suit, next to the man of my dreams being married by Hugh Jackman in his Greatest Showman outfit.'

Katy glanced over at the sales assistant, who was looking bewildered at Daniel.

'Hugh Jackman?' questioned Katy.

'Yes, of course. But as Barnum and not Wolverine. He looks great in both of course, but who else would I have officiate my wedding but the Greatest Showman?'

'Is your fiancé disabled or something?' the sales guy asked with a furrowed brow.

'Why do you ask that?' exclaimed Daniel.

'Can't he get up the hill? Is that why you're not getting married in a church at the top of a hill? Is there no disabled access or something?'

Daniel must have stared at him for at least twenty seconds before he spoke.

'No, my fiancé is not disabled. Not that it would matter if he was. I mean, Adam Hills is the definition of sexy. No, the reason we are not getting married at the top of a hill in Italy is because her mother…' At this point Daniel turned dramatically and stabbed a finger in Katy's direction. 'Her mother is marrying my fiancé's father and they are insisting we get married together. And we will celebrate in some dodgy bar on the Costa Brava. I mean, I ask you. Does this suit belong in Costa anything? Not even Costa Coffee. I think not!'

The guy gave a bewildered look to Katy. She tried to disappear into the leather couch.

'So, do you want me to show you some suits that you think might be more suitable?' he asked Daniel.

'What?' he exclaimed. 'The swimsuit section? I might as well roll up in some Speedos with an inflatable crocodile under my arm for all the class my wedding is going to have!'

The guy looked to Katy for guidance. All she could do was shake her head.

'So, will you be taking the Paul Smith then?' he asked tentatively.

Katy held her breath. It was like some weird twisted episode of *Don't Tell the Bride*, where the bride loved the dress but not where she was going to wear it.

'I suppose so,' Daniel shrugged. 'I might as well fulfil a part of my dream as nothing at all.' He looked at her so mournfully she wanted to cry or hit him.

'Can't you say no?' questioned the sales guy.

Katy and Daniel both turned to stare at him.

'Just say no,' he repeated. 'Surely?'

'This isn't a drugs campaign,' replied Katy. 'This is a wedding. The consequences of saying no could be… well… catastrophic.'

The assistant was looking blankly at her again. Of course, too young for *Grange Hill*, she thought.

But Daniel was staring at the guy, a dawning of realisation across his face.

'I could, couldn't I?' he said, turning to look at Katy. 'I could just say no. Simple as. After all, it's my wedding day too.'

Katy stared back at him. God, he was a wanker at times. Why did weddings turn people into selfish bastards? She could feel a burning anger rising up inside her. She stroked her baby bump in an effort to calm down. This was all wrong, she thought. Daniel standing there about to marry the man of his dreams and completely in the doldrums about it. Why? Why were weddings like this? Getting married was about telling someone you want to share absolutely everything and yet planning a wedding could bring out the selfish in almost anyone.

'I'm not doing it,' Daniel announced suddenly. 'I'm not doing it. I'm not having your mum's wedding, I'm having my wedding. I must have my wedding. It's the only wedding I'm going to have so I must do it my way, right?'

'Of course,' agreed the guy, who was no doubt on commission. 'Of course you must. You must do it your way. Now, do you want to take the suit off and I can get it boxed for you? I don't think there's any need for any alterations, do you? From where I'm standing, it fits like a glove.'

Daniel turned back to face the mirror and pulled down his cuffs.

'It does, doesn't it?' he agreed. 'It's a sign. It has to be a sign. Everything about this wedding should be perfect.'

Katy thought about the torment Daniel was going to put Gabriel through by forcing him to tell his father they didn't want to be part of their wedding. She thought about the grief she was going to get from Rita, distraught that she wouldn't get to play the cool stepmum.

Wedding season had just got a whole lot worse.

She heard her phone beep and hoped it would be work demanding she get back as they had an angry client needing to speak to her urgently. Anything was better than this. But it wasn't. It was a text from Matthew containing two words.

Help me!

It was like an automatic reaction. Her legs and arms started moving as if on autopilot. She pulled herself up off the deeply uncomfortable sofa and headed towards the exit.

'Where are you going?' Daniel called after her. 'I thought we would go and look round the kitchenware section next. See if there's anything we could put on a gift list. Do you think there's anyone I know who might buy us a KitchenAid? I mean, I know they're very expensive but I've got just the spot where one would look great.'

Katy stopped and turned round. She was at a loss as to what to say.

'Now that I've taken that wall down and put the cupboard in to hide all the other appliances,' continued Daniel, 'the surfaces look a bit bare but a KitchenAid would look fabulous, don't you think? Why are you looking at me like that?' he asked when he finally noticed her confused look.

'You don't bake,' she said.

'I know,' he agreed.

'So why do you need a KitchenAid?'

He sighed. 'Like I said, it would look great in my new kitchen, and to be quite honest, I've got no idea what we should put on our wedding list, so I thought a KitchenAid would be a good idea. It's not like I would ever buy one for myself, is it? I mean, they are ridiculously expensive.'

Katy said nothing.

'So, are you going to come with me to have a look? See if they have any special editions?' he asked.

'No,' she replied. 'I have no interest in going to see items for your wedding list that you are willing for your nearest and dearest to spend a small fortune on despite being something you don't need. No interest at all.'

'Aww, come on, Katy! It'll be fun. It's all part of getting married, isn't it?'

Just at that moment Katy's phone buzzed again. She looked down at her phone. It was another message from Matthew.

Desperate.

It beeped again.

I don't know what to do.

'If it's work,' said Daniel, 'tell them to piss off. We put enough hours into that place for them to give us a bit of time off to go wedding shopping.'

'It's not work,' she said. 'It's Matthew.'

'Matthew!' exclaimed Daniel. 'What's he texting you for? Surely he never wants to see you again after the fiasco at Braindead's wedding?'

'He needs help,' she said steadily. 'He needs help because his marriage has fallen apart and he's fighting to hold his family together whilst you are stood here being stroppy because you can't have your wedding exactly the way you want it. Don't you get it, Daniel? Weddings don't make marriages. It isn't the day that makes or breaks a marriage. It's the things you do on every other day, the decisions you make, that's what makes a marriage. So you go and look at KitchenAids and Norwegian spruces and Paul Smith suits or whatever else you think is important because that's clearly going to mean you have a successful marriage. Meanwhile I'll go and see if there is anything I can do for Matthew to help him piece his back together –because he's sure as hell not thinking that he's relieved they went for the aubergine shade of napkins rather than the forest green.'

She stopped for a moment, trying to catch her breath.

'Look, Daniel,' she continued, 'you have the chance to make your wedding so much more special than the fact you will get a kitchen-utensil sculpture that you will never use. Just think about that, will you? Please.'

Chapter Twenty-Nine

Matthew

He'd never thrown a sickie. Never. But after an hour of staring blankly at his screen, and feeling the rising panic that he had to go into a meeting with one of their most important clients, he just got up and started to walk. He walked over to Ian's desk first but he was on the phone. He stood next to him, willing him to finish, but he kept going on and on until eventually Matthew could stand it no longer. He leaned over and cut the call off.

'For God's sake!' said Ian. 'What the hell? That was Cartwrights. What do I tell them? We had a power cut?'

'I've got to go,' said Matthew, staring into space. 'You'll have to handle the Bittermans meeting.'

'What…? No way! You know they hate me. For some reason they only listen to you. Come on, mate.'

'Can't do it. Got to go.'

'Why? Is one of the kids sick? What happened?' asked Ian, suddenly looking panicked.

'No,' said Matthew, shaking his head. 'No. I… I just can't be here.' It felt like someone else was speaking. Like he was looking down on himself. All he knew was that he couldn't be here, he had to get out right now. He felt his heart rate start to increase. He turned to leave.

'Hang on a minute, mate,' he heard Ian say behind him. 'What about the report you were doing for Bittermans? Where is it? I can't go into that meeting without the report.'

Ian's phone rang at that point and Matthew heard him mutter 'Bollocks!' under his breath before he picked up and greeted whoever it was in his usual cheery manner.

Matthew dug his hands into his trouser pockets and put his head down. He didn't want to talk to anyone. He couldn't talk to anyone, he had to get out.

He nearly made it and then Sue grabbed him in reception.

'You got a minute?' she asked. 'I wanted to pick your brains about these new land ownership tax laws. Fancy a coffee?'

No, he wanted to scream at her. He wanted to curl up in a ball and be far away from anything and everything.

'Got to go,' he muttered and put his head down even further and headed for the door. He started breathing again when he was out on the pavement. Maybe now he wouldn't have to speak to anyone ever again.

He didn't know where to go. He didn't want to go back to Ian's. Because it was… well, it was Ian's. He'd been there three weeks but he didn't feel at home, not for a minute. And all he wanted was his home.

He wandered. He wandered down streets he never knew existed, despite having grown up in Leeds and lived there for the past six years. He discovered random industrial sites with random sheds and offices, accommodating random small businesses. Car repair, welding, pine furniture, MOTs, car washing. All small independent companies struggling to survive in the no man's land overhyped by the label 'industrial park'. He passed men with dirty faces drinking tea and eating sandwiches on low walls without a care in the world. He wished with all his heart he had a dirty face and was eating sandwiches so casually. That looked like a fine place to be.

In the end he sat on a low wall around the corner from the grubby workers and tried to get some focus.

He kept going over and over his conversation with Alison. He couldn't believe she'd hidden the fact she was on anti-depressants. Why hadn't she told him? Why would she hide that? It hurt him so badly to know that she hadn't felt she could share that with him. That their bond wasn't close enough for her to feel she could disclose her innermost dreadful feelings.

Their marriage had started with such positivity during the most epic of wedding days. It had been a perfectly orchestrated day because, after all, Alison had been involved. Never had a wedding had so many lever arch files. This was a wedding where everything was going to be perfect. And it was. Of course it was. And he was happy that it was. Alison's obsession with getting their wedding right – indeed, getting their life right – made him feel safe and secure and focused. She was most definitely in charge and that suited him just fine.

But then suddenly the plan had failed. The plan to have babies a year after they had been married to give themselves some 'fun time' hadn't come to fruition. As the plan spiralled out of control, so too had Alison, and Matthew had painfully watched his wife unravel. But he'd had no idea that she had unravelled to the point of requiring medical help.

Why hadn't she talked to him?

He knew why.

Alison saw her lack of fertility as her failure. For her to admit that her mind was failing her too would have been a step too far. Dealing publicly with more failure would have destroyed her and so she had dealt with it alone. A fact that made Matthew want to break down at the very thought of it.

The sky bore down on him as a lorry passed by too fast, nearly spattering him with water from a puddle. He instinctively pulled his feet in and watched the spray soak into the grey pavement.

All he wanted to do was look after her. He wanted to take her in his arms and tell her that none of it was her fault and that she could tell him anything and he would always stand by her. Always.

Okay, so he'd made mistakes. When the chips were down he'd seen Katy as an exit route. Some respite from his difficult relationship as it was then. He'd been weak. He'd temporarily forgotten those sacred vows he'd made on that sacred day. For all of Alison's meticulous planning of every single aspect of their wedding, the only thing that had really mattered was when they said those words that should have bound them together for ever and ever in sickness and in health, till death do us part.

*

'You all right, mate?' asked a man in a boiler suit after Matthew had been sitting there on that low wall for two hours.

'What?'

'You all right? We were just a bit worried that your lift hadn't turned up or something. Or do you just like our wall?'

'Oh,' Matthew said, looking round, bewildered. He had no idea how long he had been sitting there. 'I was just, er… er…' He looked at his watch. 'Christ, better go!' he said, jumping up and scurrying off, leaving the boiler-suited man gazing after him in wonder.

Now where?

He knew he had nowhere. That wall had held him up for the last couple of hours and now he had nowhere that could give him any kind of support.

So he walked round the next corner and found another low wall and sat down before starting to cry.

Chapter Thirty

Katy

Fortunately Katy had been here before. She'd purchased her first ever car from a dodgy dealer somewhere on this back road. Her dad had had a fit when she told him where she'd bought the Ford Ka with alloy wheels but she hadn't cared. She was twenty and buying her first car. The excitement far outweighed any caution.

She'd been back recently though, she remembered. To a tile warehouse because someone at work had said the tiles were cheap. And they were, but there was a reason for it. They were clearly tiles no-one in their right mind would want and she had spent all of twenty seconds in the place before turning round and driving straight to a tile shop in a trendy suburb of Leeds that had tiles so lovely you wanted to stroke them whilst you took out a second mortgage to be able to afford them.

Matthew had said he was outside a sign maker's, which was Unit 6. Christ, it was depressing just driving into here! There was no comfort to be sought out here amongst the corrugated iron and breeze blocks and dust blowing in the light wind.

She could see him now. Squatting on a wall. Shoulders hunched. She gasped. He looked a sorry sight, defeat written all over him.

She drew up in front of him and put the window down.

'Get in, will you,' she shouted.

He looked up slowly as if surprised to see her there. He didn't move.

'Get in, Matthew. Please,' she said.

He raised himself slowly from his seat as though it hurt and ambled over. She sighed. This was not going to be an easy afternoon.

He fell into the car as though he wasn't quite in control of all his faculties.

'Thanks,' he muttered as he reached back to secure his seatbelt.

'Where shall we go?' she asked.

He shrugged.

She didn't want to take him back to hers. Ben and Millie would be back from school soon and she didn't fancy trying to explain to her daughter why there was a man crying in the kitchen.

'Where are you staying?' she asked.

'At a mate's.'

'Shall we go there?'

He shrugged again, his eyes fixed ahead.

'Where does he live?'

'Number 4 Chapel Street.'

But they never made it to Number 4 Chapel Street.

Chapter Thirty-One

Matthew

And then he let go. It all came out. The grief, the anguish, the horror, the guilt poured out of Matthew in front of the only person he felt he could let it all out to. Because she had been there. She couldn't judge him. Because she had been there, his partner in crime.

They didn't touch or hug, they just sat facing forward, looking at a sign-production workshop as he poured his heart out and Katy listened.

He told her about the anti-depressants and she gasped. No doubt appalled as he was at how low Alison must have been when they cheated on her. It made him feel better to tell someone, even if it was Katy. It was no longer just his guilty secret that he had cheated on his wife whilst she was taking anti-depressants and undergoing IVF. He felt one per cent better, but, of course, that was not enough.

When he was done they sat in silence. Katy said nothing. What could she say? There was nothing to be said. He had screwed up his marriage in the most spectacular fashion and discarded his claim to a blissful future with his wife and four children.

The grief was almost unbearable. Suffocating. And it was all his own doing.

The road was getting busier now as 4.30 approached. Men in boiler suits started to knock off early, no doubt having been there since the crack of dawn. Cars burst into action and accelerated, their drivers eager to be released from the shackles of work.

'What do you want to do?' asked Katy eventually.

'I want to go back in time and stop what happened. I want to go back and not thump that bloke we can't remember so you didn't offer me a bag of peas, so I wouldn't need to go back to your flat and then do what we did.'

'So the buck stops with the bloke with no name, does it?' she asked.

'No. It stops with me.'

'And me,' she muttered.

'I wish we had never met,' admitted Matthew.

'Me too,' sighed Katy.

A ringing interrupted the thick atmosphere.

Matthew took out his phone and looked at it hopefully. Every time it rang, he dreamt it might be Alison. It gave him a moment's relief from the agony but then the agony flooded back instantly as her name didn't appear on the screen. This time it was Ian.

'Where are you, mate?' he said. 'Ricardo is seriously pissed with you for the no-show at the Bittermans meeting.'

Matthew sighed but didn't reply. He really couldn't give a fig about the Bittermans meeting.

'Where are you?' Ian asked again.

'On the West Meadows Estate with Katy,' Matthew replied.

Shocked silence at the end of the phone. 'I'm on my way,' Ian eventually replied and the phone went dead.

Matthew stared at his phone.

'I think Ian thinks I'm shagging you on the West Meadows Estate,' he told Katy dully.

She nodded slowly.

'Does he know I'm pregnant?' she asked.

Matthew turned to face her and stared at her bump. He'd totally forgotten that she was pregnant.

'No,' he replied. 'He's now going to think that I might have got you pregnant again, isn't he?'

Katy stroked her bump protectively and looked out of the front windscreen.

'Possibly,' she sighed.

They fell into silence again.

Next, it was Katy's phone's turn to ring.

'Daniel,' she said as she looked at the screen.

Matthew watched as she listened to whatever Daniel was saying with a blank expression on her face until she eventually said, 'I'm with Matthew on the West Meadows Estate.'

She paused again. Matthew held his breath. Five seconds later, she removed the phone from her ear and tapped the screen.

'Does he think I might have made you pregnant again?' he asked.

'Possibly,' she replied.

'Great,' said Matthew, sinking into further doom.

They sat in silence for a further ten minutes until Katy announced that she had some mints.

'Would you like one?' she asked.

'Does my breath smell?' he asked.

'No. Just, would you like one?'

'Okay then.'

She rummaged around in her bag until she found a tube of Mentos that had been half-eaten, the wrapper screwed up tight around the remaining mints.

'I don't like Mentos,' he stated.

She turned to look at him. 'But I thought you wanted a mint?'

'I do, but I thought you meant like a Polo or something. I don't like Mentos. Too chewy.'

Katy gave a huge sigh and unwrapped herself a mint before putting the rest back in her bag.

'What do we say to them when they get here?' she said.

'That I've had a breakdown and my life is over,' replied Matthew.

'Have you?' she asked, turning to face him abruptly. 'Is that what you were doing here? Having a breakdown?'

'I don't know,' he replied. 'I've no idea. I just felt like shit. I *feel* like shit. Is that a breakdown?'

Katy continued to stare at him.

'I don't know,' she replied eventually. 'But perhaps we should check.'

'Check what?'

'If you've had a breakdown.'

'How do we do that?'

Katy looked him up and down.

'Shall we Google it?' she asked.

'Google if I've had a breakdown?'

'Well, yes.' She was starting to look panicked and Matthew didn't need to add stressing out a pregnant woman to his current list of crimes against humanity.

'Why would we do that?' he had to ask.

She was shaking her head as if she didn't really know. 'Because if you've had a breakdown, like a proper one, then we should do something about it.'

'Like what?'

'Well, I don't know. If we Google it, it might say what you do. They may have a number you call or something, or a checklist. Let's just Google it and then at least we will know.'

Matthew watched as Katy got out her phone again and started tapping.

'What are you typing?' he asked.

'"What are the symptoms of a breakdown?",' she said matter-of-factly.

Matthew turned back to face the bleak outlook through the front windscreen. He wasn't sure that Katy was helping.

'Are you overeating?' she barked out suddenly.

'What?'

'Overeating? Is your eating out of control?'

'No. I just turned down a mint.'

'Right, okay, that's good. Have you lost interest in how you look?' She looked over at his crumpled shirt and grey V-necked sweater. It was hardly going to get him any adoring female admirers but then he was a middle-aged, married man.

'I've never really cared how I look,' he replied, feeling confused.

'I can see that. So perhaps that's okay? Would you say you care more or less about how you look since Alison chucked you out?'

Matthew shook his head. Was any of this relevant?

'I couldn't really give a monkey's about how I looked before or after,' he replied.

'That has to be good. No change in lack of care of appearance. Must be a good sign. Has your nose gone into overdrive?'

'My nose?'

'Yes, your nose. Are you much more sensitive to bad smells? Apparently that's a sign of severe anxiety and stress.'

'Living with Ian means my threshold for bad smells has had to be dramatically raised. But that's Ian's backside and not stress as far as I'm aware.'

'Right. Not sure how conclusive that is. Are you struggling to concentrate?'

'Yes,' replied Matthew immediately. 'Of course I am. I need to get my wife and kids back. How can I concentrate on anything other than that? I literally cannot think about anything else.' He felt angry now. Didn't she get it?

He looked over at her. She was biting her lip, looking very anxious.

'I'm not sure you're helping,' he said.

'Then why did you call me?'

His mouth dropped. He wasn't entirely sure.

'Because you are the only one who can't judge me.'

She nodded and appeared to calm down.

'Are you having a breakdown?' she asked nervously.

'I didn't think I was until you started asking me lots of stupid questions,' he replied.

'Sorry.'

'I don't think I'm having a breakdown,' he muttered eventually. 'I'm just very, very sad. I'm just so very sad and so very disappointed that I am in this situation.'

She reached out and put her hand over his. Then pulled it back abruptly.

'I shouldn't be doing that, should I?' she said. 'I mean, I know the last person both of us want right now is each other, but... well... you know what I mean.'

'I know what you mean,' he nodded, folding his arms tightly to his chest.

'So what are you going to do then?' she asked.

'There's nothing I can do, is there? Believe me, I have racked my brains. I've looked at it from every angle. I even set up a spreadsheet.'

'A spreadsheet?'

'It's what I do when I can't solve a problem – I set up a spreadsheet. Even if there are no numbers involved it just makes me see it differently sometimes. But not this time. I put in one column all the things I have done wrong and then I was going to try and put in another all the things I could do to put those things right, but I couldn't think of anything that meant my columns were balanced. There was nothing to get me out of the red. Nothing.'

'For heaven's sake, what the hell are you both doing here?' gasped Ian, climbing into the back seat. 'Hi, I'm Ian,' he continued, leaning forward and offering his hand to Katy. 'We met briefly once before but you probably don't remember me. However, I feel like you have been a part of my life for some time, owing to me being Matthew's go-to man whenever disaster strikes in the marriage department.'

Katy felt her mouth drop but she still offered her hand and shook Ian's limply.

'Ian had an affair and his wife left him,' Matthew pointed out sarcastically. 'He is now dating our nanny, which nearly caused Alison to chuck me out then. Ian has been hugely helpfully in supporting my marriage to Alison.'

'Pleased to meet you,' said Katy. 'I've never heard you mentioned before?'

'Well, that's me, I guess,' replied Ian. 'The backroom boy. I like to keep a low profile.'

'It's all your fault anyway,' muttered Matthew.

'What is?' asked Ian.

'If it hadn't been for you pestering me to go to the school reunion then none of this would have happened.'

'But you didn't go to Dove Valley, did you?' asked Katy.

'No, he bloody didn't,' said Matthew. 'But when I mentioned it, he smelt fresh meat. Women who had never met him so had not had the opportunity to realise what an idiot he is. Daisy Greenwood that night, wasn't it?'

'Who?' asked Ian.

'Daisy Greenwood. I used to sit next to her in French. Recently divorced too, wasn't she? I bet she was so glad she met you that night.'

'What was her name again?' asked Ian.

'Daisy Greenwood.'

'A bit on the plump side?' he asked.

'Yes,' said Matthew. 'I seem to remember you saying you were looking for someone who might be "amply" grateful for your affections.' He shook his head. 'There's you with that attitude towards women and it's me who's the villain!'

'I love women!' argued Ian.

'Look, this isn't getting us anywhere, is it?' interrupted Katy. 'What are we going to do?'

'Oh, you're here to help, are you?' asked Ian.

'Yes,' replied Katy.

'And is she helping?' Ian asked Matthew.

'Well, she's established I'm not having a nervous breakdown.'

'Marvellous,' he replied.

'I Googled it,' added Katy. 'Just to check.'

'Great, brilliant. Have you tried Googling how Matthew should get his wife back after he shagged his ex at a school reunion?'

'Ian!' exclaimed Matthew. 'It's not her... well...'

'Well, it is partly my fault,' agreed Katy, turning away from Ian to face forward. 'Oh God!' she exclaimed. 'That's all we need. Seriously? And who's that he's brought with him?'

The three inhabitants of the Volvo V50 estate car watched as Daniel got out of the front seat of his Tesla. Then he stepped back to open the back door and let out a pair of very long, slim legs, which angled themselves down and glided into an upright position.

'Erica!' said Katy.

'Who in the name of Jesus Lord Christ my saviour is that?' asked Ian.

'Braindead's sister,' said Matthew.

'Braindead!' exclaimed Ian. 'That shambles that took you out for a drink?'

'Braindead is no shambles,' said Katy. 'He's... he's... he's a wonderful human being.'

'No,' replied Ian. 'That is a wonderful human being.' He nodded towards Erica, who was now gliding towards them.

'What are they doing here?' muttered Matthew.

'Clearly they've come to join this little car party we have going on,' replied Katy.

Daniel walked past Katy in the driver's seat and opened the back door. 'Room for two more?' he asked.

'For fuck's sake,' muttered Matthew.

'If you've come here to ask me to go and look at decorative Hoovers for your wedding list, I'm not coming,' announced Katy.

'Budge up, will you,' Daniel said to Ian as he shuffled along. 'I'm the knight in shining armour, who are you?'

'Er, Robin Hood? Are we playing a game or something?'

'Ian, this is Daniel, Daniel, this is Ian,' said Matthew over his shoulder. 'Daniel works with Katy and…'

'He's my best friend… usually,' she added. 'Well, when he's not getting married, he is.'

'Oh, congratulations,' said Ian. 'I've been there, done that, mate. Divorced, Tindered and now happily in love with his nanny.'

'As in grandma!'

'No, the nanny who looks after his kids! Jesus, I don't look that old, do I?'

'Nothing a touch of moisturiser wouldn't fix. Let's exchange numbers and I'll send you a recommendation. How old do you think I am?'

'Well, I'd say early forties,' replied Ian.

'Bingo!' replied Daniel. 'I'm forty-eight.'

'Forty-eight! Tell me your number now.'

'Is that what you came out here for, Daniel?' asked Katy. 'To exchange beauty tips?'

'You'd be surprised how many straight men are interested in skincare, young lady. Do you want me to text you too, Matthew?'

Matthew shrugged and seconds later, his phone pinged.

'I've also sent you the contact name of my therapist,' said Daniel.

'I'm not having a breakdown,' said Matthew crossly.

'He's not,' said Katy. 'We Googled it. He's just very sad.'

'Still, give her a call,' said Daniel. 'You don't have to be on the edge of oblivion to talk to a therapist, Katy. I mean, look at me. I'm damn cheerful most of the time but everyone needs somewhere to dump their shit, as I say.'

'Where's Erica?' said Katy, suddenly realising she hadn't got in the car and yet she'd seen her get out of Daniel's.

'Having a cigarette,' replied Daniel. 'She was a bit peckish.'

'Shall I see if she's all right?' asked Ian.

'No!' said everyone.

'So, where are we at?' asked Daniel, settling himself into the seat.

'The West Meadows Industrial Estate I would say, wouldn't you?' said Matthew rather impatiently.

'I don't mean physically,' said Daniel. 'You know that's not what I mean. I mean, where are we at with your problem?'

'My problem!' said Matthew. 'You mean the end of my life as we know it?'

'Well, that attitude is not going to get you anywhere, is it?' replied Daniel. 'I take it then that you are at a deadlock. That Alison is not going to take you back. That you are not going to be forgiven.'

'I'd say that's a fair summary of the situation,' agreed Matthew. 'As I said in the first place, the end of my life as I know it.'

The back door opened.

'Ah, get in, Erica,' said Daniel, shuffling up to sit in the middle of the back seat. 'Let me introduce everyone. So, this is Matthew, the reason why we are here, the one your brother dobbed in at the wedding. And it appears we are also joined by Matthew's friend Ian, who is sat to my left and not budging up enough for my liking.'

'I'm rammed right against the door,' protested Ian.

'Well, breathe in then,' requested Daniel.

'I am breathing in!'

'When I get your number I will also text you the details of a nutritionist.'

'Christ!' exclaimed Ian. 'You really have an opinion on everything, don't you?'

'Generally, yes. And generally I find that I have a valid contribution to make, which is why I am here. To offer my services to your friend in his hour of need.'

'I think you will find that we were working through the issue. I have known Matthew a very long time,' bit back Ian.

'So you've had a proper conversation with him, have you, about the impact of his estrangement from his wife and children and offered thoughts and ideas on how to deal with that?'

'Mostly, he's moaned that I nick all the milk and then chucks me on the street when his girlfriend's coming round,' mumbled Matthew.

'Excellent,' declared Daniel. 'Thoroughly helpful.'

'I just wanted to say I'm sorry for what my brother did,' said Erica, leaning forward and squeezing Matthew's shoulder. 'He's devastated, you know that, don't you? He'd do anything to put it right. Absolutely anything. Anyway, I thought I'd come along on his behalf, just in case, you know, in case I could be of any help.'

Matthew turned round and offered his thanks.

'It's really very good of her,' said Daniel. 'She could be earning an absolute fortune from that face today if she wanted to but instead she's sat in the back of a Volvo, trying to sort your love life out.'

'I appreciate it,' mumbled Matthew.

'What's wrong with my Volvo?' asked Katy, turning round crossly.

'It's a Volvo, Katy,' replied Daniel.

'It's practical,' said Katy.

'Precisely,' said Daniel. 'So, shall we press on? I need to book some flights to Spain before the day's out.'

Katy turned round sharply.

'Have you decided to get married in Spain, with Mum?' she asked.

Daniel flashed her a grin.

'I have,' he replied. 'But let's not make this all about you and the fact that you will be smug now for some time because you were right. We are here to sort out Matthew's problem. So, let's hear what the current status is with Ali, Matthew.'

'She hates me.'

'Can you articulate exactly why your wife hates you?'

'Isn't it obvious?'

'Not necessarily, Matthew. You may be focusing on the symptoms rather than the root of the problem. So let's hear it.'

Matthew looked at Katy pleadingly.

'Go on,' she said. 'For all the twatty speak he's actually quite good at this. He might just be able to help.'

Matthew's shoulders sagged and he stared out of the window into the distance.

'Because of what happened with Katy at the school reunion my wife thinks I could have got someone pregnant whilst she was on IVF and she will never ever, ever, ever, ever forgive me for that.'

The car fell silent.

'Wow,' muttered Erica.

'Did you tell me that Alison was on IVF?' Daniel asked Katy.

'I didn't know that, did I?' exclaimed Katy. 'I didn't know any of that.'

'When you put it like that it doesn't sound good,' admitted Ian.

The car fell silent again. Only breathing could be heard.

'You're all wasting your time,' said Matthew suddenly. 'There is nothing you can do.' He opened the door and started to get out.

'Get back in the car,' said Katy as the door slammed. She began to wind down the passenger door window. 'Get back in,' she shouted after him.

'Follow him,' said Daniel. 'Come on.'

'Seriously? In the Volvo?' replied Katy.

'Come on,' urged Daniel.

Katy put the car into gear and drove less than one hundred yards to catch up with him.

'Get in,' shouted Daniel.

'Look, mate,' said Ian, winding down his window. 'Just get in, will you, and let's talk about it.'

'No,' repeated Matthew over his shoulder. 'Leave me alone.'

A man in a boiler suit was walking towards him. Matthew dropped his head down, trying to avoid eye contact.

'Are you all right, mate?' he heard the man say.

Matthew shrugged.

'Tell him to get back in the car,' shouted Ian through the open window.

'Are these people harassing you?' the man asked Matthew.

Matthew turned round and gave them a mournful look. 'Not really,' he said.

'Because I've got a garage round the corner. You know, with crowbars and mates and that. We can get rid of them for you. Is that why you've been sat on our wall all afternoon? They after you for money or something?'

'We have to get out,' declared Daniel, hustling Ian. 'Come on.'

Ian opened the door and began to climb out of the car.

'I'll go and get my mates,' the boiler-suited man said to Matthew, turning to go.

'No!' cried Katy, jumping out of the driver's seat. 'I'm pregnant, look!'

The man looked over and took in Katy's bump. His eyes about popped out of his head as he watched Erica get out of the car before he gave a passing glance to Ian and Daniel.

'Your baby?' said the man, nodding over at Katy.

'No!' shouted everyone.

'You sure you're okay?' he asked Matthew again.

He nodded.

'Right, if you're sure then I'll leave you to it.' He turned away, glancing over his shoulder with a worried look on his face.

'I'm here,' came a shout from the opposite side of the road.

'Why?' said Matthew, throwing his arms up in the air as Braindead approached at a run across the road, dodging cars along the way. Matthew lowered himself back onto the low wall whilst everyone gathered round him.

'Sorry,' said Erica. 'Daniel painted a really grim picture of you maybe hanging off a bridge somewhere so I thought he should know.'

'How come you're just sitting on a wall?' said Braindead, panting as he approached. 'I thought... I thought...' he added, sitting down next to Matthew and struggling to get his breath back. 'I thought you were about to do something stupid off, like, a really high place. I wasn't expecting a *low wall*.'

'Sorry to let you down,' muttered Matthew. 'I'll try a high wall next time.'

'You're all right, mate,' replied Braindead, throwing his arm around him. 'I've never been so pleased to see a low wall in my entire life.'

'He's not having a breakdown,' interrupted Katy. 'We Googled it and he's just very sad.'

Braindead turned to Katy. 'You can do that? You can Google it?'

'I don't know really,' she said. 'I just thought I'd check.'

'You don't need Google to tell you that I am a complete and utter failure,' muttered Matthew.

'No, you are not!' exclaimed Braindead. 'How can you say that? Look at you. You're a grown-up who does a grown-up job and has a wife and kids and who is a grown-up. You are the most grown-up man I know! How can you be a failure?'

'Because I had sex with Katy,' replied Matthew simply.

'Oh God!' said Katy, burying her head in her hands.

'So you see this is where society has it all wrong, right?' added Ian. 'Don't you think? You pretty much nailed the rest of your life apart from for what? Twenty minutes? For twenty minutes you went AWOL. Twenty fucking minutes compared to years of getting it mostly right.'

'I think it was more like ten minutes actually,' said Matthew.

'I'd have to agree,' added Katy. 'Only ten minutes.'

No-one commented.

'So are you going to let go of your whole life for the sake of ten minutes' stupidity?' asked Erica.

Everyone turned to stare at her as she sounded so impassioned.

'What is it you want?' she asked Matthew.

'I want my wife and kids back.'

'So bloody well fight for them then,' said Erica. 'You *have* to try harder. You *have* to do more. You can't just let them slip through your fingers or else you will regret it. You have to say everything that is in your heart. *Everything*, because if you don't, your heart may never recover. Ever.'

'Steady on, sis,' said Braindead.

'Just beautiful,' added Daniel.

'I just know what it's like to have regrets,' said Erica to the floor. 'It's not good.'

'Seriously!' exclaimed Katy. 'You want us to feel sorry for you? You with the international career in modelling who flies all over the world and has enough money that she can do whatever she wants, whenever she wants?'

'Career success often doesn't naturally transfer into personal success, Katy,' said Daniel. He turned to Erica. 'Did you lose someone?' he asked her. 'Did you let someone go?'

'Oh, for goodness' sake,' interrupted Braindead. 'Is this about Ben? Fetch me a bucket!'

'What about Ben?' asked Katy, turning startled to Braindead.

'Ben told me,' Braindead said to his sister. 'About the New Year's Eve party that apparently you organised just so you could kiss him. I wish he hadn't told me. That's my brother you are lusting over.'

'Ben!' said Katy.

'Katy, I… I…' stuttered Erica. 'I, well, yes, I was in love with him. But he's married to you now. And as for you, brother! Just for once can you keep that gob shut?'

Braindead looked back at her, stunned.

'I should be banned from speaking forever,' he said, looking nervously over at Katy. 'He doesn't fancy her. I can assure you of that.'

Katy looked over at the supermodel that was Erica. She didn't know what to think.

'Shall we get back to the matter in hand?' said Daniel, looking agog at Erica. Clearly he hadn't predicted that little scenario.

'Yes, let's,' said Erica, nodding eagerly. 'I was just trying to say to Matthew that he has to make her listen. He *has* to.'

'That's right,' said Braindead. 'Make her listen, Matthew. You have to.'

'What, like she listened to your speech?' bit back Matthew. 'I think that's the last time she had any interest in listening. When she heard those words come out of your mouth. In front of everyone. At a wedding, for Christ's sake! When everyone had to listen. I don't know how to get her to listen to me now.'

Braindead hung his head in shame.

They all stood in their little huddle and stared at one another, surrounding Matthew as he perched on the low wall.

'That's it,' muttered Daniel. He sighed. 'I suppose that's it.'

'What's it?' asked Katy.

'Let me say that I am only doing this for you, Katy, and… and for… well, for the celebration of marriage and all it means. And for love, I guess.'

'What the bloody hell are you talking about now?' she asked.

'I know I'm so going to regret this but, as you so ungraciously told me this afternoon, marriage is all about compromise.'

'As well as forgiveness,' said Braindead. 'It's all about forgiveness. Remember I said Ben taught me that?'

'I do,' said Daniel. 'That little nugget of insight is precisely why we are in this predicament and precisely why there is really only one thing we can do to have any chance of getting out of it.'

He looked down at Matthew then bent forward and tentatively put one knee on the pavement.

'He's not gay!' exclaimed Braindead. 'You can't marry him! You're not gay, are you?' he asked, turning to Matthew. 'Are you? Because if you were that would solve all of this because… well, you wouldn't want to be married to Alison then, would you, and…'

'Shut up, Braindead!' chorused everyone.

'May I continue?' Daniel asked Braindead.

'I'm not gay,' pointed out Matthew nervously.

'I know you aren't, you idiot,' said Daniel. 'What I wanted to ask you is, would you be my best man?'

'What!' said everyone in unison.

'Seriously, guys, I'm starting to think I'm in an off-Broadway musical about the man on the low wall,' said Daniel. 'So, would you?' he asked Matthew again.

'Why on earth would you want me?'

'Well, to be honest, I can think of a trillion more appropriate friends to have by my side on the day of reckoning, including my best girl buddy stood right beside me.'

Katy glanced over and noticed that she and Erica were standing either side of Daniel. She assumed he meant Erica as there was no way Daniel would want a pregnant mother as his best man/woman.

'But I think Katy will forgive me not asking her if there is a greater good to be had.' Katy felt her eyes fill with inexplicable tears of warmth towards her buddy. God, she hated the way he did that. One minute she couldn't stand the guy with his arrogance and his pretentiousness and the next he really was the most charming person she had ever met.

'But why me?' asked Matthew again. 'I'm no use to you as a best man.'

'You're right. You are no use to me at this present time as a best man. But being best man is of paramount use to you.'

'I have no idea what you just said,' said Braindead, 'but I'm with you. Keep going, Danny boy.'

'Don't call me Danny,' said Daniel crossly.

'Don't call him Danny,' echoed Matthew. 'Please carry on.'

'Okay, so being best man will give you something to do. A distraction, as it were, from your current woes.'

'I don't need a distraction, I just need my family back.'

'Hold on, I was just getting to that. You do need a distraction. You look terrible. And there is one thing I will not stand for in a best man and that is shabbiness. So, sort that out for a start. And then my thinking is – and forgive me as I'm kind of making this up as I go along – but my thinking is that if the last time Alison listened to you was during a wedding speech then maybe your best man's speech is how we get her to listen to you now. You see there is a kind of symmetry to it? A beautiful symmetry. Do you see what I mean?'

Everyone looked back at Daniel in stunned silence.

'Erm, so how do I explain?' he continued. 'I just think there's something about speeches at weddings that makes people sit up and listen. They seem to have weight and meaning.'

'But what do I say?'

'Now I can't help you with that. You have to say what is in your heart that will make contact with Alison's heart. But if you want her to listen, if you want her to really listen, then maybe, just maybe, that is how you do it. Then the rest is up to you.'

Matthew looked up at Daniel mournfully.

'Do you have any better ideas?' asked Daniel.

He shook his head.

'But how will you get Alison to come to your wedding?' asked Katy. 'She barely knows you and you're getting married in Spain. She can't just pop round the corner and find herself in the middle of your wedding. Don't you think it's going to be really hard to get her to go to the wedding of a virtual stranger in a foreign country? Especially if she knows that Matthew is there.'

Everyone stared at Daniel. He didn't speak for a moment.

'Danny boy knows what he is doing, don't you, Danny boy?' said Braindead hopefully.

'I think I do,' replied Daniel. 'I think I have a plan. In fact, a very cunning plan that just might just work and kill two birds with one stone, so to speak.' He glanced over at Katy slyly.

'I'm not sure I want to hear this,' she said.

'Leave it with me,' replied Daniel. 'I have an idea but I just need to think it through. Matthew, let's meet tomorrow but I need you in full-on best man mode from now on. You got it?'

Matthew swallowed. 'I don't suppose I have much choice?'

'Not really,' replied Daniel. 'Not unless Alison calls you in the middle of the night and begs you to come home.'

'I guess I'll see you tomorrow then.'

'Can I come?' asked Braindead.

'No!' said Daniel and Matthew in unison. 'You'll be called upon soon enough,' added Daniel.

'Called upon?' questioned Braindead.

'I'm sure I'll be able to find you a part. A non-speaking one, of course.'

'A part?'

'Yes,' he nodded. 'There will be parts for everyone, I think. But don't ask me now. I need to give it proper thinking time. Come on, Erica. Time to go.'

Daniel strode off towards his car, leaving the rest of them gaping behind him.

'Well, I guess that means I'm out of here,' said Erica, following him.

'Hang on a minute,' said Katy. 'I think you have some explaining to do, don't you?'

But clearly Erica didn't hear as she pulled open the door to Daniel's car and slid in gracefully.

'I'm as dumbfounded as you at the thought of Ben and my sister,' added Braindead.

Katy gazed at him. 'I really don't know what I should do with the information that an international model was in love with my husband.'

Braindead thought for a moment.

'I think you need to think that it was lucky I gave everyone food poisoning that night with pork pies. That's all you need to think about that one. You should be grateful to me.'

Katy's brain was so full of stuff she needed to think about that she decided being grateful to Braindead for his food poisoning expertise was indeed the only right way to process this new piece of information.

'Shall we all go home now?' she said, suddenly exhausted. 'Do you think you can get off that low wall?' she asked Matthew.

He raised himself up and smiled weakly.

'So that's it, is it?' asked Ian. 'That's the plan? Matthew will be best man at Daniel's wedding and that's going to move him out of my spare room back into his executive life?'

Matthew shrugged.

'Do you trust this man Daniel?' asked Ian.

Matthew thought for a while.

'Quite possibly,' he replied. 'Come on, let's go. I never ever want to come back to this place ever again.'

Chapter Thirty-Two

Ben

'Not you,' said Alison when she opened the door. 'Please don't tell me you of all people have come here to plead their case.'

'No!' said Ben. 'As if. No, not in the slightest. I come bearing gnocchi and a bottle of Frascati and an exciting job opportunity.'

'What on earth are you talking about?'

Ben's heart was pounding. Ever since Daniel had got in touch with him and asked if he would run an 'errand' for him he had felt uneasy. Seeing Alison was the last thing he felt like doing but Daniel had pleaded with him, saying his entire 'plan' depended on getting Alison to believe the things Daniel had told him to say. As usual, Daniel had talked him round but now he was standing here in front of her, he wondered what the hell he was doing.

'Please, Alison, will you just let me in,' he continued. 'I'm not here to mention anything to do with… you know what, I'm just here because I have a job opportunity for you and you really need to try this gnocchi – apparently it's the best outside of Italy. If only I knew what gnocchi is. I've brought enough for the kids. And I have an organic vegetable sauce to serve with it. You see, a friend of mine needs help with the kids' menu in his fancy restaurant and I knew that you were just the person.'

'Organic pasta sauce?' asked Alison.

'Apparently he's sourcing the vegetables from the Chatsworth estate in Derbyshire,' added Ben. 'But he needs an opinion from a discerning mum and her discerning kids.'

Alison looked back at him warily for a moment.

'He just wants an opinion, Alison. And, to be honest, he might want to sponsor your blog, given how many followers you have now, and he's keen to attract the cool family crowd to boost his lunchtime business.'

Ben hoped he'd said all the right things. Daniel had spent two hours the night before coaching him on the marketing spiel.

'The hip family crowd is where the money is at these days,' Daniel had said. 'They are striving for meaningful experiences with their young ones. They want to create those special memories that they will treasure for a lifetime but the most important thing about this demographic grouping is that they are willing to splash the cash. Upper-middle-class families have money to burn on meaningful experiences because if they don't then clearly they are very bad parents. And of course this is where social media is every business owner's wet dream in this sector as mothers are the absolute queens of posting online the very best of their most expensive and exclusive experiences with their little darlings. If you have the right product, your customers will be advertising it on Facebook and Instagram before you can say "smug mummy". That's what I told Gio. Imagine filling your carriage every lunchtime with yummy mummies and their delightful offspring queuing up to take photos of your vastly overpriced organic pasta. I thank you. Just call me genius!'

'Why are you telling me all this?' Ben had asked when Daniel had drawn breath. 'I really have no idea what you are talking about.'

'Because you are going to get Alison to come to Gio's by tempting her with the prospect of becoming his chief advisor on all things mummyish.'

'Why do you need to get her to Gio's?'

'To get her back with Matthew.'

'I don't think a candlelit dinner in a railway carriage will do the trick, to be honest.'

'It's not going to be a candlelit dinner. Give me some credit. Something entirely different. But I need you to get Alison there so listen to my marketing spiel or else she will smell a rat.'

As Ben now looked hopefully at Alison on her doorstep he wondered if she had already smelled that rat.

'Gio is keen to tap into the lucrative upper-middle-class family market,' continued Ben, 'with his totally organic menu which includes vegan options. I told him about you and he says you are just the type of person he needs advice from and he is willing to pay you the spondoolies for the privilege. Alison, please let me in so that you can at least try the gnocchi, if nothing else.'

'Come on then,' she sighed. 'I was actually just about to prepare dinner so let's hope that this gnocchi is as good as you say it is.'

It took twenty minutes to corral the children. Especially as the twins got overexcited because Ben had been their favourite teacher when he'd done a stint working at their school. But before long they were sitting around the huge table in the open-plan kitchen-diner, opening foil boxes containing Gio's carefully prepared organic gnocchi.

Ben cast his eyes around the table and felt a twinge of excitement. He couldn't wait until there were four in his family to sit round the table, arguing and bickering and winding each other up. That was what family life was all about and as far as he was concerned, dinner table chaos couldn't come soon enough.

Alison made sure they had all been served a portion before anyone was allowed to start eating.

'You shouldn't eat before everyone has been served,' George told Ben when he picked up his fork after Alison had placed a bowl in front of him.

'Of course,' he said apologetically. 'I was just so excited to eat the pasta.'

'And we have to thank someone first,' added Rebecca.

'What, like God?' Ben asked.

'No, just anyone. For something we are grateful for today,' she explained.

'I'm trying to teach them Christian values,' added Alison, 'without the religion. They can decide on religion when they are old enough to think about it for themselves.'

'Right,' nodded Ben as he thought about the daily scrum over food in his house with a general lack of appreciation of anything. He really should start reading Alison's blog again.

'Would you like to start?' asked Alison.

'Thank you,' he replied, picking up his fork again.

'I meant, start by thanking someone,' said Alison.

He placed his fork back on the table for the second time. He swallowed. 'I, er, I, er... I would like to thank Gio for making us this lovely meal.'

'Who's Gio?' asked George.

'Someone I know.'

'A friend?'

'Yes, a friend,' replied Ben, crossing his fingers that George would shut up as he had never actually met the guy.

'Is he Spanish?'

'Yes,' nodded Ben.

'But this is gnocchi,' said Alison. 'Surely he's Italian?'

Ben laughed heartily and ruffled George's hair. 'Just checking you were listening,' he said. 'Your turn.'

'I'd like to thank Mr Chapman for bringing dinner and sitting in Daddy's chair.'

'Oh gosh, I'm sorry, shall I move?' said Ben, leaping up.

'Sit down,' demanded Alison. 'Thank you, George,' she said. 'Rebecca?'

'Er, er, thank you for the unicorns on my new bedspread.'

'Excellent,' cried Alison, looking slightly relieved. 'And Harry, your turn.'

'Thank you for Danger Mouse,' he said.

Rebecca rolled her eyes. 'He says that every day,' she announced. 'He loves Danger Mouse.'

'Danger Mouse saves the world every day at five o'clock,' Harry told Ben. 'I pray to him every night to bring Daddy back because I know he can,' he added solemnly.

Ben glanced over to Alison, who let out a big sigh and looked away.

'Right, let's eat, shall we?' she said, picking her fork up.

'You didn't say thank you for anything,' protested George.

'Oh, well, er, I'd like to say thank you for, er…' she looked around the table. 'I'd like to say thank you for being able to sit around a table and eat dinner with my four wonderful children,' she said.

'She says that at least once a week,' said Rebecca.

'I want to eat dinner with Daddy again,' said Harry. 'When's he coming home?'

Alison swallowed.

'Come on, eat up,' she said, staring down at her food.

Ben looked around the table at the four sorrowful children and sighed. Grown-ups had a lot to answer for in screwing up children's lives, he thought. He selected some gnocchi with his fork and put it in his mouth.

'Fuck me,' he exclaimed, before clamping his hand over his mouth when Alison gave him a vicious stare. 'Sorry! It's just that this is bloody amazing.'

'Ben!' exclaimed Alison.

George and Rebecca giggled.

'Sorry, sorry, but I was expecting, you know, for it to taste really poor, what with it having no meat in it, but that is delicious. What do you reckon, kids?' he asked.

'Don't call them kids,' chided Alison. 'They're children.'

Ben was tempted to say that the least of their worries at the moment was being called kids and in his experience as a teacher most 'children' preferred the term 'kids' and hated the patronising tone of anyone who said 'children' to them, as though they were the Child Catcher waiting to pounce.

'It's good,' nodded Rebecca. 'Not too vegetably.'

'Exactly!' said Ben. 'It's good, really good. Like, meat-level good.'

'Almost as good as bacon,' suggested George.

'Now come on, George,' said Ben. 'We both know that nothing tastes as good as bacon.'

'Chocolate does,' said Rebecca. 'And Haribos.'

'When have you had Haribos?' asked Alison. 'You know you are not allowed Haribos.'

'At Phoebe's. Her mum gave them to me so I thought you must have said it was okay,' said Rebecca. 'Can I go to Phoebe's again soon?'

'No,' replied Alison.

'Phoebe gets all her spellings right every week,' said Rebecca. 'And gets a large packet of Haribos as a reward.'

'Well, she's going to grow up with rotten teeth then, isn't she?' said Alison.

'But she will be able to spell cucumber,' replied Rebecca.

'So, what do you think of the gnocchi?' asked Ben, seeing that the conversation was winding Alison up.

'I have to say it is excellent,' said Alison. 'I do make my own pomodoro sauce but you can tell this is cooked by a true Italian. This tastes like someone's grandmother has passed down the recipe.'

'So you would recommend it then? To your friends? To other mothers?'

'Oh yes. In passing I would. If this Gio person wants a mention on the blog, of course that is entirely different. I have a rate card now. I can't just do favours any more as that wouldn't be fair on my other sponsors.'

'Oh, he's not expecting anything like that,' said Ben. 'Of course not. I think he's considering a much bigger deal.'

He racked his brains for some of the terminology that Daniel had used.

'I think he was considering product placement and maybe sponsorship?' he said hopefully.

'Well, it's certainly something that I would consider but I think I would need to meet him first and certainly see his restaurant.'

Ben caught his breath. She had just said the magic words.

'I mean, I would need to check out his child facilities. For example, does he have Kitemark-tested highchairs and a microwave for heating up milk bottles? And I assume he has baby-changing facilities?'

Ben had no idea. He'd never been to Gio's.

'I'm sure he has,' he replied.

'And I'd need to check out his environmental policy,' she said.

'Right,' nodded Ben, thinking poor Gio was not going to know what had hit him. 'You can ask him all about that when you meet him. He would be delighted to offer you and your kids – sorry, children – a complimentary meal next Saturday,' he said.

'He wants to meet my children as well?' she asked.

'Of course,' said Ben.

'Italians are so pro-family,' said Alison. 'This country could learn a lot from the Italians in their facilitation of family life.'

'Absolutely,' nodded Ben.

'I do hope it wouldn't count as bribery?' she said. 'Me accepting a free meal from a prospective advertiser? My corporate knowledge is a little rusty. I'd need to check the compliance on that.'

'Why?' asked Ben.

'Compliance is the single biggest issue in business conduct at the moment, Ben.'

'But you are writing a blog, not running a corporation. Take the free flipping lunch! You want to go, don't you, kids – sorry, children?'

'Yay!' cheered Rebecca, George and Harry.

'Will there be a clown?' asked Harry. 'I really want to see a clown.'

'A clown?' asked Ben, astonished.

'Harry is obsessed with clowns for some reason at the moment,' explained Alison.

'More than likely then,' said Ben. 'In some sort of capacity.'

'Is that a sort of car?' asked George.

'What?' said Ben.

'A capacity?' asked George. 'Is it what you call a clown car, where everything falls off? I've always wanted to see one of those. I've never seen one of those because Mummy won't take us to a circus.'

'I will take you to the circus, George, but not one which exploits animals, children or dwarfs.'

Ben looked at George. 'You ain't ever going to a circus, mate,' he told him sadly.

'But I want to see a capacity,' he replied.

'Well, Ben just said there would be someone at the restaurant in a capacity,' said Alison with a sly smile.

'Brilliant!' exclaimed George. 'I'm going to see a clown in a capacity. When are we going?'

'Gio said next Saturday,' said Ben, looking hopefully at Alison.

'Can we go, Mummy, pleeease, and see the capacity?' begged George.

'Okay then,' sighed Alison. 'You'd better tell Gio we will be there but he needs to find a capacity or there's going to be one very disappointed little boy.'

*

Ben stayed to help wash up. Well, rinse and put the foil dishes into the recycling under Alison's careful direction.

'Coffee?' she asked when he had finished.

He looked at his watch. He'd achieved his mission and he'd have really liked to get home, but he had the impression that Alison wasn't asking if he wanted coffee. What she really wanted was company.

'Sure,' he said, sitting down as he dried his hands.

'Can I ask you how you did it?' she asked after she'd taken twenty minutes to faff around with a filter coffee jug. First, warming it, then putting the coffee in and then letting it stand. He wished he'd asked for instant.

'How I did what?'

'Forgave Katy.'

Ben's coffee cup was halfway to his mouth when she asked the question. He tried to hold his hand steady and decided to put the mug down.

'To be honest, I've thought a lot about this since, well, since Braindead opened his big mouth. And the more I think about it, the more I know I did the right thing.' He paused and rubbed his eyes. 'I look at my life and I cannot imagine it any other way. Married to Katy, little Millie, another on the way, I wouldn't be missing that for the world, and if I'd not forgiven her then I wouldn't be living this life and that would have been a tragedy. That doesn't bear thinking about.'

Alison took a sip of her coffee. 'But you weren't married. You weren't trying for a baby. You'd only just started going out together,' she said. 'We'd committed. We were married. We stood up in church and vowed not to do the very thing that he did.'

'That's true,' replied Ben, screwing his eyes up. Thinking very hard about what to say. 'We weren't married when it happened so it would have been even easier to walk away, right? A lot less to lose, right? Do you know what? I'm glad we weren't married because it wasn't a set of vows or a bit of paper that kept us together, it was just how I felt, Alison. I felt that Katy regretted it totally. I felt that she really loved me and I really loved her. That's what I felt. And that is what mattered. Not a piece of paper with some binding words on it. Not society. Not someone else telling me what to do. All I knew was that I felt in my heart of hearts we should stay together. And I was right. We have become a great family who have made mistakes and will no doubt make them in the future, but right now I feel like the luckiest guy on the planet to be married to Katy and have a beautiful daughter so I'm going to go with that.'

Alison said nothing.

'I can't tell you how you feel, Alison,' continued Ben. 'Only you know that. But listen to what your feelings are telling you, not what you think a piece of paper in your valuables box is telling you to feel.'

'It's in the safe actually,' said Alison. 'I assume you mean our marriage certificate?'

'You have a safe! What else have you got in there? You nicked the Crown Jewels or something?'

'I can tell you exactly what is in there. The wristbands each of my children got in the hospital when they were born and a locket Matthew bought me for our first wedding anniversary, in which I keep a strand of each child's hair. I wear it every anniversary when Matthew takes me away for the night. We always open the locket after dinner and look at what we made. I can tell which piece of hair belongs to which child.'

'Your most prized possession?' asked Ben.

'Yes,' she nodded. 'Unlikely we will be doing that on our next anniversary.'

'I think that is entirely up to you, Alison,' replied Ben.

Chapter Thirty-Three

Katy

'It's a bloody circus!' exclaimed Katy as she rounded the corner. Once again she found herself in the disused car park next to Gio's train carriage/restaurant except this time the entire area was taken up by the most enormous big top, resplendent in red and blue stripes and golden flapping flags.

'A circus, really?' said Ben, who was standing beside her holding Millie's hand.

'Yay, a circus!' said Millie, jumping up and down with excitement. 'I didn't know we were going to a circus, you never said. Will there be clowns?'

'What the hell?' said Katy, turning to Ben. 'What in the name of Daniel and his grand ideas is he playing at today?'

'Excuse me,' shouted a man, zipping by them on a unicycle.

'How does he do that?' exclaimed Millie.

'I thought we were meeting Daniel here for... for... well, some food or something,' said Ben.

'So did I,' replied Katy. 'Well, to be honest, I don't really know why he wanted us to meet him here. Every time I asked him, he told me to trust him. That he had a grand plan. That all our problems would be solved but he wouldn't tell me any more. He even told me to forget about weddings, that I should focus on me and you and Millie and this one coming,' she said, stroking her bump.

'You mean he wasn't demanding attention, demanding you help him organise, demanding you negotiate between him and Rita?'

'No,' said Katy. 'Every time I even mentioned the word "wedding" he would literally put his fingers to his lips and tell me to shut up about it. And I rang Mum and she was just as bad. She said that she was "delighted that plans for the double wedding were progressing and I was not to worry about it. I have enough on my hands being pregnant". It sounded like she was reading from a script, to be honest. Like that was what Daniel had told her to say. I've never known her so tight-lipped *or* considerate. It's very weird.'

'Come on, let's go in,' said Millie, tugging on their hands.

'But I'm not sure why this is here, Millie,' said Katy. 'I'm not sure we can go in. Last time I was here this was an Italian restaurant in a train carriage.'

'Don't be silly, Mummy,' replied Millie.

'Roll up, roll up,' came a shout from within the tent. 'Roll up for the greatest show on earth.'

Ben and Katy looked at each other in astonishment as out came Erica, dressed resplendently as a ringmaster in white britches, a flame-red coat with magnificent gold buttons and jet-black top hat and a cane.

'Bloody hell,' said Ben. 'Hugh Jackman, eat your heart out!'

Although the costume was very *Greatest Showman*-esque, Hugh Jackman would not have been the first person to spring to mind at the sight of this stunning woman, thought Katy. She looked gorgeous.

There was an awkward moment as they all realised that they hadn't seen each other since Katy found out about Erica's secret love for Ben.

'So this is awkward,' stated Ben, pulling a face.

'This is when I need my brother here to say something wildly inappropriate to distract everyone,' said Erica. 'Instead, I can only apologise,' she said to Katy, looking wildly embarrassed. 'I have no idea why I confessed my stupid teenage crush. I think it's just that whenever I come home I so envy everyone with their homes and kids and husbands and—'

'And mortgages and nine-till-eight jobs and nappies and toilets to clean and…' interrupted Katy.

'Okay,' said Erica. 'I get it. Grass is always greener, right?'

'Too right,' said Katy. 'And it's hard to appreciate what you have. Like the driver and the first-class travel and the exotic holidays and the sports car and the *legs* to die for.'

'I know,' Erica nodded, a small grin emerging on her face. 'We could all do with appreciating what we've got more, I guess. I'm sorry. Will you forgive me?' She stepped towards Katy and held her arms out.

'Maybe,' she replied. 'If you let me have some hand-me-downs. After I've had the baby, of course. When I've half a chance of fitting in them. Anyway, I have no need to forgive you. I know I'm the luckiest lady there is to have this man and it's not really surprising at all that one day a supermodel walks in and says she has a secret crush on my husband.'

'A supermodel though!' said Ben.

'I know. Check you out!' Katy told Ben.

'Can you just forget it?' asked Erica. 'Forget I ever said anything?'

Katy nodded and stepped forward to reciprocate the hug.

'When I'm old and wrinkly, am I allowed to remember it just to keep my spirits up?' asked Ben.

'No!' replied Katy and Erica in unison before breaking apart.

'So now we have the whole you-fancying-my-husband thing out of the way,' said Katy, 'can you tell me what the hell is going on and why you are standing outside of a big top dressed as Hugh Jackman?'

'Ah-ha,' said Erica, brandishing her cane. 'This *is* the greatest show. Now, who is the only person that you know who would have the audacity to plan the greatest show right here in Gio's car park?'

'Daniel,' the two of them said in unison.

'Correct. Now, what is the only thing that Daniel would plan the greatest show for?' she asked them both.

Katy had a slight sick feeling forming in her stomach that she was sure wasn't pregnancy related. She knew Daniel so well that the big top could mean only one thing. And hadn't he mentioned once that his dream was to have Hugh Jackman officiate at his marriage? Perhaps he thought that Erica dressed as Barnum was the next best thing. If she was right, this could be a catastrophe.

'This is his wedding, isn't it?' she said. 'Are we at his wedding?'

'Ta-dah!' said Erica, again brandishing her cane and doffing her top hat.

'But… but what about Carlos, what about the joint wedding? I don't understand. Carlos is going to be devastated,' said Katy. 'And how has Daniel managed to organise this all on his own? He doesn't know how to do this kind of thing.'

'No need to panic,' said Erica. 'This is Daniel's dream wedding. He decided to really push the boat out because—'

'But I told him,' interrupted Katy, 'I told him he had to compromise. That that was what weddings and marriage were all about.'

'Oh, and he really took that to heart,' said Erica.

'It doesn't bloody look like it! Is that a trapeze wire in there?'

'Listen, this is Daniel's dream. He decided he didn't actually want understated and sophisticated, he wanted this with all the bells and whistles. This is the wedding he's dreamed of, but… Well, maybe he wants to tell you himself.'

'I can't believe he's done this,' chuntered Katy. 'I just can't believe it. And I bet he's going to rely on me to tell my mum and Carlos. It's just typical Daniel, he's so selfish. How he ever expects his marriage to work I have no idea. What on earth has Gabriel said? I mean, it was important to him to get married with his father, wasn't it? This is a wedding disaster.'

'No, Katy,' said Erica. 'It really isn't. Honestly. You just have to wait and see. Hang on a minute…' She fished a small notebook out of her pocket and flipped some pages over. 'Daniel and Gabriel have requested that during this wedding you are instructed to… enjoy yourself. In fact, you have an asterisk next to your name. Yes, you are also guests of honour and will be seated next to the main ring. May I show you to your seats?'

Katy glanced over at Ben, who shrugged. 'I think we should just go with it,' he said. 'Do what Daniel is asking. How about we just "enjoy" this wedding?'

'Well, I don't suppose we have much choice in the matter,' grumbled Katy. She sighed. She wasn't even appropriately dressed for a wedding – she was wearing maternity jeans for goodness' sake. Guaranteed to ruin the enjoyment of anything, never mind a grand occasion. 'Come on, Millie,' she said, taking her daughter's hand, 'let's go to a wedding, shall we?'

'It's not a wedding, it's a circus,' protested Millie as they walked into the big top. 'Look, there's someone breathing fire.'

'Wedding? Circus? I guess it's all the same thing, really,' shrugged Katy.

*

'Abby?' exclaimed Ben as they approached the roped-off seating area at the edge of the ring.

'Oh, hi,' she replied, looking round from her seat. 'Boy, am I glad to see you! Braindead said to meet him in a railway carriage restaurant and I got here and all I could find was this big tent. I have no idea what's going on.'

'We've no idea either,' said Katy. 'But this could be a wedding.'

'A wedding!' exclaimed Abby. 'Whose wedding?'

'Daniel's. But it might not be. It's all very confusing.'

'But where's Braindead?' Abby asked.

'No idea,' shrugged Ben. 'He's not breathed a word to me about any of this. I guess we just have to sit here and see what happens.'

Abby shook her head in confusion. 'I cancelled my hair extensions for this. It had better be good.'

A dwarf appeared, dressed in a sliver leotard and pink-feathered headdress, and handed some popcorn and a large white balloon to Millie.

'The grooms have asked that you hold onto these and they wish for them to be released outside after the show – I mean, ceremony,' said the dwarf balloon lady.

'But I want to keep it,' said Millie.

'The well-dressed groom said that any child who said that was to be told if they keep it, it will turn into a leprechaun that will live under their bed for ever more and play Justin Bieber at full volume so you can't sleep.'

'Justin Bieber!' shrieked Millie, horrified. 'Can't I get one that plays Little Mix?'

'No,' replied the dwarf. 'The smartly dressed groom man was very clear it would be Justin Bieber the leprechaun would play.'

'Okay,' nodded Millie, 'I promise to let it go. But if you get any that play Little Mix, will you let me swap?'

'I surely will,' said the dwarf, winking at Katy.

The four of them sat in silence and stared in awe at the enormous tent and at the crowd slowly forming on the grandstand seating around the edge of the tent.

'Who are all these people?' asked Ben.

'I think over there is pretty much everyone from work but I have no idea who the rest of them are. They must all be friends of Daniel and Gabriel's, I imagine.'

'How can anyone have this many friends?' said Ben. 'I think I can count my mates on the fingers of one hand.'

'I reckon I could fill this tent with my mates,' announced Abby.

'Daniel does have an annoying habit of drawing people in and for some unknown reason everyone loves him,' said Katy. 'Never been able to work that one out, to be honest.'

'Well, it's you he's got in the VIP seats,' offered Ben.

'He's probably just put us here to stop us mixing with his trendy mates. Heaven forbid we might let him down.'

'Do you think we have other people joining us?' said Ben, looking over at the empty chairs next to him. 'His family?'

'I doubt it somehow,' said Katy. 'His parents are still in denial, can you believe? His mother still invites the local single women round when he goes to visit. Can you imagine, poor things, being faced with Daniel!'

'Oh my God,' said Ben, looking over her shoulder. 'There's a brass band arriving!'

Katy whipped her head round to see Erica marching into the big top from the entrance, followed by a full-on marching band playing 'Here Comes the Bride'.

'This is just weird now,' said Katy.

'Weird? More than weird,' said Ben.

'It's amazing!' said Millie as she licked a lollipop the size of her head. 'The best wedding I have ever been to and I have only been to yours and I can't remember it because I was a baby. Did you have elephants at your wedding?'

'No, Millie,' replied Katy. 'And I'm sorry to disappoint you but I don't think there will be any elephants here today. I'm not sure even Daniel would go that far.'

'But there *are*,' said Millie. 'Look!'

Katy had been busy watching the marching band fill up the ring in front of them. She turned back to the entrance to the tent and gasped. There were indeed two full-size elephants with Daniel and Gabriel sat astride each one, grinning from ear to ear.

'Am I seeing things?' asked Ben. 'How much did I drink last night?'

'I wish me and Braindead had had a circus wedding,' announced Abby. 'Arriving on elephants? So much better than the Bentley we had.'

Daniel caught sight of them in the VIP section and gave Katy a regal wave. He was dressed rather incongruously in the emerald green suit she'd last seen him in, in Harvey Nichols. From where she was sitting she couldn't see if it brought out the colour of Gabriel's eyes, but it contrasted nicely with the grey of the elephant skin.

He's lost it, thought Katy. Absolutely lost it.

'I believe these seats are for us?' came a voice from behind them.

Katy spun round, unable to believe her ears, but then maybe nothing could surprise her now. Alison was standing behind her with her four children, along with Ian and Lena. She looked confused and slightly cross.

'Yes, these are our seats,' said Ian. 'Sit down, everyone, the show is about to start.'

'Millie!' exclaimed Rebecca, dashing over to her friend. 'I didn't know you were coming to the circus too.'

'It's not a circus, it's a wedding,' said Millie. 'Do you want some popcorn?'

'Look, elephants!' cried George. 'Real elephants. I bet there will be clowns in a capacity car. You said there might be, didn't you, Mr Chapman?'

'I… I… did,' said Ben, recollecting his awkward supper with Alison and her kids during which his only mission had been to get them to agree to go to Gio's restaurant at a specific time. He remembered now that he'd reported back to Daniel that he'd had a successful mission but that poor George had wanted to go to the circus and see a clown in a 'capacity' car. Daniel had shown passing interest in this, no more. And he wouldn't divulge why there was a need to have Alison and her children go to Gio's. Was this circus just for George? Ben wondered.

'What's going on?' demanded Alison as Ian tried to get her to sit down.

'We don't know,' said Katy, blushing. She still felt rotten to the core about what had happened. 'We appear to be attending Daniel and Gabriel's wedding, but they are supposed to be getting married with my mother and Gabriel's father in Spain in a couple of months.'

Alison stared at her. 'I'm not sure I understand any of that,' she said.

'Daniel's fiancé's father is marrying my mother,' said Katy.

Alison blinked back at her.

'It doesn't matter,' said Katy. 'Alison, I… I…' she stuttered, with no idea what she was going to say.

'Don't say anything,' said Alison. 'I have no idea why we are here. I had been led to believe we were coming to meet Gio and eat gnocchi. I had no idea we were going to get wrapped up in this… this circus!'

She looked over at Rebecca and George, who were hanging over the perimeter of the ring, waving at the elephants.

'Just sit down, please, Alison,' said Ian. 'Let the children watch the show and then you can go, I promise you.'

'I have no idea what's going on but whatever it is I'm not happy about it. This is ridiculous. Even by your standards, Ian. Lena? Do you know why we are here?'

Lena looked at her boss, terrified. She shook her head. 'I promise you I have no idea, but… but if I may say so, Alison, I think, whatever it is, someone has gone to a huge amount of effort and so I think maybe you should just wait and see why.'

Alison stared back at her.

'Don't you want to know why?' asked Lena.

Alison glanced over to where Daniel and Gabriel were being gently lowered down from their elephant perches onto the floor. They both slid off to the ground as the crowds went wild with applause and cheering. They looked unbelievably happy. Daniel peered over to the VIP section and waved at the children still leaning over the edge of the ring in awe of the elephants right in front of them. Then he looked up and gave Alison a thumbs up before taking Gabriel's hands in his.

'We'll stay,' said Alison, sitting down abruptly. 'Until we find out what this ridiculous display is all about and then we are going home. Without eating gnocchi, if need be.'

'Ladies and gentlemen,' bellowed Erica, who was now standing on a podium in the centre of the big top, 'please give your very best welcome to our groom and groom.'

The crowd went wild, banging on the floorboards and cheering and whistling. Daniel waved at the entire audience, rotating his body slowly so he could take it all in as though he had just won an Olympic gold.

'Daniel and Gabriel are delighted to welcome you today to this very special occasion. Their not-really-a-wedding wedding!' said Erica with a flourish.

Again the crowd went wild. Katy turned to look at Ben with raised eyebrows.

'What's one of those?' he asked.

'I have no idea,' replied Katy.

'Now, I'm sure you are all thinking, "What the hell is a not-really-a-wedding wedding?"' bellowed Erica.

Everyone laughed.

'And I think there is only really one man who can explain. The man whose brainchild all of this was. May I call upon Daniel to begin the proceedings.'

'The elephant is doing a poo,' Millie shrieked. 'Look!'

Indeed, one of the elephants had decided now was the time to do its business.

'That elephant should be on the stage,' said Ben. 'Best comic timing ever.'

Out of nowhere the dwarf balloon lady appeared with a shovel and a bucket and the poo was magically spirited away.

'On behalf of my not-quite-husband and I, I wanted to thank you so much for coming,' said Daniel. 'I know the invitation was purposefully vague and very short notice so the fact you have all turned up to a big top in the middle of nowhere for some strange reason is really quite lovely.'

There was a low ripple of applause. Katy heard Alison sigh heavily behind her.

'The first thing to tell you is that myself and Gabriel are not getting married today.'

'Ahhhhhh,' murmured the crowd.

'We shall get married in Spain in a couple of months in the bosom of Gabriel's family. Exactly where we should get married.'

'Yay!' shouted the crowd.

'Thank Christ for that,' muttered Katy.

'But today is *our* celebration of *our* marriage, in exactly the way we want to do it rather than the way we ought to do it,' announced Daniel. 'Because you know me, I like to do things a certain way.'

The crowd mumbled its agreement.

'So we have ditched the endless discussions around our wedding about things that have no consequence on our marriage. We have decided that the type of cake you have won't make your marriage any stronger, for example, or the colour of the napkins, or the number of flowers.' Daniel paused and glanced over at Katy before he continued. 'A very dear friend of mine pointed this out to me quite bluntly and without any finesse, I must say, but she was so right. And so myself and Gabriel have decided to choose a different way of displaying our love. Our way.'

He turned round and took Gabriel's hand. 'This is how much I love you,' said Daniel, sweeping his hand around the tent. 'Enough to fill a big top with people who care about us as well as two elephants. That is how much I love you.'

The roar from the crowd was quite deafening. Everyone was on their feet, cheering and clapping as Gabriel blushed a deep red and stepped forward to hug his future husband. Katy found that she too was on her feet, applauding and cheering. It wasn't often that you got to witness such an unbridled declaration of love. A display that left you in absolutely no doubt whatsoever of what this person meant to someone. Daniel had achieved something quite special: he'd totally exposed his feelings for Gabriel in the most spectacular way, in full and glorious technicolor.

'This is how much I love you,' continued Daniel when finally there was a lull in the cheering. 'My love could fill an entire big top. My love for you is like a circus, full of joy and laughter and wonder and awe and amazing experiences. It is full of variety, from the giddiness and silliness of the clowns to the elegance and poise of the tightrope walkers. It is broad and all-encompassing, and when I am with you we have so much that I know I will never visit another circus because this is the best ever circus that came to town!'

'Daniel!' exclaimed Gabriel. 'I don't know what to say, this is so… so… so you?'

The crowd laughed and cheered.

'And look,' declared Daniel, swirling round. 'Look, we have an audience. An audience who are willing us on. Wanting us to do well.'

The noise from the crowd increased to a crescendo.

'This lot are totally behind us and will be there for us whenever we need them.'

The cheering continued as Gabriel looked around him in awe.

Wow, thought Katy, this was incredible. She looked over to Ben, who was shouting and hollering with the rest of them. Daniel had created the most fantastic start to his marriage. It might not be conventional but it sure was impactful. He and Gabriel were going to remember this moment for the rest of their lives, surrounded by their friends, cheering on their love. It was one of the loveliest things she had ever been a part of.

She suddenly remembered Alison sitting behind her and turned to see how she was rating this alternative wedding celebration. She was standing and she was clapping, the smallest of smiles on her face. The glow from Daniel and Gabriel had got through even to her.

Then suddenly there was an enormous explosion. A massive bang and a cloud of smoke erupted from the entrance. For a moment there was a gasp of shock and then a horn beeped and a shower of glittering confetti erupted out of the smoke.

'I've invited a couple of friends to join us,' announced Daniel over the microphone. 'A couple of clowns wanted to have their say on this very special day.'

He indicated to the conductor of the band and the ensemble immediately burst into action and a rendition of 'The Entertainer' filled the tent. The cloud of smoke started to settle and racing into the ring at a very slow speed came a...

'It's a capacity car!' screamed George. 'Look, Mr Chapman. A capacity car and some clowns!'

And there it was. A classic clown car with enormous headlights and a bright red bonnet rolled into the middle of the ring with its two clown passengers in spotted costumes and huge red noses.

They pulled the car up in front of Daniel and Gabriel and then stopped, the band still playing their hearts out. There then ensued what looked like an argument between the two clowns as they struggled to extract themselves from the car. They pushed and pulled at the door but to no avail, turning to each other every few seconds to wag an accusing finger and to reach across and try each other's doors. It was clear this was going nowhere until Daniel leaned forward and calmly opened the door, much to the clowns' amazement.

All of the children were in hysterics as if it was the funniest thing they had ever seen: two clowns unable to get out of a car.

First, one clown got out and dusted himself down and then walked around and opened the door for the other clown. However, the minute he turned the door handle, the entire door fell off and the rest of the car collapsed, leaving the remaining clown sat on his chair holding onto a steering wheel, the rest of the contraption lying in a heap around him.

'It's a capacity car!' screamed George again. 'Did you see it, Mum? It collapsed all around that poor clown. Can I have a capacity car, Mum? Perleeeeese? Oh look, he's trying to drive it away,' he said, pointing. He cupped his hands around his mouth and shouted, 'There's no car!' at the top of his voice. 'You can't drive no car!'

The clown looked over at him and scratched his head.

'There's no car!' George, Millie and Rebecca screamed.

The clown looked around him and jumped in surprise as though he had only just realised that his car had vanished around him. He scrambled to get out of his remaining seat, still holding onto the steering wheel, then walked over towards George.

'He's coming!' shrieked George, his eyes wide. 'Hello,' he said, waving frantically. 'Do you need a lift home?'

The clown continued to walk silently towards him, then bent forwards and handed him the steering wheel from the capacity car.

'Can I have it?' George gasped.

The clown nodded, then pulled aside his enormous red nose so his face could be seen.

'Daddy!' exclaimed George and Rebecca.

'It's Daddy!' squealed Rebecca, turning to tell her mother. 'Look, it's Daddy!'

'Is this what you've been doing?' asked George. 'Are you a clown now?'

Matthew cocked his head and said nothing.

'Is that your capacity car?' asked George. 'Can we keep it?'

Matthew grinned and ruffled his hair. He glanced up at Alison and took a deep breath before turning round and walking back towards the centre of the ring.

'Has Daddy been training to be a clown?' Rebecca asked her mum. 'Is that why he's been away?'

Alison looked grimly back at her but didn't reply.

'Look,' said George, pulling on his sister's sleeve, 'Daddy's going to say something.'

'Clowns aren't supposed to talk,' said Rebecca. 'Hasn't he even learnt that yet?'

Matthew was now standing on the podium next to the happy couple with the other clown. It had to be Braindead, thought Katy. What was Daniel thinking, getting those two up on stage with him? It had all been going so well so far. Those two could kill any happy occasion stone dead.

'I'd like to introduce you all to two very special people,' announced Daniel. 'I decided we didn't want readings or poems or words of wisdom from people we'd never met. Instead, I invited the two men in my life who I know would be the ones most likely to talk honestly and earnestly about the meaning of love and marriage. Now, these are two unusual men as they have decided to go down a different path to me, i.e. they married women! But despite that, I know whatever they tell you now will come from the heart. And that is what I wanted for today: flamboyance and honesty. Take it away, guys!'

Daniel handed the microphone over to Braindead first and took a step back, putting his arm around Gabriel's shoulders.

Braindead stepped forward and took a piece of paper out of his blue and yellow spotted jacket pocket. He cleared his throat.

'Hello, everyone,' he said, looking up. 'I only got married a few weeks ago and I completely ballsed up my speech.'

The crowd giggled.

'Like, off-the-scale ballsed it up, so when Daniel asked me to speak today, I decided that I'd try and say what I should have said at my own wedding. And I hope you'll forgive me if I read it to you because, believe me, you don't want me speaking off the cuff. That's where I went epically wrong last time. So here we go…'

Katy glanced over at Abby, who was mesmerised. She had never known her so quiet.

Braindead swallowed and looked down at his paper.

'Love is complicated,' he stated. 'Really bloody complicated. That's what I thought. You meet someone and you kind of like the look of them. Well, probably really like the look of them, so you try and pluck up the courage to talk to them and in the meantime your entire personality changes because suddenly you think you should try and be this perfect person so that this person you like will like you and so you try and talk to them but you kind of talk to them in a weird voice and you say really weird things you would never say to anyone else, like I once asked this woman… do you prefer cheese crispy pancakes or ham *and* cheese? That didn't last long. Anyway, usually when you like someone you change to suit them and hope they will like the changed you and then if they like this new weird, you then hopefully spend some more time together and you have to keep it up and it's really hard work. And then you have to do things together to see if you like doing things together, like going to the pub – obviously – and going to the cinema, and then it moves on to going shopping, which is like a *major* test. But if you pass those tests then other stuff happens, like you meet their friends and maybe end up going to a wedding together, which to be quite honest is enough to break up most couples. Anyway, the point I am trying to make is that relationships take a lot of work. Well, that's what I used to think. That love is complicated. And then I met Abby, my wife, who is sat over there, look. Stand up, Abby, and wave or something.'

Abby stood up and excitedly waved at the crowd.

'So I thought love was complicated until I met Abby. But I met her and I realised that love was dead simple. I'd got it all wrong. Love is simple, it's life that's complicated. When I met Abby it was so obvious what love was. It's knowing that whatever complications life throws at you that the love bit is always there. Always there to fall back on. Always there to rely on. Always there to guide you through. It's just a thing that's there that stops you giving in to the shit life throws at you.'

A low cheer started to emerge.

'So I just wanted to say right here, right now, dressed as a clown… Why am I dressed as a clown, Danny boy, by the way?' said Braindead, turning back towards Daniel.

Daniel shook his head, refusing to comment.

'I just wanted to say, because I met Abby, she made me realise that love is dead simple. It's just a feeling here.' He held his fist to his chest. 'The best feeling in the world.'

You could have heard a pin drop in the silence that followed Braindead's final thoughts on love and then the entire tent went crazy. Everyone was on their feet again, stamping and cheering. Abby leapt out of her seat and ran into Braindead's arms on the podium, where he swept her off the ground and swung her around, much to the delight of the onlookers.

'Oh,' he said, leaning back towards the microphone, 'I also wanted to apologise publicly for not having sex with you on our wedding day because—'

'Thank you, Braindead,' said Daniel, grabbing the microphone out of his hand. 'Let's not ruin a fantastic speech, hey? Big round of applause for Braindead, everyone, and his words of wisdom on love.'

Again the crowd erupted, causing Braindead to blush deeply before Abby forced him to take a bow. They stepped off the podium and walked back to the VIP area together.

'Nice one, buddy,' Ben said to Braindead.

'Very succinct,' added Katy, grinning with pride as any stand-in mother would.

'I wanted to do it right this time,' said Braindead, gazing adoringly at Abby.

'Now, ladies and gentlemen,' said Erica, stepping up to the mike again, 'we have another very special guest at Daniel's request here to give his thoughts on love and marriage.'

Katy gasped as she watched Matthew walk forward, remove his clown hat and nose, and look nervously out at the crowd. She glanced over at Alison, who had crossed her arms very firmly across her chest.

'Love,' began Matthew, wringing his hands and looking nervously out into the spotlights. 'To be perfectly honest with you, I think I really only knew what love has meant to me in the last few weeks... What I mean is that the feeling was always there but, you see, my life got complicated. Like, really complicated, and unlike my good friend here who seems to know already to let love guide him through, I didn't. I let my complicated life take over. Big time.' He swallowed and looked out into the crowd into the spotlights. Searching for Alison probably.

'You see, when you get married your future seems so straightforward. You have your life mapped out before you,' he continued, turning to smile at Daniel and Gabriel before returning to face the audience. 'But living that life can be much more complicated. Hazards will inevitably be thrown in your way and throw you off-plan into places you weren't prepared for. You may react in the right way and return to plan quickly or you might find yourselves in dangerous territory, where the route back might be the hardest challenge you ever face.'

He swallowed again.

'And whilst these two wonderful gentlemen are at the beginning of their perfect plan I am right in the middle of the dangerous territory, fighting for my life to get back in the game.'

A quiet and sympathetic 'aaaaah' whispered its way around the tent.

'I'm sorry to tell you I'm *not* actually a clown, I'm an accountant,' he announced.

Some low-level booing erupted before it died down into light laughter.

'The accountant in me has done his best to get us back on track but it hasn't worked. I haven't managed to tell the person that I adore and love most in the world what I need to. I need them to understand what is inside here,' he said, clutching his hands to his chest in exactly the same spot as Braindead had. 'I haven't managed to tell them that all I want to do for the rest of my life is to make them happy.'

Another 'aaaaah' skipped around the audience.

'There are no other words I can say,' continued Matthew. 'I have racked my brain for words to express what love means to me and that is it in a nutshell.' He looked out into the crowd, directly at Alison.

'All I want to do for the rest of my life is to make you happy,' he said into the microphone.

Everyone was now silent. All that could be heard was the shuffling feet of two elephants.

'As an accountant I have failed to get this message across so I have decided to communicate as a clown would. Give that a go. Quite frankly, I'm willing to try anything.' Matthew reached up and placed his red nose back on his face and put on his silly hat.

'It's got to be worth a shot, hasn't it?' he said, raising his hands and beginning a slow hand clap, encouraging the crowd to join in.

'Speaking of shots,' he continued. 'I would like to announce that the way I wish to display how I feel in my heart about my beautiful wife and family will be in the form of... drum roll, please...'

A young man in the band started to beat at his drum with two sticks.

'...being fired out of a cannon!'

Matthew took a step back and bowed as everyone gasped.

'Oh no!' Katy heard Alison murmur.

'Ladies and gentlemen,' announced Erica, stepping forward to speak into the microphone, 'for one night only, *Captain Catastrophe* here will be performing as a human cannonball. Yes, I did say human cannonball. He will be fired in a death-defying fashion out of the cannon you see before you.'

As she spoke a red, white and blue painted cannon was wheeled into the ring by two technicians dressed in black. The whole crowd was stunned into silence as they rolled it towards the podium, where Matthew was now donning a red cape and replacing his clown's hat with a shiny red balaclava.

'What's Daddy doing?' asked Harry.

'He's going to get fired out of that big tube,' said Ben helpfully.

Katy had her mouth open in shock.

'Wow,' said Harry. 'Awesome! Go, Daddy!' he shouted at the top of his voice. 'Go really far.'

Matthew turned and gave Harry a wave.

'Is he really going to do it?' said Rebecca. 'I didn't think daddies were supposed to do things like this. Don't you have to be an expert proper clown to be blown out of a cannon?'

Katy turned round to look at Alison, who was staring blankly at her husband, possibly in shock.

Matthew was now being helped into the contraption by Daniel and Gabriel.

'We love you, Daddy!' cried out Rebecca, getting up and running to sit on her mother's knee. 'He will be all right, won't he?' she asked her. Alison didn't reply.

The drummer from the band started to bang with all his might on the drum suspended round his neck in an ominous fashion. He started slow as the entire audience took up the beat and started to clap in time. After a few moments he sped up, taking the audience with him until he was banging frantically and the audience were once again vigorously stamping their feet and clapping their hands.

Erica stepped forward with a lit torch and made a show of bending over to light the cannon. Katy covered her eyes. Was this really happening? At a not-really-a-wedding wedding? A man being fired out of a cannon? This was insane.

Suddenly there was a massive boom and a cloud of smoke billowed up from the cannon. The audience went deathly quiet as a ball of red billowing satin containing Matthew flew through the air, high over the centre of the ring, and landed in a net strategically placed on the other side.

There was a moment's silence before Matthew threw his arms in the air in victory. The crowd went wild as the band struck up with a version of 'Happy Days Are Here Again'.

'Daddy, Daddy, Daddy, Daddy!' chanted George and Harry. 'That was our daddy!' said George, turning round to explain to Ben. 'Our daddy,' he repeated in amazement. 'He just got fired out of a cannon!'

Braindead had run back into the ring and was over by the net, helping a somewhat dazed-looking Matthew to scramble out. He lowered himself onto the floor and bent over double for a minute to catch his breath. Everyone was on their feet cheering as he raised himself up, thrusting his arms in the air to wave at the crowd before breaking into a trot and heading towards his wife and children, his red cape billowing behind him.

'Daddy, you are the best!' shrieked George. 'How did you do that? Did they set fire to your bottom?'

'Circus secrets,' said Matthew, tapping his nose and scooping Harry and George up into his arms. He looked over towards Alison expectantly.

'*Why* did you do that?' she asked, a look of utter amazement on her face.

He put the children down and stepped towards her, taking both her hands in his.

'To attempt to show you how massively sorry I am,' he said. 'That I realise what I have done but I want to put it right. I'm asking you to let me try. I will do anything, and I mean anything, for permission from you to let me try to spend the rest of my life making you happy. Please just let me try, Alison. That's all I'm asking. Please just give me the chance to make us a family again and make us all happy.'

She said nothing.

'Please let Daddy come home now he's finished his clown training,' pleaded Rebecca. 'Will you teach me how to do it, Daddy?'

'Will you, Alison, please?' repeated Matthew. 'I'm begging you.'

Alison looked down at her children and then looked back up at him.

'Okay,' she said eventually. 'I will.'

Chapter Thirty-Four

Katy

Two Months Later

'You're going to be a great husband, you know,' said Katy as she watched Daniel straighten his blue tie in the hotel bedroom mirror.

'Finally you realise what a catch I am!' said Daniel, shaking his head.

'You're only a catch since I had a word,' replied Katy, sipping a glass of iced water. She looked out over the balcony at the glittering sea of the glorious Catalonian coastline. It was utterly breathtaking. She got up steadily, clutching her now enormous belly, and walked to the edge of the balcony to where she could look down at the guests gathering on the beach for the impending nuptials of Daniel and Gabriel and Rita and Carlos.

'So it's all down to you, is it?' said Daniel, joining her and putting his arm around her shoulders. 'I'm only great husband material because of you?'

'Obviously,' replied Katy. 'If I hadn't lost it, well, who knows what kind of selfish bastard partner you would have become?'

'I like to think that the makings of me being a great partner were all there, you just needed to point out a few things,' he replied.

'Like the fact that it isn't all about you,' said Katy.

'Correct,' nodded Daniel with a small smile. 'In fact, I did need that pointing out to me, quite bluntly I seem to recall.'

'Well, you came good in the end. Especially with your not-really-a-wedding wedding. It was pretty spectacular.'

'I did it all for Matthew,' said Daniel.

'Of course you did,' replied Katy. 'Putting yourself at the centre of a huge circus is the most unselfish act I have ever seen you perform.'

'Thank you,' he nodded. 'Matthew texted me to say good luck, by the way.'

'Did he? How are they doing – did he say?'

'Well, he's moved back into the spare room. But I told him that's a good thing – the slower the better. It's going to take time.'

'Does he realise he wouldn't be anywhere near the spare room if it wasn't for you?' said Katy.

'Oh, I think he does. He keeps calling for advice on how he can show Alison how much he loves her. So far I've advised he learns to cook and takes her ballroom dancing. I'm thinking of telling him to take up knitting. You know, just to wind him up – because quite frankly, he will do whatever I tell him to at the moment.'

'Please don't be mean, Daniel.'

'I'm trying not to, but I've been so nice for soo long. Surely I deserve some fun?'

'Go on then. I guess you've earned it.'

'Really!' said Daniel, already reaching into his pocket to get his phone. He began to tap away, speaking his words out as he went.

'News just in,' he said. 'Knitting is the new must-have hobby for today's hunk. Sexiest thing since a six-pack, says Claudia Winkleman. Get knitting, Matthew!'

He waited a few seconds and sure enough, a ping rang out.

'"Seriously?"' he read. '"I'll see if I can buy some wool on the way home from work. Enjoy your day!"'

'You are evil,' announced Katy.

'I know, but I'm worth it. Is it time to go yet?'

'Not quite. We're meeting Ben and Mum in the foyer at four thirty sharp. We'll go down in a few minutes.'

'Oh, look,' said Daniel, pointing down towards the beach, 'Carlos and Gabriel have just arrived.'

'Are you supposed to look?' said Katy. 'Isn't that bad luck?'

Daniel was quiet for a moment, mesmerised. 'How can it be bad luck to see that?' he murmured.

Katy looked down at the gathering and watched as Gabriel and his father walked down the flower-lined aisle, their arms around each other, laughing and joking with the guests as they went. They couldn't have looked happier or more at ease.

'That has to make a double wedding worth it, doesn't it?' she asked.

'Of course it does,' he replied. 'You were right. And, to be honest, this place is pretty perfect. I couldn't believe it when Carlos rang and suggested we get married here rather than his bar.'

Katy smiled to herself.

'Don't say I never do anything for you,' she said.

'What do you mean?'

'Let's just say, after all the trouble you went to with the not-really-a-wedding circus, I decided you deserved a bit of help with making sure your actual wedding wasn't something totally horrific. So I sent pictures of this hotel and beach to my mother, telling her this is where we were going to stay, knowing she wouldn't be able to resist going for a look. And when she did, I made sure Miguel, the general manager, was ready for her.'

'You set all this up!'

'It only took a few phone calls.'

'You set all this up for me? I thought Rita must have stamped her feet or something.'

'Well, she did, after she'd seen this hotel and Miguel had hinted that the Spanish royal family often stay and they just so happened to have had a cancellation for the day of her wedding. She was done then. Getting married where royalty stay even trumps getting married with her gay stepson!'

'You are a very clever lady, Katy Chapman. I knew when I asked you to give me away that you would come up trumps.'

She turned to look at Daniel suspiciously.

'You mean you only asked me to give you away knowing that I'd then step in and get you the wedding you wanted?'

'Not at all,' said Daniel. 'Of course not. I just knew that you'd look after me. Like you always do.'

'Well,' said Katy, suddenly feeling teary. 'That's what mates do, isn't it, I guess. Look after each other.'

'You're not going to tell me you love me, are you?' asked Daniel, stepping back. 'And don't hug me. The last thing I need on my wedding day is to be seen being hugged by a heavily pregnant woman just before I walk down the aisle. It would be nice if this wedding went off without any gossip or rumour or revelations. I'm so over that kind of wedding.'

'Don't worry,' laughed Katy. 'I've told Braindead not to speak to anyone all day. He's under strict instructions to be on his best behaviour.'

'And I've sat Erica next to Gabriel's cousin, who is quite frankly to die for,' announced Daniel. 'There's no way she's lusting after your husband sat next to that Adonis, believe me!'

'But my husband is an Adonis,' complained Katy.

'If you say so,' he replied. 'Now, can we please get going. I have my own Adonis waiting downstairs and I'd really like to go and get married to him now.'

*

Ben was waiting for them in the hotel lobby but there was no sign of Katy's mother.

'She's not happy with her make-up apparently,' he said. 'The woman had done it twice before Rita threw her out and is now doing it herself.'

'Sounds like she's nervous,' said Katy. 'There's no pleasing her when she's nervous. Poor Carlos, I hope he knows what he's letting himself in for.'

'That's my future stepmother-in-law you are talking about,' said Daniel.

'Lucky, lucky you!' said Katy. 'At least now you can share my pain.'

'Are you okay?' Ben asked her. 'You're not overdoing it, are you? You need to be careful today. We don't want you going into early labour.'

'Oh my God,' said Daniel, slapping his forehead, 'I'd forgotten about that potential catastrophe. It's not Braindead's mouth we should be worrying about keeping shut today, it's your cervix.'

'Daniel!' exclaimed Katy. 'This is not the moment to be discussing my cervix.'

'Nor my mouth,' said Braindead, coming up behind them.

'What are you doing here?' said Katy. 'You promised me you would sit at the back and not speak to anyone. Remember what I said, you are *not* allowed to speak at weddings ever again!'

'But I had to come and find you,' he said in hushed tones, looking over his shoulder nervously. 'I have something to tell you but don't tell anyone, it's a secret. Especially not Abby.'

Ben, Katy and Daniel all looked at him, horrified.

Daniel covered his ears and started singing in a desperate attempt to avoid whatever it was that Braindead was about to disclose.

'Can't it wait till tomorrow, mate?' said Ben. 'You and secrets and weddings are a disaster waiting to happen.'

'No!' he exclaimed. 'I have to tell you. I can't keep it to myself, even though Abby has made me swear not to tell anyone.'

'Please don't tell, Braindead,' urged Katy. 'Listen to Abby.'

'But we're pregnant!' cried Braindead. 'I'm going to be a dad!'

'What!' exclaimed Katy and Ben.

'That's amazing,' said Ben, embracing his friend, grinning from ear to ear.

'Congratulations,' said Daniel, slapping him on the back. 'Honeymoon baby then? You don't mess about, do you?'

'No,' said Braindead, shaking his head. 'We didn't have sex on our honeymoon.'

'What do you mean, you didn't have *sex*?' asked Daniel. 'Isn't that what honeymoons are for? Don't tell me this now.'

'We didn't have sex because Alison haunted me throughout my honeymoon and for some time afterwards. You try and have sex whilst the ghost of Alison is watching you. But we reckon that it all cracked off after your circus wedding. Let's just say there was a certain sense of release seeing Matthew back with Alison!'

'Too much information, Braindead,' said Katy.

'So not so much a honeymoon baby as a circus baby then?' asked Daniel.

'Exactly,' exclaimed Braindead. 'Perhaps we should name it Clown? What do you think?'

'I think you've got plenty of time to work out names,' interrupted Katy. 'Now do you think you should go back to Abby and try and pretend you haven't told us so she doesn't end up killing the father of her unborn child?'

'Good thinking,' he replied. 'I just, I just wanted to share it, you know. How happy I am. And if you ever need to ask for a pregnancy test in Spanish, you know where to come.'

'You did the test here,' gasped Katy. 'And you've already told us?'

Braindead looked at them, bewildered.

'But it's good news, isn't it? It's not wedding-ruining news?'

'What's wedding-ruining news?' boomed a voice from behind them. Everyone turned and then gasped when they found Rita standing there. There was complete silence for a moment.

'Wow!' Braindead suddenly exclaimed. 'You are the most beautiful bride I have ever set eyes on. Apart from my wife, of course,' he said.

'Really?' said Rita, instantly relaxing. 'Do I look okay?'

'Stunning,' said Braindead. 'Carlos is a lucky man.'

'Divine,' added Daniel. 'You put us all in the shade.'

'Why thank you,' giggled Rita, fiddling with her hair.

'You look really lovely, Mum,' added Katy.

Rita turned to look at her daughter. Katy sucked in her breath, preparing for an insult.

'And you look utterly glorious,' her mother told her.

'Braindead was just coming to see if we were ready, weren't you?' said Katy, keen not to give any space for a put-down line. She glanced across at him but he was staring at her bump, a soppy smile on his face.

'Braindead, why don't you go and tell them we are ready,' she said.

'What?' he said, looking up, oblivious.

'Go tell them we are ready now. Off you go,' she said.

'Right, right, of course,' he muttered. 'Break a leg, guys,' he added, giving them all a thumbs up, then walking backwards into a large pot plant and falling over.

'I'm fine,' he gasped, leaping up. 'Absolutely fine, nothing broken.'

'Just go!' said Katy.

'Right, yes, bye, see you on the other side.'

Finally, he walked away and the four of them were left looking at each other, wondering what to do next.

'We should go first, don't you think?' said Rita. 'I mean, Carlos is paying for most of this.'

Katy tried to stifle a gasp and looked over at Daniel nervously.

'Of course,' smiled Daniel. 'After you, Mother-in-Law.'

*

Daniel and Katy paused at the top of the aisle to allow Rita her moment, laughing and waving at her gathered friends and relatives.

'Now may I have the honour of giving you away on your wedding day?' Katy asked Daniel.

'Of course. It is indeed an honour to have you by my side on this auspicious day that—'

'Shut up, Daniel,' said Katy.

'Okay,' he replied. 'I'm ready.'

'Good.'

'For sex on the beach.'

'What?'

'I've provided the post-wedding drinks and I thought it only appropriate in this setting that we have cocktails. Sex on the beach, to be precise.'

'Bloody hell!' said Katy, rubbing her baby bump. 'I get to miss out again!'

'What, on sex on the beach?'

'Yeah, that as well,' she replied glumly. 'Anyway, no-one ever has sex on the beach, do they? I mean… the *sand*?'

'Well, I can assure you that I'm going to enjoy my sex on the beach,' said Daniel with a grin. 'One way or another. This is my wedding day after all.'

A Letter from Tracy

Dear Reader

I want to say a huge thank you for choosing to read *No-one Ever Has Sex at a Wedding*. If you enjoyed reading it and want to keep up to date with all my latest releases just sign up at the following link. Your email address will never be shared and you can unsubscribe at any time.

www.bookouture.com/tracy-bloom

I really hope you enjoyed *No-one Ever Has Sex at a Wedding* and if you did, I would be hugely grateful if you could write a review on your seller's website. I'd love to hear what you thought and it makes such a difference helping new readers to discover my books for the first time.

I would love to hear from you directly and you can get in touch on my Facebook page, via Twitter, Goodreads or my website.

Many thanks
Tracy

www.tracybloom.com

tracybloomwrites

@TracyBBloom

7075043.Tracy_Bloom

Acknowledgements

Acknowledgements are a bit like wedding speeches, aren't they? A unique opportunity to thank people for helping you with stuff. So I thought I'd take this unique opportunity to use my acknowledgements to thank those who helped me with my wedding!

I'll start with my sister Helen, who is always brilliant but was the best bridesmaid I could wish for, and her hunch-backed walk down the aisle, holding the hands of my two-year-old nieces, Rebecca and Laura, is an image I will never forget! Thank you to my BFF Helen for a beautiful reading in church and for not getting her heel stuck in the grate, Tony and Gemma for their spectacular rendition of 'When I'm 64' by The Beatles and Rosie and Phil for being the best of friends to us and guiding us all through it. Alastair, you were a faultless best man at the wedding – no idea about the stag do! Mum and Dad, Chris and David, thank you for your love and support and for paying for stuff. Very much appreciated! Oh, and thank you, Bruce, for asking me to marry you. Good call!

So now I have thanked the people I should have thanked over thirteen years ago, I'll thank Madeleine Milburn and her great team at the Madeleine Milburn Agency, as well as Jenny Geras, Peta Nightingale, Kim Nash, Alex Crow and all the other hard workers at Bookouture, for helping make this book happen. And as ever, thank you to everyone who has read it and told other people to read it and made it all worthwhile. You are the best!

Printed in Great Britain
by Amazon